THE WHISPER SOUL

A NICK DRAKE NOVEL

DWIGHT HOLING

The Whisper Soul
A Nick Drake Novel

Print Edition
Copyright 2020 by Dwight Holing

Published by Jackdaw Press
All Rights Reserved

ISBN: 978-1-7347404-1-7

For More Information, please visit dwightholing.com.

See how you can **Get a Free Book** at the end of this novel.

For John & Terry Holing
Who read Oregon rivers as ably as they do mystery novels

"Gaze not too long into the abyss, lest the abyss gaze into thee."

— EDWARD ABBEY

1

Summer storm clouds were veined with lightning, but no rain fell. It hadn't rained for weeks and the parching sun had cracked the playas into puzzle pieces with gaps wide enough to trap a man's boot. Brittlebush bore no yellow blossoms, sagebrush faded from silver to brown, and tumbleweeds snapped free from their roots in hope of fleeing the heat. Pronghorn and wild horses were forced to paw at the thick crust that topped soda lakes. When the longing animals uncovered a trapped puddle to drink, salt would ring their muzzles like hoarfrost.

I was speeding along a gravel road that ran parallel to the northern border of Hart Mountain National Antelope Refuge. The newest recruit in the US Fish and Wildlife Service's special ranger program for Vietnam combat veterans like me rode shotgun. Loq was a much-decorated Marine who'd been hired in the spring to help patrol several wildlife refuges scattered across southeastern Oregon. Our orders were to divide the sprawling territory between us. Loq was to take the refuges near his Klamath Indian tribal home due west and I was to keep watch over the Hart, Malheur, Sheldon, and Deer Flat refuges from my base in the one-blink town of No Mountain in Harney County.

While our military training had taught us to obey the chain of command, we'd spent enough time in country to make decisions based on what was actually going down in the field rather than adhering to battle lines drawn on a map by officers far from the action. As wildlife rangers, we took the same approach, and for that reason, we teamed up more often than not.

This was shaping up to be one of those times.

The road ran straight at a horizon crimson with flames and muddled by smoke. Dry lightning had ignited a sea of sagebrush that surrounded a woodland of old-growth western junipers. Large mammals—predators and prey alike—routinely sought refuge from the blistering sun in the grove of thousand-year-old trees because it provided shade around a perennial waterhole. It was the high desert equivalent of Switzerland, a place where mortal enemies temporarily united by an even more powerful enemy honored an uneasy truce.

The fire had created its own weather, a superheated storm of whipsaw winds that sent columns of twisting, swirling soot and embers taller than any dust devil I'd witnessed since exchanging the confines of Walter Reed Hospital's special ward for soldiers suffering from combat fatigue for the wide open spaces of the tenth largest county in the country. I could feel the firestorm's furnace grow hotter as we neared.

Loq glanced over his shoulder, past the rack in the rear window that cradled my long guns, and checked on the flatbed trailer swaying behind the government-issued white pickup. Strapped to it was a 500-gallon plastic storage tank that we'd commandeered from a cattle ranch along with gear that would turn the four-wheel-drive into a jury-rigged firetruck: a gas-powered generator, pump, and 200-foot coil of hose. Picks, axes, and shovels skittered around the bed each time we hit a pothole.

The *Maklak*—how the Klamath referred to themselves in their native tongue—turned back to stare at the fire ahead. "Reminds me of a time in the Central Highlands. We were moving fast with only light arms and ran straight into an NVA division dug in with field artillery."

"But you didn't turn back, did you?" I said as I tightened my grip on the steering wheel and kept my boot on the gas.

He looked down his high cheekbones. "How come white men always ask questions they already know the answer to?"

"To make us feel superior," I said.

Loq grunted. "Thing about you, Nick, when you tell a joke, I can't always tell you're joking."

"This road goes straight by the woodlands. People use it as a shortcut between Lakeview and points south of Burns. If we go past the fire, we'll be able to see how wide it is."

"And then what?"

"There's a dirt track that circles the trees. Hunters in their four-bys made it. If we can find a spot where we can get close, we can lay down water to create an escape route for any animals trapped in there. The *Nuwuddu*," I said, using the Paiute word for the first people. Humans were the second people.

"Why bother going around it?" Loq said. "We know what we got to do. Go straight at it. And faster too before the heat melts the big bucket we're toting and all we end up doing is giving each other a bath."

"Roger that," I said and cranked the wheel.

We swerved off the gravel road and bounced across the desert. I intercepted the smaller dirt track near the north end of the grove of ancient trees.

"There!" I shouted over the roar of the fire and rattle of the tools. "That game trail must lead to the waterhole. The *Nuwuddu* will be bunched around it."

Knee-high flames were already licking both sides of the trail.

The burning branches of a downed juniper blocked it a few yards past the entrance. The tree's cones were popping like gunfire from the heat. I backed the trailer toward the entrance to put the water tank closer as well as give us a running start in case we needed to beat a hasty retreat.

Loq jumped out of the pickup. There was so much static electricity in the air from the lightning, his long mohawk stood straight up. When he'd been issued his allotment of Fish and Wildlife uniforms, he'd torn the sleeves off the khaki shirts to give his biceps more room. Now he yanked off the shirt, exposing the bear tooth that hung from a leather thong around his neck and the *Semper Fi* tattoo on his chest.

"You handle the hose. I'll get rid of that tree." He grabbed an axe and strode toward the blazing juniper.

I connected the pump to the generator and started uncoiling the makeshift firehose. I had the drill down pat. This wasn't the first fire of the summer. Far from it. A new round of lightning strikes had ignited blazes like this one to join wildfires already underway in the high lonesome. For the past month, a deathly pallor of thick smoke had settled over Harney County, a 10,000-square-mile expanse of basin and range country bounded by the Blue Mountains to the north and Steens Mountain to the southeast. Unless the fires were in valuable stands of pine and fir managed by the Forest Service or threatened towns and ranch buildings, they were left to burn themselves out. That included any on Fish and Wildlife land. At least that was the agency's official policy. It wasn't mine and it wasn't Loq's either.

I got the pump going, grabbed the hose, and chased after him. Loq was swinging the axe at the burning tree. The blade sliced through flames and hacked off limbs. I trained the nozzle as the hose stiffened behind me. The water gushed out. I kept the spray up as I reached his side. Using the axe as a pike, Loq dragged the now-smoldering trunk to the side and we continued our march.

The fire's noxious gases seemed ablaze and made breathing difficult. I pulled up a wet blue bandana I wore tied around my neck to cover my nose and mouth. I doused more spot fires and Loq kept swinging the axe at branches crowding the game trail and dragging them away to create an unimpeded path.

"It'll be a trick to get the animals to leave. They're bound to be panicked," I said.

"I got a plan for that," Loq grunted.

"What is it?"

"Stand to the side unless you want to get trampled."

The hose grew taut and wouldn't stretch any farther no matter how hard I yanked. I arced the spray as high as it would go to provide a sheltering curtain of water. Loq dashed beneath it to get behind the waterhole. He was soon swallowed by smoke. The tank ran dry. I stepped off the trail and waited.

The bark on the trees shriveled from the heat and made the trunks and boughs groan. The hiss of flames sounded like snakes slithering fast through tall grass. Cones continued to rat-a-tat-tat. Rising hot air rustled the crowns of the trees. "There's no escape," they seemed to moan. I steeled myself to prevent falling into a flashback of a running gun battle with Viet Cong as napalm incinerated the jungle around me. I didn't drop the now-flaccid hose. It could prove to be a lifeline to lead us out of the eye-watering smoke.

A new noise sounded. At first I mistook it for a tree engulfed by flames rubbing against other trunks as it slowly toppled, but then it intensified. I leaned forward. There was no mistaking it now. It wasn't the rumble of fast-approaching flames, but the warning growl of a large animal. The deep, primeval call grew in volume as it thundered from the vocal folds of a mohawked

Klamath who took his name from the *Maklak* word for grizzly bear.

Loq's roar thundered through the ancient woods. I felt the ground shake before I saw any animals. First came a half-dozen fleet-footed pronghorn springing down the trail. Right on their heels were two, no, three, no, four panicked mule deer. They passed so close I could've reached out and stroked their hides. A bobcat driven by fear and not hunger scampered close behind. I made eye contact with a cougar, but she never broke stride as she raced by.

The echo of Loq's roar followed the big cat, but she was not the last refugee to abandon the waterhole. A two-legged figure emerged from the smoky gloom. It was a woman. She wore a torn white dress and was soaking wet. Watery soot left dark trails running down her face. Deep, straight wounds marred her forearms and thighs. Twigs and juniper needles littered her black hair. One of her braids had been hacked off above the shoulder.

I stepped out to intercept her. Her coal-black eyes widened and she shrieked. She threw her hands up to scratch my face, but before her nails could rake me, Loq appeared behind her and threw his arms around her, pinning hers to her side.

"Shh, sister," he shushed. "You're safe now."

2

Nothing more was to be done to save the western junipers. Either the old-growth forest would survive as it had for millennia or it would be destroyed by flames and the scattered seeds would lie dormant in the ashes until the rains returned to bring life anew. But we could save the woman who'd sought refuge there. Loq and I held her between us as we fast-stepped down the game trail and out of the burning woods. When she kept faltering, Loq scooped her up and carried her.

We finally reached my pickup. I cut the makeshift firehose and got behind the wheel. Loq placed the woman on the front seat and slid in beside her. I didn't waste any time driving away. The rig's side mirrors reflected the molten edges of doom. Loq and I tried talking with the woman, but she stared ahead, glassy eyed and mute, before closing her eyes and slumping between us with her chin resting on her chest. Every time she started to topple forward, Loq stuck his arm out and gently pushed her back.

I plucked the microphone to the police band radio from its

cradle. Deputy Pudge Warbler answered my call from his office at the Harney County sheriff's department in Burns.

"Say again?" the old lawman said.

"I said we were trying to free some wildlife from a fire at the Hart Mountain refuge when we came across her. She was hiding in a waterhole surrounded by a stand of old junipers."

"Who's 'we' and who's 'she'?" he said.

"I'm with Loq, the new ranger. And she's, well, we don't know who she is. I'd say she's in her early twenties and American Indian, but I don't know which tribe. She didn't respond when I spoke to her in English and then I tried *Numu*. Nothing. Loq spoke to her in *Maklak*, but she didn't answer. She's probably in shock." I paused. "There's more. She looks like she's been attacked."

The sound of the deputy sucking in air came across loud and clear. "You mean, like, violated?"

"She has slashes down her arms and legs and someone hacked off a hank of her hair."

"No," Loq said. "Her wounds are her own. They're the marks of a wife in mourning."

Pudge could hear him because he said, "Paiute women used to do that in the old days when their husbands died. They'd draw blood with a flint knife and cut off a braid. You say she didn't respond to you speaking *Numu*?"

I was getting better with the Paiute language and my vocabulary and pronunciation were improving, but I was far from fluent. And then there was the matter of all the different dialects, one for each of the more than two dozen different bands of Paiute who roamed the Great Basin.

"If she's from another band, November might be able to communicate with her to find out who she is and where she comes from," I said, naming the tribal elder and healer who lived with Pudge and his daughter. "We could take her straight to your ranch."

"Good idea. I'll meet you there." The lawman signed off.

As I hung up the mike, the woman grabbed my arm and screeched. "Stop!"

I slammed on the brakes. Loq stretched his arm out to keep her from pitching forward and striking the dashboard. "Easy, sister," he said.

"Let me out. My babies!"

Bile raced up my throat. "Your babies are back at the water-hole? Why didn't you say so?"

I started cranking the steering wheel to make a U-turn.

"Wait!" Loq said. "Let her speak. If her children were there, she wouldn't have left them." He continued to pin her with his arm. "Am I right, sister? Where are they?"

"I do not know. I have been looking for them everywhere."

My eyes met Loq's. We didn't have to say anything to express what we thought. We'd both seen it on the battlefield. Soldiers and rice farmers alike said all sorts of things when they were in shock. There was no way of knowing what happened to her children or even if they were still alive. The self-inflicted mourning wounds were impossible to ignore.

I asked her when she'd last seen them.

"I have lost track of time."

"Okay, where was it?" I said.

"Chewaucan."

"That's a river and marsh northwest of Lakeview, not a town. Do you mean Paisley?" It was the largest settlement of any kind near there, a community of hardworking farmers and ranchers.

"No, we lived at the edge of the marsh, not in town. We made camp there."

"You and your kids."

"And my husband. He worked at a ranch nearby."

I glanced at the wounds on her legs and forearms again. They were starting to scab. I judged them to be no more than a couple of days old.

"Where's your husband now?" I asked, already knowing the answer.

"He is dead. A horse threw him."

"Did you work on the ranch too?"

"I stayed in camp to look after my babies." She took a breath. "We were living the old ways, abiding by the old customs. I wanted my babies to live like their ancestors so they would be safe." Her voice drifted off.

"How old are your kids?"

"Six. They are twins. A girl and a boy." She started weeping again.

"What's your name, sister?" Loq said.

"Wanda. Wanda Manybaskets."

She buried her face in her hands and started rocking. "I do not know what to do. I do not know where my babies are."

"Chewaucan is a couple of hours away," I said. "How did you get here?"

"I drove."

"Why did you come this way?"

"I searched everywhere around our camp, and then I asked for help."

"Chewaucan is in Lake County. Did you ask the sheriff in Lakeview?"

"No, I asked my ancestors and they told me to listen for my babies' cries." She patted her heart. "They led me to drive north and then to turn off the main road, but the truck ran out of gas. I started walking. I saw the deer and they led me to the water. I thought my babies might be there, but they were not. When the trees caught on fire and the animals ran, I did too."

I told Loq we needed to take her back to Lakeview and talk

to the sheriff there. "We'll have to drive the long way around because of the fire."

"They are not there anymore," Wanda Manybaskets insisted.

"How do you know?"

"Their cries tell me so."

I swallowed exasperation. "Okay, we'll stick to the plan and take you to a friend's ranch. He's a lawman. He'll know what to do about contacting Lake County sheriff's and the state police."

A dirt road shortcut ran along the western base of Jackass Mountain. I counted two separate fires crackling through the sagebrush as we drove. Both were still under one hundred acres in size, but if the wind picked up, it wouldn't take long before they joined forces. The resulting conflagration would produce its own energy and create a firestorm that could easily double in size every hour. Without rain or an organized battle waged by trained firefighters on the ground and aerial tankers, there would be no stopping it. Anything in its path, including fences, corrals, barns, ranch houses, livestock, and the town of No Mountain would be consumed.

Wanda's chin was pointed at her chest again. Her shallow breathing signaled sleep.

"What do you think about her story?" I whispered. "Could've young kids just wandered off or were they kidnapped?"

"Hard to say, but it wouldn't be the first time native children were taken against their will," Loq said.

"How so?"

"When my ancestors walked the land, it was tribal enemies like the Achomawi who needed brides for their sons or slaves for their camps. When white men came, it was them. Missionaries took our children to save their souls, farmers for laborers, and childless couples as their own." He grunted. "Mostly it was the government. The Bureau of Indian Affairs set up boarding schools for them."

"Like the school November went to sixty years ago," I said. "They changed her name from Girl Born in Snow. She told me the teachers forbid her to speak *Numu*. They'd punish her if she did."

A grimace creased Loq's usually stoic face. "You heard of Brigadier General Richard Henry Pratt?"

"I take it he has nothing to do with the Vietnam War."

"He founded the Carlisle Indian School in Pennsylvania in the 1870s. Pratt's slogan was 'Kill the Indian and save the man.'"

"Carlisle is where the US Army War College is now."

"The war college took over the property after the school was shut down," Loq said. "New buildings were constructed over a graveyard where more than two hundred Indian children were buried. Those boarding schools were deathtraps. November probably went to Chemawa School here in Oregon."

"She learned English and how to read, all right, but if they were trying to kill the Indian in her, they got an F. Did Chemawa close too?"

"It's still open. Some say it's not the way it used to be, but I don't know for sure."

"Did you go there?"

Loq snorted. "I went to a one-room schoolhouse in Chiloquin, but I spent most of my time fishing and hunting rather than sitting at a desk. I joined the Marines as soon as I could pass for eighteen."

"Which was what, when you were fifteen years old?"

"Maybe a little bit older than that." He said it without a chuckle.

I checked the rearview mirror. Despite the height of the storage tank we were towing, it couldn't block out the cloud of dust my rig was kicking up. I looked west and saw a similar cloud paralleling us.

"Over there," I said. "Wild horses are on the move."

"That's a killing pace considering there's no water for miles," Loq said. "Something must be chasing them."

I braked to a stop and grabbed my binoculars. The herd of mustangs numbered around twenty. I panned the horizon and saw plumes of smoke. "There's multiple brushfires behind them."

I panned again and picked up another plume between the horses and fires, but it wasn't smoke. It was a dust devil kicked up by a speeding pickup. It drove for a while and then stopped and then started up again. I followed it with my binoculars and then panned back to where it had stopped. A new, smaller plume was rising. It was smoke, not dust. I panned south to the other brushfires. They were evenly spaced apart.

I handed the binoculars to Loq. "There's a dark-colored pickup over there. Take a look and tell me what you think."

He thumbed the focus wheel. "It's turning west now, away from the horses and us. Must be a rancher who got caught out in the open and is trying to outrun the fires." He kept the binoculars pressed to his eyes. "Wait, he's stopping."

"What's he doing?"

"It looks like he chucked something out the window. Now he's driving again. Hold on, whatever he threw burst into flames when it hit."

Loq lowered the binoculars. The top of his long mohawk brushed the headliner of the pickup as he shook his head. "He's tossing Molotov cocktails. He must think starting a backfire will stop the ones already burning."

"No, he started all those too. He's no rancher. He's a firebug."

"Then we got to stop him."

"Our first priority has to be Wanda's missing kids," I said.

"Agreed, but if he lit those, he might light more. Maybe he gets off on it."

"Then that's how we'll catch him."

3

We hit asphalt south of No Mountain and soon passed by the old lineman's shack I'd called home since taking the job with Fish and Wildlife. If my pickup had been a horse, it would've smelled the barn and balked when I didn't turn into the familiar drive. The wooden shack with its cockeyed stovepipe looked especially forlorn in smoky light that was more dusk than noon. The fires to the south were still miles away, but the shack wouldn't last long in a blaze. It would combust as surely as aged kindling touched by a match and blown by a breath.

Loq must have read my mind. "You sure you don't want to stop and put your motorcycle in the back? Replacing a Triumph like yours won't be easy around here."

"We need to get Wanda to the Warbler ranch. There's plenty of time to come back and get it."

His silence said he thought otherwise.

As I slowed going through town, Wanda Manybaskets finally stirred. "Where are we?"

"No Mountain."

"Where is that?"

"About thirty minutes south of Burns."

"Is Burns a big city?"

"Biggest in the county, but that's not saying much since Harney's only got seventy-five hundred people living in it. You're not from Oregon, are you?"

"No, Nevada."

"And you're not Paiute."

"I am Washoe."

Loq grunted. "That explains why you didn't understand *Numu* or *Maklak*. Was your husband Washoe?"

Wanda nodded. "We had been living at the Indian Colony in Reno. My husband was a janitor at a casino. He always wanted to be a rancher. A man he met at the casino told him about a ranch near Chewaucan that was looking for hands."

She tugged at what was left of her hacked-off braid. "It is my fault my babies are missing. When my husband was thrown from the horse, the rancher took him to the hospital in Lakeview. His wife drove to our camp to tell me. She took us to be with him. We stayed by his bed all night. When the doctor said he had died, we went back to our camp and fell asleep. When I woke the next day, my babies were gone."

We passed Blackpowder Smith's. The combination dry goods store and tavern was No Mountain's most popular business in the one-block-long stretch of sagging storefronts that made up the main street. A line of people snaked out the front door. A stampede for supplies was underway.

The thought of flames sweeping through No Mountain raised the taste of bile again. The town had withstood droughts, freezes, windstorms, and collapsing cattle prices. The townspeople were a hardy, self-sufficient lot with big hearts. They'd welcomed a stranger like me with no questions asked. Losing No Mountain to a wildfire would hurt, but an arsonist burning it down would hurt even worse. I might not be able to stop a firestorm, but I sure as hell could try to stop a firebug.

I sped up as we passed the last of the storefronts and then turned off the main road, clattering over a metal cattle guard that marked the entrance to Deputy Warbler's ranch. His rig wasn't parked in front of the house, but his daughter's red Jeep Wagoneer was. Gemma Warbler was getting something out of the back. Whatever it was, she left it when I pulled to a stop. She wore jeans and a pearl-snap shirt. She marched over, leaned through the open window, and kissed me on the lips.

Her eyes sparkled and her ponytail swished when she pushed away. "I read an article in *Cosmopolitan* that said firemen were hot. Now I know what it was talking about."

The only thing I could think of saying was, "Since when did you read anything besides veterinarian journals?"

Loq leaned forward to make eye contact with the horse doctor. "See, when you tell a joke, I know you're joking, but when Nick does—" He made a slashing motion with the flat of his hand.

Gemma winked conspiratorially and was about to say something when she caught sight of the woman squeezed between us. "Oh, you poor thing. You look like you've been caught in a fire."

Wanda put a hand to her face. "I need a—"

"Bath and clean clothes," Gemma finished for her. She grabbed the door handle before I could open it. "Get out, Nick. Hurry."

I gave Wanda my hand to help her out of the cab. As soon as her feet touched the ground, Gemma put her arm around her and ushered her toward the ranch house. Loq joined me and we watched them go.

"While we're waiting for the deputy to show, you think you could ask November if we can have something to eat?" he said.

"Why don't you ask her yourself?"

"I don't dare."

"November is in her seventies and half your size, and you're scared of asking her for a favor?"

"It's like in my people's story of *loq* and *moq'ooga*."

"That being *Maklak* for what?"

"Mouse."

"Ah, like Aesop's fable, only his was about a lion and mouse, not a grizzly bear and one. I know how your story goes."

"Then you know why I can't ask her. I got to save it up until when I really need her help."

"Looks like neither one of us will have time. Here comes Pudge now."

The old deputy parked his pickup with a gold star on the door and bar of Christmas lights on the roof. He took his time getting out. His uniform was yoked with sweat and his bulldog jowls flushed from heat. He tugged down the short brim of his Stetson.

"I'm surprised the back of my shirt and the seat of my britches didn't tear clean off, they were glued to the seat so hard," he growled.

"The fires don't help the temperature any," I said.

"I've lived in Harney County all my life except the years I served in the Pacific, but I don't recall a summer this hot ever." He wiped his face with a bandana. "Let's get out of the sun and I can meet this woman you found. See if we can place her."

"Gemma took her. She's probably in the bath by now."

"Okay, we'll wait."

"There's something else you need to know. She says her two children are missing. Six-year-old twins."

"What the Sam Hill? You didn't mention that on the radio."

"We didn't find out until later. She speaks English."

"Missing kids. Just what I don't need with all these wildfires going on."

"You're not going to want to hear about those either. We spotted a firebug tossing Molotov cocktails west of Jackass Mountain."

"Oh Lord, what is it about you, son, that attracts trouble like cow flop does flies? Let's get inside so I can be sitting down when I hear it all."

Loq and I followed him into the ranch house and down the hall to an office that served as a sheriff's department substation. The old deputy had been semi-retired ever since he lost his longtime job as sheriff in the last election. He loosened the gun belt holding a holstered .45 and settled into an oak swivel chair.

"First things first," he said. "The children. What's the woman's name and when was the last time she saw her youngsters?"

"Wanda Manybaskets. She and her husband were living north of Lakeview alongside Chewaucan Marsh." I told him about them being Washoe and the husband being thrown by a horse and dying in the Lakeview hospital and what happened afterward.

"And when was this?"

"No more than a couple of days ago, but you can ask her yourself when she's finished cleaning up."

"The youngsters must've woke up before her and wandered off," the old lawman said. "Children do that all the time. When Gemma was little, she'd be outside playing and a butterfly would land near her and the next thing you know, I get a call from two ranches over to come fetch her. Hers could be nearby their camp."

"Wanda is insistent her children aren't there anymore," I said.

"Why is she so sure?"

"She says she can hear them crying for her. Their cries led her up here."

Pudge sighed. "Oh Lord. I tell anyone that, it's not gonna make it any easier getting other law enforcement agencies to agree to help her out."

"I'll find her kids," Loq said. "And the people who took them."

"Now, hold on big fella," the old deputy said. "You and me have only met a couple of times, but there's some things we need to get straight. If there has been a kidnapping—and we don't even know that yet—but if there has, the law's in charge and I can't have someone running around taking matters into their own hands."

"Are you saying that because I'm *Maklak*?"

"Heck no. I'm saying it because you're a leatherneck, same as me. We might've fought in different wars during different decades and were attached to different divisions, but once a Marine always a Marine. Am I right? I don't expect you'll grin and bear it if someone was to give you a hard time."

Loq's expression confirmed Pudge's theory. "Okay," the lawman said. "Tell me again how she discovered her offspring were gone? I'm gonna ask her myself, but I want to see if anything changes when she tells me."

I glanced around Pudge's office. It was the same as always. Shelves full of books, a cabinet full of long guns, and a couch used for napping. A police band radio, facsimile machine, and telephone allowed him to keep in contact when he wasn't at the sheriff's office in Burns.

"She didn't provide any details beyond what I already told you. When she couldn't find them, she asked her ancestors for help. They told her to listen for them. She did and wound up driving through the Hart refuge. When her pickup crapped out, she jumped in the waterhole during the fire."

"Do you believe her or is she, maybe, touched?"

I shrugged. "I believe she had or has children, but what happened to them, I don't know."

He asked if she mentioned a ransom note or talked to the sheriff in Lakeview. I told him no on both accounts.

Pudge puffed his cheeks and blew out air. "Well, she wouldn't be the first Indian who didn't trust white man law. I know the sheriff down there. He can be a lazy sonofabitch, but a straight shooter when it counts. I'll give him a call since this happened in his jurisdiction."

"I know it did, but we found her on the refuge's boundary more in Harney than Lake County. She insists she was following her kids. They could still be here."

"Or anywhere else in the state by now," Pudge said. "I'll ask the college boy to put together missing person reports and send them to the Oregon State Police and every county sheriff's department in the state."

"What about the FBI?"

Pudge shook his head. "They won't get involved until there's proof the children have been taken across state lines. Why, do you have reason to believe they have?"

"There's no way of knowing."

"Well, that's the FBI's rule, not mine."

"No exceptions?"

The deputy rubbed his chin. "I suppose we could make a special request. It'll have to come from Bust'em." He meant Sheriff Buster Burton, an up and comer who won the top job thanks to a campaign flyer showing Pudge being wheeled away after he'd been shot breaking up a domestic dispute. The tagline read, "Vote Bust'em. He'll never be slow on the draw."

"Will he listen to you now that you've announced you're challenging him in the upcoming election?" I said.

"This isn't about Bust'em or me. It's about two little children.

And I got to warn you, odds are it won't have a happy ending if there's no hide nor hair of them and no one's asking for a ransom. The longer a child is gone, the surer it gets they're not gonna be found alive."

Loq stiffened. "And if they're not, then whoever snatched them won't be for long either."

Pudge sighed. "Let me do my job, okay? If I need your help, I'll ask."

Loq didn't answer, but I knew Pudge didn't expect one.

"I'll get the investigation wheels turning here and across the state," the deputy said. "I need to get more information from Mrs. Manybaskets. I also want to tell her that there's folks out there who could lend a hand. Social worker types. When I was on my way here, I saw a motorhome set up like a bloodmobile parked alongside the county health building. It has a sign on it that says Indian Services. I don't know what they offer, but seeing she's widowed and in need, it couldn't hurt for her to talk with them."

"I doubt she'll go on her own, but Loq or I could take her," I said.

"Fair enough. Now about this firebug. You sure what you saw was intentional?"

"No doubt about it. He was tossing lit bottles of fuel."

Pudge rubbed his jaw. "Can't say I have much experience with arsonists outside of the time a dress store owner got mad at a rival from Bend who'd opened a branch in Burns. One night he took a brick to the new store's front window and then shoved in a lit wad of newspaper soaked in kerosene. When I finally got him in the interrogation room, he broke down and said he was only trying to mess up his rival's picture window display of fancy dresses on sale. The entire building went up. Cost him five years in the state pen."

"Is he still behind bars?"

"No, he did his time and came on home about a year ago. His wife even took him back. He's been quiet as a hen's egg ever since. Walks with a stoop now from always hanging his head in shame."

"It could be more than storefront dummies that go up in smoke if the guy we spotted isn't stopped."

Pudge frowned. "I saw what fire does to a person up close and personal when we were clearing out those caves on Iwo Jima with the help of flamethrowers. It sure wasn't pretty." He swiveled in his chair. "I do know somebody who might know a thing or two. He's what you call an expert when it comes to anything and everything about fire."

"Who is he?"

"Colonel Marcus Aurelius Davies."

"I didn't know fire departments had ranks other than chiefs, captains, and lieutenants."

"The colonel's not with any fire department. He was with the US Army Airborne during World War Two. His parachute battalion was the 555th, better known as the Triple Nickles. For some reason, they didn't spell it the same way as a five-cent piece. The Triple Nickles didn't fight overseas. They fought the Japanese Imperial Army right here in Oregon."

"What are you talking about?"

"A piece of forgotten history. In November of '44, Tokyo started launching hydrogen balloons carrying fire bombs at us. Hundreds made their way across the Pacific and reached the mainland, mostly in the Pacific Northwest. Many still haven't been accounted for. Only people ever killed by Tojo and his boys on US of A continental soil lived not far from where we're sitting. Outside of Bly."

"I've driven through that town plenty of times on my way back and forth to the refuges in Klamath County, but I never heard about that. What happened?"

"Tell you what. Let me concentrate on the missing kids. In the meantime, go talk to Colonel Davies about fires and catching arsonists. He can tell you about Bly while he's at it. He's got a place up on Riddle Mountain. You know where that is?"

"East of Diamond Craters."

"That's right. Take Lava Bed Road and then hang a left on a rough-and-ready track that winds up the side of the mountain. You can't miss the colonel's place. It's a stone tower and there's not a tree for miles. He doesn't like wood of any sort. When you meet him, you'll see why."

"I'll say hello to him for you."

"Okay, son, but whatever you do, don't stare at him. Makes him skittish."

4

November brought out a pot of stew, platter of roasted ears of corn, and a basket of buttermilk biscuits for lunch. The old healer sat down at the table with Pudge, Loq, and me while we waited for Wanda Manybaskets and Gemma. When they finally joined us, the Washoe woman looked refreshed. She'd bathed and put on a borrowed blouse and skirt. Her hair was pinned back with one of Gemma's pretty Paiute glass bead barrettes. It helped mask the handful she'd cut off.

Gemma introduced her father. "Pudge is the best lawman there is," she said. "He'll help you find your children."

"I hope so," Wanda said softly.

"Sit," November said. "The food will not eat itself."

We passed around the pot, platter, and basket. Loq filled his plate until it resembled the peak of Jackass Mountain. Wanda only took a biscuit. Pudge asked her questions while we ate. She answered plainly, but didn't provide any more details than what she'd already told Loq and me.

"Do you have a photograph of your youngsters I can borrow?" Pudge said. "I can send it by facsimile to the main office in Burns and it would help out on the missing person reports."

She shook her head and touched her heart. "I keep a picture of my babies here."

"Well, I still need their names and descriptions so law enforcement can be on the lookout for them."

"My daughter's name is *Dawgakákitgiš*. Calm Water. I call her Daisy. She is gentle and joyful with a shy smile. My son's name is *Dahá aš*. Rainstorm. I call him Danny. He is noisy and impish."

"That's not as good as a photo, but I suppose it's better than nothing," Pudge said. "I'll get the word out."

November never took her eyes off the young woman. The flinty Paiute elder finally said, "Who are your people?"

"I am Washoe."

"Yes, I heard you are *Washeshu*," November said. "But who is your family and how did it come by its English name?"

"From my great-aunt, *Dats'ai lo lee*. She passed into the spirit world many years ago."

November's eyebrows rose, a rare show of reaction from the old healer. "You are related to Young Willow, the basket maker?"

"She is family. Washoe do not follow only the father's line. Nor are we like Paiute who follow the mother's line. Everyone in the community is family."

"What are your children's last name?"

"It is also Manybaskets. It is a good name and honors a great Washoe leader."

"And your husband, what was his name?" Pudge said.

"Tom Piñon." Wanda turned backed to November. "Did you ever meet my great-aunt?"

"When I was a young girl. My mother had cousins who lived at Pyramid Lake and we went to visit them. It was a long journey. *Dats'ai lo lee* was there to teach weaving to *Numu*. Hers was a visit of peace."

The old woman stared off as if seeing the scene from long ago. "*Numu* and *Washeshu* were not always friends. We even fought battles long ago. *Washeshu* say they were living in the brown world before us and that is why they speak a language that is all their own."

"Do you speak some of their language?" Gemma asked.

"I know a few words and some of their ways from the time I met *Dats'ai lo lee*. Her people are known for their baskets, but Young Willow was the best weaver of all. People came from far away to buy hers. Her fingers were so nimble, it was like watching a thousand grasshoppers spring from a field at once."

November picked up the basket that held buttermilk biscuits. It had a pattern of black triangles woven into it. "I made this basket. I have been making baskets all my long life, but I will never make one as beautiful as Young Willow. She could see the story she was weaving as she wove it. She sang a song to help her remember the pattern, a different song for each pattern, each story."

A smile joined the furrows in her face. "She was a very large woman to have such nimble fingers. I had never seen a bigger woman. Some say her name translated to Big Hips, not Young Willow." She turned her gaze on Wanda. "You do not have big hips like your great-aunt. You are slender, like the strips of willow she used for weaving. Perhaps she wove you."

The young Washoe woman dipped her head. "I am honored you think so."

November's gaze turned into a blank stare. After a few moments, she said, "I see you. I see you among the flames. You are standing beside the water. You are calling for your babies. You are always calling for them."

Wanda raised her chin. "You are wise, old one," she said, her voice no longer soft.

"Hm," November said, and then looked back at her basket of biscuits. "Where did you live before you came to our land?"

"The Reno-Sparks Indian Colony."

"*Numu* and *Newe*—the Shoshone—also live there with *Washeshu*. My husband, Shoots While Running, was *Newe*. He is in the spirit world now, along with my daughter, Breathes Like Gentle Wind. But you are not from Reno," November said. "You speak as a lake person like Young Willow spoke. She called her home *Dá' ah*, what white men call Tahoe." Her eyes searched Wanda's face. "You named your babies in honor of water."

"Yes, I was born at the edge of *Dá' ah*, but we had to move when I was very young so my parents could find work." Wanda brushed her cheek with her fingertips as if it still had soot on it. "My mother never learned how to make baskets like *Dats'ai lo lee* because she was always working. She took in laundry and cleaned hotel rooms. My father could not keep a job. If anything went wrong at work, the boss would blame him and fire him. We lived in fear and shame."

"Hm," November said and began rocking as if her chair had curved rails attached to their legs. "Hm," she said again. "Were your children born on the shores of *Dá' ah* also?" Wanda said yes. "And will you go back to *Dá' ah* now that your husband has made the journey to the spirit world?"

The yellow, blue, and black glass beads in the barrette Gemma had lent Wanda danced as the Washoe woman shook her head. "You know I cannot until I find my babies."

November closed her eyes and rocked some more. Her gnarled fingers moved as if she were weaving a basket. "I am *Tsua'a Numudooa Nubabe*, Girl Born in Snow. I am a healer and an elder of my people, the *Wadadökadö*, wada root and grass-seed eaters." Her eyes opened and she bowed. "I welcome you, honored grandniece of *Dats'ai lo lee*. Pudge Warbler will look for your babies because he is a great lawman while you stay here

with me so that I can look after you. Nick Drake is a soldier who
won much honor fighting many battles and tracking the enemy
in the war in the green world. He will look for your babies also.
These men will not rest until they find them."

The old woman pointed her chin at Loq. "Him, I do not
know much about him except that he is *Maklak* and *Maklak* are
very stubborn people. They show no fear because they have
none. *Numu* say *Mu naa'a*, Wolf, our Great Creator, took *Maklak's*
fear from them to give to Cottontail, *Taboo'oo*, so that Cottontail
would always know to run away from Fox, *Wane'e*." November
paused. "It remains to be seen if this *Maklak* will make a difference finding your babies for you."

Wanda got up and walked over to November. Loq glanced at
me and muttered, "What did I tell you."

The young Washoe woman put her hand on the old healer's
shoulder, bent down and whispered into her ear for a while.
None of us could hear her words, but November nodded and
finally said, "Yes, *lebík'iyi*. I can talk to *we muhu*."

Pudge left for Burns right after lunch to make sure the missing
person reports were going out and to brief Sheriff Burton and
the other deputies. I backed the flat trailer carrying the empty
water tank alongside the stable and unhitched it. When I was
finished, I joined Loq, who was standing next to the corral. I
clicked the inside of my cheeks. A buckskin stallion trotted over.
A sorrel mare followed. I scratched the buckskin between his
ears. "Attaboy. Attaboy."

Wovoka pawed the ground and snorted. His original owner,
a horse breeder named Lyle Rides Alone, named him that in
honor of a famous Paiute holy man who'd founded the Ghost
Dance religion. The sorrel mare drew closer and shouldered

Wovoka aside so she could get a pat too. She whinnied content-
edly when I stroked her muzzle. Lyle Rides Alone had named
her Sarah in honor of the great Paiute leader, Sarah
Winnemucca. Now, the pair of cutting horses belonged to
Gemma, but I'd learned how to ride on Wovoka and treated him
as my own.

"We need to divide up the work if we're going to look for
missing kids and a firebug at the same time," I said.

"What about what the deputy told me?" Loq said.

"And what about the NVA regulars who were dug in with
heavy artillery?"

Loq grunted. "All right, I'll backtrack Wanda, starting where
we found her, and then her camp at Chewaucan, the ranch her
husband Tom Piñon worked at, and all the way to the hospital
where he died. I'll find out if anybody knows anything about
Daisy and Danny Manybaskets."

"Do you plan on talking with the Lake County sheriff too?"

"Someone has to."

"Then watch your step. He's likely to be protective of his
turf."

"I'll keep it in mind, but I need to check out everything to see
if anything tells a story that we haven't heard."

"You say that like you don't buy Wanda's story completely. Is
it because she doesn't remember details or because of the way
November reacted to her?"

The *Maklak* shrugged. "I don't know what to make of
November, but we need to find out what happened in Lake
County with her husband getting killed and everything that
followed. You were in country as long as me. You know how it is.
Things get foggy in war whenever there's killing going on. The
same is true out of war. Maybe somebody's not as foggy as
Wanda."

"While you're doing that, I'll go have a talk with that colonel

Pudge mentioned, see what he knows about arsonists. Do you want a ride back to your rig?"

Whenever Loq traveled to No Mountain from his home in Klamath County, he made camp not far from the old lineman's shack and parked his government-issued vehicle there. Loq never slept indoors. He told me he didn't use a tent when he was in Vietnam, not wanting even a layer of canvas to delay him a second from hearing and responding to enemy soldiers sneaking up. The first night after he'd ridden the Freedom Bird home, he'd tried to sleep in his mother's house in Chiloquin, but the walls and roof closed in on him. He moved into the woods and lived like his namesakes until one spring morning when they woke up from hibernation and he did too and joined the Fish and Wildlife Service.

"I'll walk," he said. "Helps me think."

"We need to stay in touch."

"The range of the radios in our pickups isn't very good."

"Payphones work too. Take some dimes with you."

"We could use smoke signals if you knew how to read them."

His face didn't betray a grin, but I returned one anyway. "See, I know when you're joking."

Loq started walking. He didn't say goodbye or see you later or anything like that. He never did. I went back to the ranch house to tell Gemma I was leaving. She beat me to it. She was coming out the front door carrying a small overnight bag.

"Walk me to my plane," she said.

Gemma had taken up flying so she could reach sick and injured livestock on the far-flung ranches scattered across Harney County more quickly. Earlier that summer, her father and I borrowed an earthmover from the highway department to turn a field behind their ranch house into a dirt strip. It saved her from having to drive to and from the airport in Burns.

"Horse, cow, or sheep?" I said. "Caught in barbed wire, bloat from eating clover, or a case of blackleg?"

Gemma nudged me with her hip. "Maybe I have taught you something, after all. A herd of calves have come down with shipping fever."

"What's that?"

"It's another name for bovine respiratory disease. Ranchers call it shipping fever because calves often get it when they get stressed being loaded into a stock trailer. I'll bet you anything the stress is coming from all the fires."

"Four-leggeds aren't the only ones who are on edge because of them," I said.

"Guess what? I've been drafted as a fire lookout by the state Emergency Services. If I see a wildfire getting close to a ranch house while I'm making my rounds, I'm to radio it in and then land and alert the owner to evacuate."

"I haven't met a rancher yet who'd abandon their house or stock unless they were already in flames."

"Ranchers work hard for everything they have, but all I can do is tell them what I see."

"What did you make of November at lunch?" I said.

"What do you mean?"

"She was giving Wanda the third-degree and then changed her tune so quickly and started acting, I don't know, deferential to her."

"You know November. She lives with one foot still in the old ways. Sometimes she puts both feet back in."

"What were those words she said at the end, *lebík'iyi* and *we muhu*?"

"I've never heard them before. They're not *Numu*. They must be Washoe terms of endearment, like honored guest or granddaughter. Why don't you ask her?"

"It's no big deal. I was curious, is all."

We reached the airstrip. Gemma's single-engine plane was tied down and its wheels were blocked. I helped her remove the canvas tarp that covered the windshield.

"Loq and I saw someone throwing Molotov cocktails west of Jackass Mountain when we were driving here with Wanda," I said.

Gemma stopped rolling the tarp. "Only a sick person would do that with everything that's going on. Did you report it?"

"I told your father. He gave me the name of an Army colonel who's a fire expert. I'm on my way to talk to him."

Gemma conducted a visual of her plane and then opened the pilot's door. She got behind the stick and starting going through a check-off. I slid her overnight bag behind the seat.

"I can fly by Jackass Mountain and take a look for your arsonist. It's on my way," she said.

"Way to where?"

The horse doctor put on gold wire-rimmed aviator sunglasses. "Oh, didn't I say? The Rocking H."

The ranch was the largest in Harney County and had been founded a century prior by a family who'd adopted the name of the county as their own. The owner was Gemma's ex-husband. She'd lived on the ranch the six months they were married.

"No, you didn't say," I said.

She grinned. "I know I didn't. I wanted to see how you'd react. You know, if you'd get jealous."

"And why would I do that? I've met Blaine Harney. He's a good man."

"Yes, but that was before you and I became an item."

"An item? Is that what we are? And here I thought all we were doing was spending the night together now and then."

Gemma gawped. "Are you serious?" And then she started laughing. "You got me, hotshot."

It was my turn to lean into a vehicle and plant a kiss. "Fly safe."

"I will. I'll come over when I get back tomorrow or the next day and we can, well, be an item." Though I couldn't see them behind the aviator glasses, I knew her eyes were sparkling.

I shut the cockpit door for her, removed the wheel blocks, and then stepped back from the airstrip. With the engine warmed and prop spinning, Gemma let off the brakes, turned into the wind, and took off. I watched as the little plane climbed. Soon it was lost in a sky turned hellscape from the fires scorching the earth below.

5

Lava Bed Road wound around sunken craters and tongues of black lava that had been spewed from the vents of an ancient volcano. Mirage-like heat waves the color of firelight danced above them. The sun wore a halo as it burned a hole through the smoky haze, but there was nothing angelic about its searing rays.

Pudge was right about the paucity of trees when I turned onto the dirt track that switchbacked up Riddle Mountain. Nothing grew taller than the wheels of my pickup as it bucked over potholes and rocks. I used the shimmer cast by the spinning blades of a windmill atop a distant ridge as a guidepost. It was the only thing for miles that spoke of human habitation.

By the time a structure came into view, I was trying to raise saliva to quench a thirst brought on more by imagination than deprivation. The main building resembled a fire lookout. The walls were made of cut slabs of pale limestone. It was perched on a raised foundation and surrounded by a veranda that provided a canopy of shade as well as a 360-degree view.

An adjoining structure about half the size of a normal barn also sported walls made of stacked stone capped by a sheet-metal roof. It had no windows, only vents below the eaves. I guessed its floor was rock and I imagined the interior was dark and cool, a welcome refuge from the punishing sun for any animal lucky enough to be granted entry or whatever else might be stored inside. A beige International Harvester Travelall was parked beneath another metal roof held up at the corners by steel poles that matched the material of the derrick that supported the windmill. A sheet of cardboard had been placed over the windshield and was pinned in place by the wiper blades.

A man was sitting in a rocking chair to the right of the front door of the main building, but the veranda kept his features in shadow. I didn't venture past my pickup when I got out. I hailed him and told him who I was. "Deputy Warbler said I should come talk to you, Colonel. It's about the fires."

"What else would it be about." The tenor in his voice told me he was used to giving orders to men who never questioned, only obeyed.

"Do you mind if I join you, sir?"

"What did Pudge tell you about me?"

The question held me in my tracks. "He said you served with distinction with the 555th, sir."

"That all?"

"He said when you were with the Triple Nickles, you and your men battled the Japanese here at home after they launched balloons carrying firebombs that killed some people near Bly." That was met with a silence as stony as the house's walls. I gave it a ten-count. "I saw somebody throwing firebombs west of Jackass Mountain. There's an arsonist on the loose and the deputy and I need your help so we can stop him."

The sound of Colonel Davies uh-huhing to himself carried from the veranda. "Then, come on up and tell me about it. I expect you're thirsty. I have a pitcher of lemonade. It's plenty cold."

I climbed the steep steps to the veranda. When I got beneath the shading roof, my eyes adjusted to the change in light. Colonel Marcus Aurelius Davies was an older black man with steel gray hair that was missing in spots. The patches of exposed scalp were rubbery with burn scars. His face and hands were similarly marred.

I realized I was staring and quickly averted my gaze. "It's an honor to meet you, sir."

He uh-huhed again. "You have a soldier's bearing about you, except for that haircut, or lack of one."

"Yes, sir. I was a sergeant with the First Cav in Vietnam."

"A long reconnaissance patrol scout, uh-huh. You did more than your share, I bet. Maybe you should be the one telling me war stories."

"I don't talk about the war, sir, but if I did, I doubt I'd have anything to tell you that you didn't experience yourself."

The colonel thought on that some before saying, "Go on, Sergeant, sit down. Help yourself to the lemonade."

He waved at the pitcher set on a table between his chair and another. The thumb and forefinger on his right hand were stubs and the swirly flesh looked as if it had melted and then hardened again. It reminded me of the lava down the road. I sat and poured myself a glass, wondering if he'd been expecting someone all along, having set out a second glass and chair.

"Have you lived here long?" I asked as I took in the view. It included most of Harney Basin.

"I built this place ten years ago."

"With your permission, Colonel, I'd venture to say you're not from Oregon. You don't sound like it."

"Mississippi, a little town on the Chickasawhay River called Quitman, but no one from there ever had quit in them."

"What made you want to settle this far from home?"

"Saw the wide-open spaces when I was with the Triple Nickles and promised myself I'd move here after I retired from active duty. The high desert is a lot less woody than the bottom-land back home."

I asked him where he was last stationed.

"I led jumps into Korea with the 187th Airborne. After that war ended, I was assigned to Fort Benning, Georgia, to train a new crop of airborne infantrymen. Truth be told, I mostly rode a desk. Didn't like that at all. Not one bit."

"My father was stationed there for a little while too," I said. "He was career military. We lived in base housing."

"You don't say? That was my second stint there. The first was in '43 when they transferred a group of us to train as airborne infantry."

"I'd never heard about the balloon bombs until Deputy Warbler told me."

"Not many people have. That's because the government kept it hush-hush to keep the public from panicking over the home-land being under attack. When the war was over and the news got out, well, people moved on. Most people, not all." He uh-huhed again. "They put up a monument where those folks were killed. I lay flowers there on the anniversary, May 5, 1945. Haven't missed a year yet."

"Outside of Bly."

"That's right. In the forest, about ten miles away."

"What happened?"

The ice cubes clinked against a tall glass as Colonel Davies sipped his lemonade. "There was a young preacher name of Archie Mitchell. One morning, he and his pregnant wife Elsie took five Sunday School students on a picnic. When they got to a nice sunny spot along Leonard Creek, Elsie and the children got out of the car while Reverend Mitchell parked it. She called to him they'd found something strange. He looked over and saw one of the children reaching for it. Before he could shout don't touch it, ka-boom! Killed Elsie and the five kids on the spot. Trees still bear scars from the shrapnel."

He took another sip of lemonade before continuing. "A couple of years later, Reverend Mitchell married the older sister of two of the children who were killed that day. The couple went to Vietnam as missionaries and worked in a leper colony there. One night in 1962, a band of Viet Cong invaded the colony and marched the preacher off at gunpoint, probably to have him treat their own sick and wounded. He's never been seen since."

The story settled over me like the pall of smoke cloaking the desert. "Pudge said as many as a thousand of the balloons made it across the Pacific. Is that what you and the Triple Nickles were doing, a search and destroy mission?"

The colonel didn't answer right away. "Did you serve with any Negroes in your war, Sergeant?"

I said I had. When my squad was ambushed, leaving me the sole survivor, two of the soldiers who died that day were black. One was the squad's radio operator, DJ, and the other a sniper.

"World War Two was different," Colonel Davies said. "Soldiers were segregated. Seventeen of us from the 95th Infantry, the old Buffalo Soldiers unit, were sent to Fort Benning for training. The US War Department wanted an all-Negro paratrooper battalion, I suppose because how good the Red Tails were working out. You know, the Tuskegee airmen. I was one of the officers, a first lieutenant. By the end of '44, our battalion was fully trained and ready to ship out."

He frowned. "But the War Department had different ideas. We waited for months for our orders to come through. Some thought it was racial politics, others said it was because we didn't have enough personnel to make up a full battalion. All I knew was the war was going to pass us by and all we wanted to do was fight for our country."

I tried not to look directly at him again, but out of the corner of my eye I could see his mouth had puckered. It tugged at one of the thicker scars that ran along his jawline. I couldn't decide if it made him look mad or sad.

"Finally, in May of '45, our orders came through. It was all top secret. Operation Firefly. We shipped out thinking we were going to invade Tokyo, but instead we landed in Pendleton, Oregon. That's when we found out what our mission was. The Forest Service gave us additional training, handed each of us a leather football helmet with a wire mask on it, and a coil of let-down rope."

"You had to jump into forests where the balloons had come down like the one near Bly," I said.

Colonel Davies uh-huhed. "That was our mission and we found some too. We became the nation's first military smoke-jumper battalion. We responded to whatever kind of forest fire there was, whether it was started by a fugo or not. Over thirty fires in the year we were active. We made twelve-hundred jumps and only lost one man. That doesn't mean some of us didn't break bones or get burnt. Some got broken and burnt pretty bad."

"There's a lot of forestland in the west. How were you able to find the balloons?"

"Needles in a haystack, Sergeant, that's what it was. Lots and lots of haystacks and needles that would do more than prick you if you found one."

I glanced around to avoid looking directly at the fire-scarred colonel. The stone walls of the building, the metal roofs, and the rocky perimeter denuded of all vegetation told me fire was an enemy that he treated with respect.

"Deputy Warbler says you're an expert when it comes to fires and fighting them, that you keep in touch with the heads of fire-fighting teams throughout the west."

"I do. That steel derrick holding up my windmill does more than pump water from a well. It's an antenna for my shortwave. I monitor all the channels. I talk regularly to everyone, from Forest Service fire battalion commanders to rangers stationed in fire lookout towers like mine."

"Does your knowledge include insights into the sort of people who light fires on purpose?"

"Pyromaniacs, you mean. It does. I've studied up on them. Do you know where the word comes from? It's Greek. *Pyr* for 'fire' and *mania* for 'rage.'" The colonel let it sink in. "Pyromaniacs are motivated more by fear than rage. They're scared of fire. They're scared of themselves. They're scared of everything. It's fear that drives them to do what they do."

"What is it about fire that scares them?"

"Because it's a living, breathing entity, a monster bigger and hungrier than anything they imagine lives under their bed or in their head. Anybody who doesn't fear fire, hasn't seen what it can do. Hasn't heard it talk. Oh, it does, all right. Everything from a gentle whisper to a murderous scream. Those who don't fear it, haven't breathed its flames. Haven't felt its caress on their face and hands and arms as it lulls you into believing its warmth is the same as clinging to your mama's breast." He looked off into the distance. "Believe me, fire is not your mama. It's anything but."

I finished my lemonade. The ice cubes had all melted. "This person could do more harm to Harney County than the lightning-strike fires. He could burn up everything in it. Towns, cities, ranches, animals, and people too."

"Tell me what you saw."

I described the desolate scrubland where the arsonist was

driving. I told him it looked like he was following a diagram he'd drawn up with the fires set in measured distances apart.

Colonel Davies uh-huhed. "Sounds to me like he was training, the same as in boot camp or a war game."

"Training for what?"

"Battle, Sergeant. Battle."

"How do we stop him?"

"It's the same as war. You need to put your enemy in a position where his fear is greater than your own. Make his fear consume him the same as a fire would."

He put his glass down and pulled a chrome Zippo lighter from his pocket with his left hand. He flicked it and then held his burn-scarred right hand directly over the blue tip of the flame. Seconds passed and he didn't waver.

"You can't be afraid to fight fire with fire," Colonel Davies said. "The same is true with fighting a pyromaniac. You got to make your flame bigger and brighter than his. You got to let him know you won't put yours out until he's burnt to a crisp."

6

I thought about my experiences with deadly fires on the drive down Riddle Mountain. All were when I was a soldier in Vietnam. I'd called in napalm strikes, felt the searing heat from a fuel bomb that transformed the sky into flame, and was temporarily blinded by M34 phosphorus grenades I'd hurled in close quarters when our position was overrun at night. But what scared me more than fire those times was the thought of what would happen to my men without it.

Instead of going straight back to No Mountain, I detoured to Burns. The town had its lights turned on even though night wouldn't fall for another couple of hours. The sidewalks were empty as residents spared themselves from having to breathe smoke. I drove to the county public health building and spotted a white Winnebago with a trademark brown *W* and matching stripe running the length of the boxy motorhome. "Indian Services" was lettered on a canvas awning that stretched above the side door.

I parked behind it and knocked. A young woman wearing a dull blue jumper with a white apron opened the door and greeted me with a prim smile. Her hair was pulled back in a tight bun. She wore no makeup.

"Are you still open?" I asked.

"We are always open for those in need. Pardon us, but we have to keep the door closed because of the smoke. Please, come in." She beckoned me with pale blue eyes.

The interior was as austere as her clothing. A center aisle ended at a closed door. I assumed a bedroom was on the other side of it. A brown vinyl bench seat faced a matching vinyl dinette booth and kitchenette. A man wearing a black suit jacket over a white shirt but with no tie was sitting at a Formica-topped table. He had a wispy beard and longish hair that fell over his collar. A stack of manila folders was at his elbow. He looked up from a form he'd been filling out in blue ink.

"Nick Drake," I said. "I'm with Fish and Wildlife, but I'm here on behalf of a Washoe woman who was caught in a wildfire."

The woman gasped. "Oh, the poor dear."

"Did she suffer any injuries?" the man asked.

"She wasn't burned. And you are?"

"We're the Parkers," he said. "Cameron and Arabelle. Tell us more about the woman."

"She's originally from Nevada. Her name is Wanda Manybaskets. She and her husband were living near Lakeview. They have two children, twins."

Arabelle blurted, "Children! Were they caught in the fire too?"

"No."

"Praise the Lord," she said.

"And the husband?" Parker said.

"He died in an accident. Mrs. Manybaskets was alone when we found her. She was looking for her children. They're missing."

Arabelle gasped again. Her husband frowned before saying, "I assume you've contacted law enforcement."

"Yes. Harney County sheriff's department is transmitting missing person reports to the Oregon State Police and other county sheriff's departments."

"Hopefully, they'll locate the children," he said. "What are their names?"

"Daisy and Danny Manybaskets."

Parker pointed his pen. "And where's the mother now?"

"She's staying at a ranch belonging to a sheriff's deputy. I've been told you might be able to provide her some assistance. You know, access to state and federal programs set up to help people in her situation."

"You need to understand we're not a government agency," Parker said quickly. "We're completely independent. We're not an arm of the Bureau of Indian Affairs, nor are we associated with any law enforcement organization. I stress that because it's important for us to keep the trust of the people we serve."

"Then what do you do?"

"We act as a liaison between American Indian people and health and social service providers. We offer information. We've been at it for some time now and in doing so we've earned their trust which allows us to help them. We travel to communities where Indian people don't have established health clinics on or off their reservations or have any way to learn about programs that can help them."

Parker used the pen to push back a boyish lock of hair that had fallen across his forehead. "We conduct basic health screening right here—blood pressure tests and the like. My wife is a nurse's aide and I worked in public health while we were in the Peace Corps in South America. We also provide information on proper nutrition and the dangers of substance abuse. Depending on the assessment and on the patient's willingness, we make referrals to medical professionals. We also provide basic information about Social Security, Medicare, and unemployment benefits. We help people fill out all the forms."

I asked if their services included emotional counseling.

"To a limited degree," Parker replied. "We make basic assessments, and then depending on what we learn, either give informational handouts or make a referral to trained counselors."

"Mrs. Manybaskets needs more than a brochure," I said. "Her husband died and her children are missing. She appears to be in shock."

His eyes narrowed. "Are you saying she's clinically depressed, maybe even suicidal? American Indian people have one of the highest suicides rates in the country."

"She could use someone to talk to," I said.

"Is that a professional judgement or do you have personal experience with counseling?"

It wasn't the time nor the place—nor did I have any inclination—to talk about the months I'd spent with counselors working to come to terms with what happened in Vietnam and to kick a heroin addiction I'd picked up there.

"How much do you charge to make an assessment?" I said.

"No, no, you misunderstand. Our services are free. We're a charity."

"Like the Ford Foundation or Catholic Charities?"

"Ours is more modest than that. We're an outreach mission of a church in Spokane. New Faith Directions Community Ministry."

Arabelle Parker smiled. "We are blessed."

I asked if they'd still be there the next day. "I'd like to bring her by to see you."

"We're scheduled to be here for another—" Parker turned to his wife. "How long, dear?"

"Two more days before we go back to Spokane. We are at the

end of a two-month rotation through the Great Basin. We started in Idaho and went to Utah and then Nevada and now here."

"What's the woman's name again?" Parker asked.

"Wanda Manybaskets."

He jotted it down. "And you said she's originally from Nevada?"

"The Reno area."

"And where was the family living in Oregon?"

"Near Lakeview. You may have passed through it on your way here from Nevada."

Parker looked up from making a note. "Why don't you bring Mrs. Manybaskets by and we'll see what we can do. Now, if you'll excuse me, I have a mountain of paperwork to climb."

Arabelle escorted me to the sidewalk. She clutched my hand. "Please tell Mrs. Manybaskets I'll be praying for Daisy and Danny. Will you? Please?"

"I'll let her know."

As I walked to my rig, I wondered why she'd neglected to say she'd include Wanda in her prayers too.

When I got home to the old lineman's shack, I shut the door behind me and breathed in the lingering smell of smoke. It wasn't from the wildfires; it had been baked into the walls by the woodburning stove. The aroma was redolent with history and told a tale of a succession of working men who'd lived in the shack before me. They'd been watchmen for a now-defunct shorthaul railroad built to ferry timber to a mill near Burns. The stove had thawed their frozen hands after having to clear snowdrifts from the rails and kept their supper warm when they ran outside in midmeal to shoo cattle off the tracks.

The stove had always welcomed me home too, the first real one I'd had after three years of soldiering in Vietnam followed by six months in a locked ward trying to get over it. It provided more than warmth during a long winter's night after a cold day spent patrolling the wildlife refuges. The crackle from the quarter-rounds of burning pine and the light flickering from its load door left ajar were companions while eating alone or reading a book. More recently, I'd discovered another side to it. It cast a romantic glow on the nights Gemma and I would pull the mattress off the narrow bunk and snuggle next to the stove.

I watched the moon rise through the kitchen window as I cooked dinner. Its pale light was muddied by the smoke from wildfires. Ever since men first walked on its surface earlier that summer, the moon seemed to have grown much closer and the world it shined upon that much smaller. The thought was unsettling because a smaller world meant the war still raging in Vietnam had come that much closer to the high lonesome where I'd fled to find peace.

No stars were as close as the moon, and they were unable to burn through the smoke. I knew my Paiute neighbors would miss seeing them. The constellations told them stories that had been passed on through the generations to help explain the world they lived in and how to survive in a harsh land. With no stars and stories to guide them, the Paiute were in danger of becoming as lost as the children whose Indianness had been beaten out of them at schools like the one run by Brigadier General Richard Henry Pratt.

I placed my dinner plate on a rickety wooden table and sat down to eat. My dining companion wouldn't be the unlit stove or Gemma that night, but a book she'd given me. It had been published the previous year and was written by an author I'd never heard of, a fellow named Edward Abbey. The book was titled *Desert Solitaire*. The horse doctor assured me I'd relate to it.

It was composed of personal essays and a memoir of the years he spent as a park ranger in southeastern Utah. Abbey's words were direct and his opinions provocative. His descriptions of the plants and animals that inhabited a land not unlike the high desert of Harney County had me feeling the poke of cactus spines, seeing lizards scurrying across the pages, and marveling at red sandstone arches that magically appeared beside me as I read.

After dinner, I crawled into the narrow bunk and drifted off to sleep. My dreams soon turned from visions of a tranquil red-rock desert in Utah to red flames devouring the desert on the other side of my door. I woke and bolted outside. The wind was up and rattling the windows. I walked into the open, cupped my hands, and held them out.

I was soon holding ashes as big as the snowflakes that fell in winter.

7

At first light, or what passed for it, I loaded my Triumph 650cc motorcycle into the back of the pickup for safe-keeping and drove to Blackpowder Smith's. The dry goods store owner and barkeep had shadows under his eyes. Ashes clung to his white billy-goat beard as if he had been smoking a cigar.

"You look like you got about as much sleep as I did, which amounts for less than nothing," Blackpowder greeted me in a gravelly voice.

"The wind woke me," I said. "It's blowing this way."

His black cowboy hat with a rattlesnake-skin band bobbed. "I been burned down before. It was when I was half-growed. My family was living east of here in a town that don't exist no more. By the time the wildfire was done with it, there wasn't nothing left, not even a single drop of water in the bottom of the well."

"You're not resigned to losing your business here, are you?"

"Hell no. I'm the chief of No Mountain's volunteer fire department. I got more people willing to save the town than I got hooks and ladders."

"Sign me up," I said.

The old codger cackled. "I already did, young fella. Same as I did everyone else. We got a meeting this afternoon to go over battle plans. Don't be late."

"I won't. While I'm here, do you have some already-made coffee?"

"You know I do. Goes with running a tavern where sometimes you got a customer who refuses to sleep it off in the bunkroom I keep for them in the back. When that happens, I persuade them to have a couple of cups of Joe before they drive home. The sawed-off behind the bar helps with the persuading."

Blackpowder filled two brown enamel mugs from a percolator that could use some polish. He slid one across to me and added a healthy dollop of whisky to his.

"What I call a nooner only sooner," he said with a wink.

The coffee tasted as if it had been brewing since yesterday, maybe even longer. "You've lived here a long time and know everybody," I said.

"True as a cow chews cud. Who is it you want to know about?"

"I'm looking for answers to a couple of things. I'll start with the easy one first. Have you ever heard of someone who takes a particular interest in lighting fires?"

Blackpowder's bushy eyebrows rose. "You talking about arson-type fires, a pyro?"

I told him what Loq and I had seen near Jackass Mountain and my conversation with Colonel Davies.

"The only ones who spring to mind are a couple of kids who got in trouble lighting stuff, but most every kid plays with matches at one time or another. Part of growing up."

"Tell me about them."

His face scrunched. "The first one I'm thinking about was a kid name of Freddie. This was maybe ten years ago, so he wouldn't be a kid no more. Freddie Saunders. No make that

Sanderson. Or was it Sondheimer? Freddie Somethingorother, anyway. He lived on a ranch outside of town and rode a mule to school. He was scrawny for his age and wore hand-me-down bibs with patches. Got teased for being more of a hayseed than any of the other hayseeds. He was always in playground scuffles. One of them amounted to more than name calling and making the one you pinned cry uncle. I don't remember the particulars outside of Freddie picked up a rock and whaled on the bigger kid's skull. Teacher sent him home. That night the schoolhouse got splashed with gasoline and torched."

"Did they have proof Freddie did it?"

"Nothing for certain, though everyone suspected him because of the scuffle and him saying I'll show you to the teacher who sent him home. Thing of it is, he never came back to school after the fire."

"Does he still live around here?"

"His folks moved on right away. Where, I don't know. They were sharecropping a ranch, tending to the hayfields and a few head of cows and splitting the profits with the landowner, which couldn't've been much given the paltry profit margins on hay and beef."

"Even though it was a decade ago, the teacher should remember his last name," I said.

Blackpowder scratched his beard. "You got to remember No Mountain School only goes up to eighth grade. After that the kids got to go to Burns for high school. The student body is so small all the grades get mixed together. Teachers don't last but a couple of years or so before they're ready for something new. Might also be hard to find anyone who recollects him. He wasn't here long and weren't never voted Mr. Popularity neither."

"What about the second kid?"

"Now that's a horse of a different color. Everybody around could name Judd Hollister. This happened about five years ago.

Judd and his folks lived on a real nice spread. It had a year-round spring that kept their fields lush, their stock watered, and their pockets well lined. Judd was an only child. Some would call him a spoiled rich kid. The night of his high school graduation, the Hollister ranch house went up in flames. Judd managed to get out. His folks did not. Burned alive in their beds, at least that's what the insurance investigator found. He said they probably never woke up. Smoke inhalation."

"Did the investigator figure out how the fire started?"

"A combination of faulty wiring and propane leaking from the stove. The company paid off the claim."

"What makes you think the son had anything to do with it?"

"I didn't at the time. Despite Judd being a snot nose, people felt sorry for him becoming an orphan. They passed the hat and even brought him casseroles and pies."

The tavern owner took a sip of his fortified coffee. "But a lot of times in life actions speak louder than words. Judd cashed that big insurance check lickety-split, sold off the family's entire herd of prized Angus along with a dozen fine cutting horses. He hired a construction crew and built a new house. Looks like one of those Malibu beach houses the movie stars live in. Judd also dammed up the spring and built a swimming pool. Didn't help make him any friends with his downstream neighbors, except their daughters who he invited over for swim parties. I stopped selling him kegs of beer once I got wind of what was goin' on. Last year he bought himself a souped-up Ford Mustang fastback. The Shelby GT500 model."

"What's he do for work?"

Blackpowder polished off his coffee. "Not a lick. You may have run into him when you're out speeding down the back roads on your Steve McQueen motorcycle. He's got a reputation for doing the same in that Shelby Mustang. Maybe Judd's got demons he's trying to outrun too." He gave me a wink.

"I'm surprised Pudge didn't mention him or Freddie when I asked him if he had any experience with arsonists. He only talked about a dress store owner."

Blackpowder shrugged. "No surprise there. The first fire happened right after Gemma left for college in Corvallis and the second when she was still there goin' to vet school. This was before Pudge lost the election and became semi-retired. With Gemma gone, he'd buried himself alive being sheriff in Burns even more than he done after his wife died. Spent all his time at the office while November stayed at the ranch waiting for Gemma to come home. Pudge couldn't be bothered by kids playing with matches. No siree Bob. He needed what comes with chasing killers and bank robbers to keep himself busy. No lawman in all of Oregon ever caught more bad guys than Pudge, and he never let county lines stop him if he was in pursuit. He also never let anybody who drew on him get away with it neither. There's more than a few on the wrong side of the sage-brush who tried."

The old codger put his mug in the sink. "What's the second thing you need answers to?"

"Kidnappers." I gave him the rundown on Wanda Many-baskets.

"Now I understand why you left that to last. That is a harder one to answer, and much sadder too. I don't know if I can be much help there. I've heard stories over the years about a Paiute kid or two who've gone missing, but it's often wrapped up in a husband and wife who stopped seeing eye to eye and one packs up the tots and moves away without leaving a forwarding address. Or there's the older kid who watches too much TV and starts thinking the grass is greener in the big city and goes gets himself lost in Portland." He stroked his beard. "What did November have to say?"

"Not a whole lot. She told Wanda Manybaskets that Pudge

and I would find her kids for her, but as to where we should start looking, she didn't say."

"Well, she's the expert on all things Indian. Tell you what, I'll put the word out on my grapevine. Anybody and everybody from these parts comes in here for gossip, groceries, and grog. Maybe somebody heard something. I'll do the same with any news about a pyro."

I pushed my empty coffee mug toward him. "I'm on my way to the Warbler ranch to collect Wanda Manybaskets and take her to talk to some social worker folks. I'll be back for the volunteer fire department meeting."

"I'm counting on it. And if you see Pudge, tell him to get his sorry behind back down here too. He don't know it yet, but I already volunteered him."

A cackle followed me out Blackpowder's front door.

November was sitting on the front porch making a basket. Its shape resembled a hot-air balloon, and I pictured the drooping bottom as a gondola laden with fuel bombs.

"That's an unusual-looking basket. What's it used for?" I asked.

"*Kida*, that means to carry water," she said as her gnarled fingers wrapped and twisted thin, horizontal strips of willow around vertical willow strips. More strips of willow and sumac were heaped in a pile at her feet along with plant fibers with horsehair loops that had been twisted into what looked like a handle that could be attached to the completed basket.

"Did Wanda Manybaskets' great-aunt teach you how to make it?"

November tsked. "Not *Dats'ai lo lee*, but my mother. *Numu* have been making this basket ever since we came into the brown world. How else are we to carry *paa'a* with us as we hunt for food? My mother taught me and her mother taught her and hers before her. Perhaps I will teach Gemma if she would sit down long enough to learn."

"She's not back yet?"

"No. As a little girl, she was like *Sonoe'e*, Hummingbird, always moving, going from flower to flower, but now with her airplane she is becoming more like *Kwe'na'a*, Eagle. She flies higher, farther, and stays away longer." The old healer eyed me. "She needs a nest of her own to settle down in and roost."

I let that slide. "What will you do with the *kida* when you finish making it?"

"I will give it to the rainmaker to carry *paa'a* in it to bring the rain. *Nuwuddu* and *Numu* both need the fires to stop so they can build nests and life can continue in the brown world."

"Who's the rainmaker?"

"You will see."

"And when is he getting here?"

"When it is time."

"If you have a way of reaching him, reach now. The fires are growing bigger to the south and they said on the radio this morning that a forest fire was spotted near King Mountain north of Burns. We're half surrounded."

November tsked. "Can you not see I am weaving as fast as my old fingers can twist the willows? Wanda Manybaskets is inside. That is why you are here. Go help her and leave me to my weaving."

The young Washoe woman was sitting in the living room. She was staring into space, her eyes unblinking, her lips barely parted as her breath came and went.

"Good morning," I said.

She jumped up with a start. "My babies! Have you found them?"

"Not yet, but we're searching. I know it's hard, but you have to be patient."

"I can hear them." She put her palm against her chest. "They are telling me I need to find them soon or they will be lost forever."

"Trust us, we're doing what we can. It's why I'm here. I want to take you to Burns to speak with some people who might be able to help."

"Have they seen my babies?"

"No, but they can help you in other ways. Will you come with me?"

"Maybe I will see Daisy and Danny on the way."

"It's possible," I said, hearing the disbelief in my own voice.

8

Wanda Manybaskets sat as close as she could to the pickup's door and kept her forehead pressed against the glass. She started humming and then singing softly. I didn't recognize the words.

"Is that a Washoe song?" I asked when she finished.

"My mother sang it to me when I was little to get me to fall asleep and I sing it to my babies. I hope they hear it and tell me where they are."

"A lullaby. What do the words mean in English?"

Wanda didn't turn to face me, but kept her eyes trained on the passing landscape. "Water carries the boat. Water carries the baby. Water carries the boat. Water carries the baby. Across the big lake. Toward the big mountain. Swirling, swirling. The baby and boat swirl. Across the big lake. Toward the big mountain. Swirling, swirling."

"That's beautiful," I said.

"So is our great lake. *Dá' ah* is the center of our world and the mountains that guard it are sacred."

Wanda started singing the lullaby again. I found myself

humming along. Water carries the boat. Water carries the baby. Swirling, swirling, across the big lake, toward the big mountain.

"Tell me about your children," I said.

"They are the light of my life, for they are the past, present, and future. They connect me to my yesterdays, brighten today, and promise tomorrow. Washoe families include blood relatives, spirit relatives, and all people in the community where we live. That way everyone is connected to a child no matter who gave birth to him or her."

"And what kind of man was your husband?"

"How do you mean?"

"Was he a hard worker, a good father, a good husband?"

Wanda kept her forehead pressed to the glass. "Tom Piñon was all of those things despite always struggling for a decent job and respect. Things never came easy for him. He had courage even though some might think he did not. He had never ridden a horse before, but was not afraid to try when he took the job at the ranch."

"Was the man who told him about the job a friend?"

"No, he was a gambler at the casino. He spilled a drink while playing cards and Tom Piñon was sent to clean it up. The man tried to give him a gambling chip worth twenty dollars as a tip, but my husband would not take it. The man found him later and asked why. He told him he was only doing his job. The man asked if he liked being a janitor and my husband said he always wanted to be a rancher. That is when the man told him about the ranch near Chewaucan looking for hands."

"Did the man own the ranch?"

"I am not sure."

The Winnebago was parked in the same spot. I pulled in behind it. Arabelle Parker answered the door when I knocked. She rushed out and grasped the Washoe woman's hands.

"You must be Wanda Manybaskets. Do not be frightened.

We are here to help you." Arabelle's voice turned sing-song, as if she were speaking to a child. "Please, come in. Would you like some water? Juice, perhaps? I have cookies. They are yummy."

Cameron Parker was still sitting in the brown vinyl booth with stacks of forms and manila reports next to him. It looked like he hadn't moved all night.

"Ranger Drake has brought Mrs. Manybaskets to see us," Arabelle said, still using the sing-song voice.

Parker gestured with his pen. "Please, take a seat and make yourself comfortable." He turned to me. "I'm sure you have some errands you'd like to run while we speak with Mrs. Many-baskets."

"That's okay. I'll stay here and keep her company."

Parker maintained a level gaze. "Actually, it would be better if you didn't. A private conversation can be more fruitful."

I didn't want to leave her alone, but I knew from my own experience with counseling he had a point. I told Wanda I'd wait outside.

I left my rig where it was and trotted three blocks to the sheriff's office to get an update on the missing children investigation. Pudge Warbler wasn't at his desk. I walked down the hall and found Orville Nelson in the file room that had doubled as his office ever since he'd started as an intern. The college boy, as Pudge called him, wore the buttoned-down white shirt and narrow black-tie uniform of an FBI agent because he'd always hoped to become one. He'd been interning at the sheriff's office while awaiting admission to Quantico when a cattle rustler shot him in the back last spring. It left him paralyzed from the waist down.

On Pudge's insistence, the sheriff's department hired Orville full time. The file room had been reconfigured to accommodate his wheelchair. The four-drawer metal file cabinets had been relocated. The pyramid of Shasta cola cans that once adorned his desk had been relegated to a bookshelf. In its place stood a clunky device that looked like a cross between an electric typewriter and an adding machine the size of an old-fashioned cash register. I asked him what it was.

While his boyish face showed the pallor of someone who'd spent weeks in a hospital followed by months in a physical rehabilitation facility, Orville Nelson's eyes still shined with gee-whiz excitement.

"It is a Hewlett-Packard 9100A programmable scientific calculator," he explained. "It has a built-in logic circuit, CRT readout, and magnetic card storage. There are multiple calculating functions, including trigonometric, logarithmic, and exponential. You would not believe how much it cost. The Cattlemen's Association bought it for me. It was extremely generous of them."

"You helped solve a big problem for them. It was the least they could do. What do you use it for?"

"Among my new duties are keeping track of the department's budget and expenses, along with time sheets for the sheriff and his deputies. The 9100A makes that a snap and leaves me plenty of extra time. I have programmed it to help make calculations for the databases I am creating."

I asked him what those were.

"I am compiling the county's crime statistics for sorting and searching. Another database I started is for known offenders. It has categories for allegations, convictions, sentences, and parole dates. I am still working on that one. Once I complete them, I will send them to the FBI so they can input them into their mainframe computer system. Who knows? Maybe someone at the bureau will take notice of me in a new way and make an exception for this." Orville patted the arm of his wheelchair.

He glanced around as if someone could be hiding in the tiny room. "Another thing I am working on—off the clock, mind you

—is a database of all the voters in the county. Not only have I inputted their addresses, but their voting records too. I am a Pudge Warbler for Sheriff man. Once I identify his likely supporters along with the issues they are most concerned about, I can develop targeted messages for his mailers, speeches, and billboards. The 9100A calculated that if I can increase voter turnout by two point one percent, Deputy Warbler will win his old job back."

"Your secret is safe with me," I said.

"The 9100A is only the beginning. I read an article by the engineer who developed the prototype for Hewlett-Packard. He is already building a new and improved model. I sent him a letter with my ideas on how to make it more useful for law enforcement work. He wrote right back. He is calling his new invention a desktop computer and asked me to be what he refers to as a beta tester." Orville beamed. "I cannot wait to beta test the heck out of it."

"Until you do, can you tell me if there's anything new on the missing Manybaskets children, Daisy and Danny?"

Orville's enthusiasm dimmed. "I sent out the missing person reports and have created a database for responses, but so far, we have not fielded a single call."

"Pudge said he was going to ask Sheriff Burton to make a special request to the FBI to ask for their help."

"I am afraid that did not come to anything because there is no evidence they were taken into another state. The FBI's authority remains very limited on such cases. They were not even authorized to investigate kidnappings until the Lindbergh baby abduction in 1932."

"But these children are six years old."

"Age does not matter. The Lindbergh baby was only twenty months old. The FBI's policy might change some day, but until then, all they will do is monitor the situation and offer laboratory assistance if requested. As of now, there is nothing we can give them to analyze."

"That means we'll have to redouble our efforts to track the kids ourselves."

"I can help by searching my known-offenders database for child molesters and kidnappers. I am afraid it still has plenty of gaps because everything has to be entered by hand, but there could be something there."

"Does your database happen to include people who've been suspected, charged, or arrested for arson?"

"I would have to take a closer look since all the entries are by penal code and not common usage descriptive words. Why?"

"There's a firebug on the loose. I saw him in action west of Jackass Mountain."

"Did you get a physical description?"

"He was too far away to ID, but I spoke with Blackpowder Smith this morning and he remembers a couple of boys associated with suspicious fires. Both incidents took place years ago, but it's worth checking out. The fact that Harney County's population is so small and people are moving out, not in—not to mention everyone knows everyone—really narrows down likely suspects. I figure our best shot is to look at people with a history."

"That makes sense," Orville said. "Who are they?"

"One of the boys is named Judd Hollister." I told him what I knew about the fire that killed Judd's parents. "The other boy will be trickier to find info on. His first name is Freddie and the last name starts with S and could be Saunders or something like it. His family moved ten years ago right after a fire was set at the No Mountain school the day Freddie was suspended."

"One was in grade school ten years ago, the other in high school a few years later. That means the boys are about the same age." Orville patted his calculator. "I like a challenge. I will see what I can turn up."

"There's a third person too. I don't have his name, but he owned a dress store and went to prison for burning down a rival's store. I would've asked Pudge for it when I got here, but he's not at his desk."

"Sheriff Burton sent him to a ranch near Drewsey to serve a warrant."

"Must be for a big offense to have the senior deputy drive over there. What was the crime?"

"A missed court appearance for a speeding ticket." The FBI hopeful lowered his voice. "The sheriff has been doing that ever since Deputy Warbler told him he was going to run against him in the upcoming election."

"If he thinks that's going to tire Pudge out and make him drop out of the race, he's got another thing coming. Do me a favor and don't slack up on your voter database work. The county is depending on you."

"You can count on me."

"Thanks. I got to run. I dropped Wanda Manybaskets off at a mobile Indian Services office and don't want to leave her waiting."

"The Winnebago parked by the county health building? I saw it when Lucy drove me to work," Orville said.

"Who's Lucy?"

"Lucy Lorriaga. She is a physical therapist I met at the rehabilitation center. I told her I needed to find a new apartment because my old one had stairs and she said her mother had a ground-floor vacancy at the boarding house she owns. Did you know that most of the boarding houses in the Great Basin are owed by Basque women like Lucy's mom? They were built to house Basque sheepherders. Lucy lives there too."

"That's convenient," I said.

"It is. I am in line to get a car with hand controls, but the waiting list is very long. Lucy offered to give me a lift since it is on her way to work."

"She sounds nice. I take it you two have become close."

Orville's pallor suddenly reddened. "If you are inferring romantically, it is nothing of the sort. Ours is strictly a platonic relationship. That is a friendship based on Plato's theory about people rising above carnal attraction through levels of closeness to wisdom and true beauty to achieve closeness to the soul and truth."

"And here I thought Plato was Socrates's foxhole buddy during the Peloponnesian War."

"No. Socrates was Plato's teacher, and Plato was Aristotle's. The three of them were— Wait, you were joking, right?"

"I hope you and Lucy can teach each other some things too. I'll see you later."

As I headed down the hallway, Sheriff Burton stepped out of his office and intercepted me. His hair was freshly barbered and his mustache neatly trimmed. He was the only one in the department who paid to have his uniform dry cleaned.

"What are you doing here?" he said.

"Looking into missing children and arson. Didn't Deputy Warbler tell you about it or is he too busy writing parking tickets?"

Burton's mustache twitched. "I know about the Washoe woman. My staff originated the missing person reports and then I handed the investigation over to its rightful jurisdiction, Lake County. Since there's been no mention of the mother being contacted about a ransom, the sheriff there is treating it like a domestic dispute."

"Her kids went missing there, but we found her on the Harney County side of the line at Hart Mountain. She believes they may be here or at least passed through. That puts it square in your camp, Sheriff."

Burton's chin rose. "Don't tell me my business. Now what's this about arson?"

"Another ranger and I spotted someone throwing flammables out of a pickup. He started a number of brush fires. All this was in Harney too."

"Did you obtain any evidence? What about a description of the alleged perpetrator or a license plate of the vehicle?" When I shook my head to his questions, the sheriff issued a smug smile. "As I thought. Let me remind you that your authority starts and ends at the boundaries of the national wildlife refuges. Try and insert yourself into a sheriff's department investigation again and I'll charge you with interfering with an officer."

"I'll keep that in mind when it comes time to punch my ballot in November."

Burton scoffed. "As if I need your vote. You'll discover that the day of the election when I win in a landslide. That's also when you'll learn Deputy Warbler has been permanently relieved of duty."

The sheriff left me burning, but there were more important fires to tend to. I trotted back to the Winnebago.

"Perfect timing," Cameron Parker said as I entered. "Arabelle, would you please help Mrs. Manybaskets finish with the questionnaire while the ranger and I step outside?"

As soon as the motorhome's door closed behind us, I asked him what Wanda was filling out.

"It's a standard questionnaire to measure intelligence, cognitive dissonance, and emotional stability." Parker took a deep breath. "You were right to be concerned about Mrs. Manybaskets being in a state of emotional distress. I believe she's severely depressed. She's also exhibiting signs of being detached from reality. I can't even be certain that everything she believes to be true is real. That goes for her husband's death, her missing children, and, well, almost everything."

"But you're not a trained psychiatrist," I said.

"No, I'm not. But I do have experience with indigenous people who've suffered emotional trauma, both when I was in South America and here in the Great Basin." He handed me a form that had already been filled out. "This is my referral to a psychiatric clinic I work with. It specializes in American Indian patients. The chief psychiatrist is writing a medical text book on it. The clinic is based in Spokane and admits patients on a charity basis."

"Spokane, as in where your church is."

"Yes. It's how I know about the clinic."

"What's it called?"

"Bright Rivers Behavioral Treatment Center. They've pioneered progressive treatments that have achieved a notable rate of favorable outcomes."

I held up the form. "What am I supposed to do with this?"

"Nothing. I only wanted you to see it. I plan on calling the clinic to discuss Mrs. Manybaskets' case. If they were to agree to take her, I'll need to submit that form."

I glanced at it. The checkmark in the box next to the word "Suicidal" was bolder than the others. "If you think Wanda's in danger of taking her own life, why don't we walk her over to the county health clinic next door and have her evaluated immediately?"

"It's an option, but not a preferred one. No one there is a specialist like the psychiatrist at Bright Rivers. If the county diagnosed her as suicidal, they'd have no choice but to place her in an immediate seventy-two-hour psychiatric hold. That would entail physical and chemical restraints. If they still deemed her a risk to herself at the end of the hold period, they would have to transfer her to a state hospital. Once that occurred, it would take weeks, if not months, to have her released. It would cause irreparable damage to her psyche." He paused. "Is that something you want to risk?"

Parker didn't wait for an answer. He pushed back the lock of fallen hair with his pen. "The best course of action is for me to call Bright Rivers and urge them to see her. If they agree, we can work out transportation."

"And what do you suggest Wanda do in the meantime?"

"Return to the ranch with you, of course. Mrs. Manybaskets clearly trusts you and she spoke favorably of a Paiute woman there who's befriended her. Remaining at the ranch will cause less stress and make for an easier transition. Obviously, it'll be up to you to convince her that getting help at Bright Rivers is the right thing to do for herself and her family."

"But we don't know where her children are, or, as you said, if they even exist."

"That's true, but they're real to her and that can be used as strong motivation for her to agree to get help. I'll do everything in my power to impress upon Bright Rivers to make a speedy decision. If they agree, Mrs. Manybaskets could be in their care as early as the day after tomorrow."

"And if they won't admit her?"

"Then you'll have to take her to county health. You don't want to risk her taking her own life."

9

Wanda seemed as exhausted as she had when Loq and I found her. She slumped against the pickup's seat and stared straight ahead as I drove back to No Mountain. When I asked if she was feeling okay, she didn't respond. Thinking she may not have heard me, I was set to ask again, when she snapped, "Why did you take me to see those people?"

"I thought the Parkers might be able to help. Why, is there something they said you didn't understand?"

"I understood them. They think I am crazy. They do not believe me about my babies."

"Cameron told me he and his wife Arabelle are very concerned about your well-being. He believes the best thing he can do to help you is to have you talk with a doctor he knows."

"A doctor who treats crazy people. Do you think I am crazy?"

"I think you suffered something very traumatic. Your husband died. Daisy and Danny are missing. You nearly got burned up in a fire."

"How would you know how I feel?"

"I've been where you are," I said.

"You lost a loved one, your babies too?" she said mockingly.

"I lost men I loved whose lives I was responsible for. I saw children die because I got there too late to save them."

We drove in silence until she said, "I do not trust the Parkers."

"They seem friendly enough."

"So is *Mák'i* when she hides her rattle and fangs from *P'ušála*."

"I can guess the Washoe word for rattlesnake, but what's the other one mean?"

"Mouse."

It made me think of Aesop's fable again, but there was no way the mouse in her story was going to get the upper hand. "What makes you think that?"

"A mother always knows."

I'd often wondered if my mother really knew what war would do to me. She was a woman of quiet resolve and little formal education, never complaining every time my father announced he'd been reassigned and we'd have to move to yet another military base. As soon as we were unpacked, she'd sign up to work at the school cafeteria or volunteer for playground duty. One time at the base swimming pool when I started to founder, she jumped in with all her clothes on and push-pulled me to the side even though she didn't know how to swim. She never tried to talk me out of enlisting, nor did she tell me when I shipped out that she'd been diagnosed with leukemia. She didn't tell my father either. I got the news of her death toward the end of my first tour. The counselors at Walter Reed took lots of notes when they learned I'd re-upped for another tour instead of taking emergency leave to go home for the funeral.

"You could be wrong about the Parkers," I said.

Wanda made fangs with her index fingers and then shot them forward and jabbed her nails in my forearm.

"Ouch," I said, more surprised than hurt.

"See, *Mák'i* does not always rattle before she strikes. You cannot make me go to Spokane."

"I'm not making you do anything."

"Good, because I have already made up my mind I will not go. I cannot. I need to find my babies."

"What makes you think they're still in Oregon?"

"They told me."

"When they spoke to your heart."

"Why do you doubt me? Do you not listen to your own heart?"

"Maybe it's best if you don't worry about Spokane for now," I said. "Pudge, Loq, and I won't stop looking for your children. We can leave the clinic and the doctor there for another time."

We arrived at the Warbler's ranch. By the time we got out of the pickup, November had opened the front door and was waiting on the front porch.

"You look tired, *lebík'iyi*," she said. "Come inside. I will draw a bath for you. The water will soothe you."

The Washoe woman disappeared inside. November said, "Gemma called. A fire is growing close to the Rocking H Ranch. She is not sure if it can be saved, but she will not leave."

"What about the rainmaker you promised?" I said. "We need him now."

"The rainmaker will come. You will see."

"Don't let Wanda leave. I'll tell you why when I get back."

The old healer harrumphed. "You do not have anything to tell me that I have not already seen with my own eyes. Now go help Gemma, and go quickly."

10

Cattle were stampeding straight at me. They were using the dirt road and the shoulders of desert scrub on either side to flee the crackle of burning sagebrush and plumes of oily smoke. I braked to a stop, but didn't tap the horn. I'd driven on country roads filled with cow-calf pairs before and knew better than to spook them more than they were already spooked. The herd leader lowered her head and butted my front bumper. A couple more took on my fenders. The wave of bawling beef that followed started parting like a river meeting a big boulder. My pickup rocked from side to side as the cattle jostled past.

Hoots and hollers added counterpoint to the thunder of pounding hooves. A trio of cowboys—one on each side of the herd and one behind—was urging them on. The left rider's style and skill were as graceful as they were practiced. They were also very familiar. This was no cowboy, but a cowgirl. The swish of a ponytail beneath a flat-brimmed tan Stetson matched that of the bay mare's tail. Like the barrel racer she was, Gemma controlled the borrowed cutting horse effortlessly by leaning, reining, and calling, guiding her to make quick turns to head off any panicked cow trying to separate from the herd and bolt back toward the fire.

The cowboy in the middle was recognizable too. Blaine Harney rode tall in the saddle aboard a muscular gray stallion that matched his own stature. He was wielding a stock whip, making the leather tip snap and pop as he drove the herd. When the last cow had passed my pickup, he reined to a stop. He touched the straw brim of his sweat-stained Trail Rider by way of greeting.

"You're pointed toward fire, not away from it," he drawled.

"Has the blaze reached your buildings yet?"

"No, it started in a pasture a mile downwind from the ranch house."

I hadn't seen Blaine since his father died. Zachariah Harney was a legend. He'd been as single-minded as he'd been ruthless when it came to acquiring ranchland and grazing rights to expand the family's empire and maintain his iron grip on the county's economy. Pudge Warbler and the old cattle baron had been nemeses since kindergarten until a series of strokes did what the law and no enemy could.

"I heard about your father's passing," I said. "Condolences."

"Much obliged. Dad always said good pastureland was hard to come by and never waste any, so I buried him on a rocky hill behind the house. I'm pretty sure he'd approve."

"Are you moving this herd down to the reservoir I passed?"

"Yep. Cows can tread water a long time if they're forced to."

"This looks to be only a couple hundred head. Where's the rest of your stock?" The Rocking H Ranch's herd numbered in the thousands.

"Most are still in the high pastures or on leased land on the other side of the basin. What are you doing here?"

"Offering to lend a hand."

His lips tightened. "Gemma called you. Figures." He glanced

at the Triumph tied down in my pickup's bed. "There's a corporate ranch in Diamond Valley that herds its cattle with a helicopter. I've yet to see anybody do it on a motorbike."

"If you have a spare horse, I've learned to ride."

"We're almost finished here. Why don't you go on up to the house. We'll be there shortly and can get something to eat while we're waiting for my fence riders to report in. They're out looking for more lightning strikes. We can figure out what needs doing next depending on what they find."

"Okay, and I can tell you about an arsonist on the loose. He wasn't that far from here when I saw him."

"Gemma told me about that, but nobody started this one. Dry lightning did."

"Are you sure about that?"

"I was born and raised here. I know what a lightning bolt looks like."

Gemma rode up on the bay mare. Rings of trail dust gave the horse doctor raccoon eyes. "I see November gave you my message." She sneaked a peek at Blaine. "It was very gallant of you to rush over here."

"Or gullible," I said under my breath before driving away.

The headquarters of the Rocking H Ranch were nestled in a sea of threshed grass that stretched for miles. Deep wells and year-round springs accounted for much of the ranch's wealth. The ample supply of water flowed through a sophisticated irrigation system that featured steel wheel-lines with lateral water pipes and sprinkler heads. Bales of alfalfa and rolls of hay dotted manicured fields that surrounded a sprawling ranch house set among shade trees, fruit orchards, and flowerbeds. A bunkhouse, barn, and stable were nearby.

I parked in the circular drive and used a boot scraper on the porch before opening the front door. It was unlocked as was the custom throughout Harney County. The interior was dark and cool. All the drapes were pulled to block out the sun's rays. I'd been to the house before and knew where the kitchen was. I filled a glass from the tap. I also knew from a previous visit that Blaine still kept a wedding photograph of him and Gemma on his nightstand.

The pair didn't keep me waiting long. The clip-clop of horse-shoes on the gravel drive brought me to the porch. Gemma and Blaine rode side-by-side. The horse doctor waved when she saw me.

"That was the most fun I've had in a long time," she said. "I miss cowpunching."

Blaine dismounted the gray stallion and reached over to hold the bay mare's cheekpiece as Gemma got off. The Rocking H was the kind of spread that had stable hands. A teenager wearing a green ballcap advertising a farm supply store appeared and led the two horses away.

"He'll give them a good rubdown and an extra handful of oats," Blaine said. "They'll be ready to ride at any time, fire depending."

"Where's the cowboy that was with you?" I asked.

"He's keeping watch over the herd at the reservoir. Come on, let's get in the house. I need to wash up and have something to eat."

Blaine climbed the stairs to the bedrooms on the second floor. Gemma held back at the foot of the staircase. "I should-n't've said anything to November that led you to drive all the way out here, but when I woke up and saw the sun rise and realized it wasn't the sun but fire, I got worried. The cattle and horses are still my patients and Blaine is still my friend, but I'm glad I'm not married to him anymore." She looked down at her boots and then up at me. "Do you understand?"

"You never really leave a place behind. It always follows you, both the good in it and the bad."

"You don't always have to be so damn understanding." She threw her arms around me and squeezed. "And since you won't ask, I'll tell you. I slept upstairs in the guestroom last night. Alone." She wheeled around and clomped up the stairs.

I returned to the kitchen to put the glass back. A comely young woman with thick long hair as black as a raven and eyes to match was busy with cookware. "Need any help?" I said.

She waved me off with a spatula. I backed up quickly. As I headed to the living room, I passed an open door to a wood-paneled study. A map was spread out on a heavy oak table, its corners held down by bronze statuettes. One was a cowboy on a bucking bronco and another a cowboy twirling a lariat. The other pair were Indians, one, with a bow and arrow, astride a war pony and another on horseback lancing a buffalo.

"They're Frederic Remingtons," Blaine said as he found me admiring them. "My grandfather met the artist and became a collector. That painting above the study's fireplace is a Remington too." It depicted a blue-shirted cavalry soldier wearing a white hat with a turned-up brim firing a rifle from a galloping horse at a band of Indians chasing him. "So's that one." He pointed to the opposite wall. The painting was of an Indian boy wrapped in a blanket sitting on a horse in a snowy field. There's a couple more hanging in my father's bedroom."

"These have to be priceless," I said. "You sure you want to keep them here with all the fires?"

"My grandfather didn't believe in banks and my father wouldn't trust one he didn't control. This place is safer than any vault. Besides, I have plenty of Remington's cousin's creations around here to protect them."

Blaine opened the glass door to a gun cabinet that contained several long guns, including a rolling block rifle, a .30-caliber pump-action rifle, and a .35-caliber semi-automatic. "Eliphalet Remington founded the oldest gun manufacturing company in the country. My family's stuck by his brand since day one."

"Those antiques might stop thieves, but not flames," I said.

"I see Blaine's showing off the family treasures," Gemma said as she joined us. She'd washed her face and changed her pearl-snap shirt. "I love this one the most." She pointed at the portrait of the boy on the horse in the snow. "He looks so alone, but so resolute. He reminds me of Nagah Will." She was referring to a young Paiute who, along with his grandfather Tuhudda Will, I'd befriended. "Remington makes you feel the chill in the air by the way he painted the slope in the boy's shoulders and the horse's head hanging down with his tail between his legs."

I looked at the topographic map held in place by the bronzes. A black marker had been used to outline the Rocking H's boundaries. A couple of spots were shaded in red.

"Those must show where you've had fires," I said.

Blaine nodded. "You own as much land as us, you got to keep track of everything, including lightning strikes. The sections with numbers penciled on them are where we currently have herds pastured."

"Your map reminds me of a chess board," I said. "You can try and move your herds to stay one square ahead of the flames, but the trouble is, you don't know which square will ignite next."

"You can't predict lightning," he said.

"But maybe you can a firebug." I told him about the blazes I'd seen and what Colonel Marcus Aurelius Davies had said about how the arsonist was in training.

"Training for what?"

"Who knows, but whatever it is, it can't be good."

Blaine pulled a bolt-action Remington with a mounted scope from the glass-fronted cabinet and snugged the rifle to his shoulder. "I'll be in my rights if I spot him on my property," he growled.

Gemma placed her palm familiarly on her ex-husband's arm. "Now, now, Blaine. Let's go have some lunch. I bet Elena cooked up a feast."

He put the gun back immediately. "Sorry," he said, his head hanging down like the horse in the snow in the Remington painting.

The fence riders reported in after lunch. There were no other fires on Rocking H land. Gemma finished administering anti-inflammatories to calves exhibiting signs of shipping fever and gave a preventive dose of antibiotics to those who didn't.

"Any news about Wanda's children?" she asked.

"Nothing yet. I took her to Burns to talk with the social services people. Your father is coordinating a statewide search with state troopers and every sheriff's department in Oregon. Orville is putting his new calculating machine to work."

I asked her where she was off to next as she finished packing up her medical kit.

"The Big X. They have a horse who got spooked by lightning and was injured trying to bust through a corral. Are you headed back to No Mountain?"

"Eventually. Since I'm out this way, I'll take a run at Foster Flat Road and see what I can see. It leads in the same direction as where the firebug was headed."

She hoisted her kit. "Come on, I'll take you."

"What?"

"Ever since I earned my pilot's license, you haven't gone flying with me. Now's your chance. I'll fly you over Foster Flat so you can have your looksee and drop you off back here. It'll save you time."

"Do you have enough gas for that?"

"Sure. Blaine keeps an unlocked tank of aviation fuel next to his airstrip."

"Just for his favorite flying doctor?"

"For any pilot. If they get in a pinch, they know they can always land here and help themselves. It's the neighborly thing to do."

"Thoughtful guy," I said.

Gemma cocked her head which made her grin grow even wider. "You're not scared of flying are you?"

"Of course not."

"Are you scared of flying with me?"

"There's nothing I don't think you can handle."

"Aw, you're making me blush."

"Let me fetch my binoculars." What I really wanted to grab was my sidearm and Winchester that were still in the pickup. I'd learned the hard way that an ounce of lead could be more helpful than a pound of prevention.

Gemma was wearing her aviator sunglasses and had the plane already flight checked and warmed up by the time I let Blaine know I'd be back later for my pickup. If the big rancher was jealous of me flying off with his ex-wife, he kept it to himself.

The airstrip was short and our takeoff steep. The ranch's headquarters quickly fell away as we finished climbing and leveled out. Gemma handed me headphones equipped with a mic.

"There are The Narrows," she said, pointing to a pinched strip of land that was usually underwater. It ran between Malheur Lake and Mud Lake. Malheur was shallow and freshwater; it cast a blue reflection despite the smoky air. Mud Lake was dry and the color of a scab. Touching its western shore was the alkaline surface of Harney Lake. The usually bright expanse was more pepper than salt because of fallen ash. The trio of lakes were the low spot in Harney Basin and served as a drain.

Gemma banked to the right and found the dirt road to Foster Flat. Gullies etched the desolate scrubland. Waterholes were far and few between, and those that hadn't dried up were nearing their bottoms. A lone coyote was using the dirt road as a trail. When the shadow of the plane passed over him, he dove into the nearest thicket of brittlebush. I scanned the ground to the left, right, and straight ahead. There were some four-wheel-drive tracks, but none looked fresh.

"That's Keg Springs Valley over there," Gemma said.

I swiveled my binoculars. "I don't see any ranch houses."

"Outside of a fence rider's shack or two, there aren't any. The whole area is about as desolate as it gets."

"Where does Foster Flat Road end up?"

"If you stay on it long enough, Warner Valley in Lake County. Before you reach that, there are cutoffs to a half dozen other dirt roads that will take you to Mule Springs Valley, Dry Valley, and Rabbit Basin, among others. They're not exactly bustling with people and ranch houses either. Most of those roads eventually connect to the Lakeview-Burns Highway."

"Which connects to a two-lane to Chewaucan Marsh," I said.

"Where Wanda Manybaskets lived," Gemma said, finishing my thought for me. "I feel terrible for her. Nothing could be worse than not knowing where your children are. If I were her, I'd do anything, give anything, to find them. I'd trade my life for theirs without a blink. The only thing worse for a mother than finding them dead would be never finding them at all."

I mulled that over and then said, "Was having children the reason you married Blaine?"

Gemma issued an indignant snort. "How come you're asking me that now? Is it because I spent the night at the Rocking H?"

"It's because what you said about mothers, I wondered if—"

"That the only reason women get married is to have children?" The headphones magnified the sound of her spitting air. "It's *a* reason, but not the only reason. I'm certainly not seeing you because all I want is to be barefoot and pregnant." Gemma snorted even louder.

"Wanda told me that her heart is leading her to find her children," I said. "She said it tells her they're in Harney County and a mother always knows. I'm trying to help her, but I need a woman's point of view. I need to know what's driving her. The people I took her to at the mobile Indian Services office said she's out of touch with reality, that maybe her children don't even exist. I don't know what she is except that she's a woman. I need help figuring her out and you're the smartest woman I know to ask for it."

Gemma took her eyes off the windshield for a moment to lock eyes with mine. "I'm sorry, I misread you. I'm not a mother, at least not yet, but I can tell you there's nothing stronger than a mother's love. Look at my mom? There she was in incredible agony while she was dying and she went out and found November and talked her into taking her place. That's a mother's love for you. Strong, unbreakable. I see it all the time with the animals I treat. There's nothing a mare won't do for her foal, a heifer for her calf. Same is true in the wild. A mama bear, a mama moose? Get between them and their offspring and you're in for a world of hurt."

We flew on for another ten minutes without speaking. I didn't spot any vehicles, structures, or evidence of man-made fires. We crossed over a butte. At its base was a grove of old-growth junipers like the one where Loq and I found Wanda Manybaskets. A dirt road led to it. It was short, narrow, and rocky. I looked back at Gemma. Her ponytail had fallen over her shoulder. She had missed a smudge of dirt on her jaw when she'd washed her face after herding the fire-spooked cows. The big lenses of her aviator glasses reflected the sky out the cockpit window.

"Look. Down there," I said.

"Do you see something? Where?" Gemma banked the plane so she would have a better view out her side window. "What am I supposed to be looking for?"

"That dirt road. Do you think you can land on it?"

"Why? Is there someone down there? Do you think it's the arsonist?" She began circling.

"As your father would say, I need to talk to a man about a horse."

"You didn't go before we left the ranch? I can't believe it. It's the first rule of flying in a small plane. You always go to the bathroom before takeoff." She blew at a wisp of hair that had gotten loose from her ponytail. "Just wiggle your toes."

"Does that mean you can't land on the road or are you—?"

"Scared? Ha. Nothing frightens me. I'll have you know I've landed at ranches that don't have airstrips, not even a plowed field to put down on. Why, I've landed on desert scrub, butte tops, and even right in front of Blackpowder's store when I stopped to pick up groceries on the way home. I can land anywhere." Gemma cranked her head at me. "What are you grinning at?"

"You."

"Why?"

"For believing me." I gave it a few seconds. "If there are trees down there, there's probably a waterhole or at least a spring. I thought we could take a swim and, you know, see what happens."

"Well, I'll be darned, hotshot. You do know how to put one over."

Gemma's laughter filled the headphones as she pushed the stick forward, dropped the flaps, and we braced for contact.

11

I t was dusk when I got back to the old lineman's shack. The sky was the color of a three-day-old bruise. Two pickups were parked out front. One was a twin to mine. The other was older, rustier, and had mismatched front fenders, one blue, one green. Loq was sitting on the front porch sharpening a skinning knife on a gray whetstone.

"Looks like you found Wanda Manybaskets' pickup," I said.

"It was out of gas like she said and so I tied down the steering wheel, hitched it to the back of my rig, and towed it." He spit on the whetstone and kept sharpening the blade.

"Did you find any stories in it?"

"There was no registration in the glove box. No maps either. No hamburger wrappers on the floor, no cracker crumbs on the seat."

"How about a license plate?"

"Nevada, but the bolts are newer than the tags."

"I'll ask Orville to run it for us."

"How come?"

"It's the only thing we have of the family's unless you turned up something else. Were you able to find the ranch where Wanda's husband worked?"

"You got a lot of questions. You got any water inside?"

"Runs fresh out of the tap same as always. The door's never locked. You could've helped yourself, but you didn't want to go inside, did you?"

Loq grunted. "There's that question you already know the answer to thing again."

I sensed something was up, and it wasn't only because I didn't recognize the skinning knife he continued to sharpen. "Something happened down there. What was it?"

"Water first, story second."

I went inside, filled two glasses, and carried them to the front porch. I handed the *Maklak* one. He drained it in a single gulp. I gave him the second glass. He emptied that one too. I sat down and he started talking.

Loq told me the pickup with the mismatched fenders was parked in the middle of the gravel road about a quarter mile past the waterhole where we'd found Wanda Manybaskets. The key was still in the ignition. He pushed her rig to the side so other vehicles could get past it and then followed Wanda's footprints that led across the ash-covered pebbly sand, between charred stumps of sagebrush, and into the burnt grove of ancient junipers.

He knelt at the waterhole, formed a cup with his palms, and scooped. The water was clear and cold and clean. As he took a sip, he noticed two small basket-like items on the bank. They were baby rattles woven out of willow. Given the look of their age, he wondered if Wanda's great-aunt, Young Willow, had made them. He carried them out of the grove.

Loq left Wanda's pickup where it was with the intent of coming back for it later and followed the gravel road to where it met the Lakeview-Burns Highway. From there, he drove to the

Chewaucan Marsh, a remnant of a lake that once covered the region when mastodons last walked in Oregon. Farmers had drained most of the marsh during the past century to irrigate their crops and converted the rich soil to hayfields.

He had to search hard to find the Washoe family's camp, but finally spotted the top of a wickiup made of dried cattails. Steps away from the wickiup was a small pool of freshwater. Tiny bubbles rising to the surface told him it was fed by an underground spring. He knelt and sipped some water. It was fresh and didn't taste of dead plants like most marsh water did. Inside the wickiup was a bed made of gunnysacks stuffed with straw. A blanket was spread over them. It was handloomed and depicted a sapphire lake surrounded by snowcapped mountains. "*Dá' ah*," he said to himself.

There was a fire ring with a clean cast-iron pot and fry pan next to it. Four hand-carved wooden bowls were stacked alongside four sets of wooden spoons. Everything was neat and orderly as if the wickiup's occupants had eaten breakfast, washed up, and gone out for a stroll. Loq removed nothing, not even the blanket.

He drove to the nearest ranch. No one there knew anything about a Washoe family living alongside the marsh. They'd never heard of Tom Piñon or any ranch hand who'd recently been thrown by a horse and died. Loq drove to the next ranch and then the next. It was the same story at all of them.

Doors were slammed in his face more than once. Loq wasn't surprised by it. What were they supposed to think when a mohawked *Maklak* showed up at their front door asking about a dead man and missing children? A couple of ranchers had kids of their own. Loq could tell by the toys in the front yard. A teeter-totter made by laying a plank across a 55-gallon drum turned on its side. An old tractor tire hanging by a rope from the limb of a cottonwood. He thought those families would know something. Maybe their kids had played with Daisy and Danny. But they proved even more tightlipped than the rest, keeping their children hidden inside while keeping him on the front porch.

It was 45 miles from the marsh to Lakeview. The distance between ranch houses thinned the farther away he got from the marsh. He waved at the occasional oncoming driver in the traditional country fashion of raising two fingers while clutching the top of the steering wheel. On a long, straight stretch of blacktop far from any ranch house or settlement, a pickup appeared in his rearview mirror. The driver was in a hurry because in no time he was tailgating him. That's when the *Maklak* noticed a second pickup right behind the first. The first pickup pulled out to pass. When it came alongside him, a hand stuck out of the passenger window and gestured for him to pull over. The pickup whipped in front and slowed. The second pickup closed the gap behind him.

Loq told himself that word had gotten out among the ranchers about his inquiries and maybe these fellows knew something. When the lead pickup came to a stop on the shoulder, he pulled in behind it. The second pickup boxed him in. There was no license plate on the rear bumper of the lead pickup and none on the front bumper of the pickup behind.

Like every Fish and Wildlife ranger, Loq had been issued a Smith and Wesson .357 Magnum, a lever-action Winchester .30-30, and a 12-gauge pump shotgun. The long guns were in the rack behind his head. He wasn't wearing the heavy two-pound sidearm while he drove. It was on the seat next to him in a holster. The two men in the lead pickup got out and approached on either side of his rig. One was armed with a shotgun, the other held a deer rifle.

"Help you?" he said as the man holding the shotgun reached his cab.

"Word is you've been asking around about a man who was working on a ranch and got hisself killed."

"That's right. Tom Piñon. I'm helping out his wife."

"How's that?"

"Her kids are lost. Why, do you know something about the family?"

"We don't know you and the closest law around here is down in Lakeview. Stranger starts knocking on doors and asking questions, we get real vigilant real quick."

"Fair enough, but I don't bite. I see the man in the pickup behind me is in charge. If he wants to talk to me, what's he waiting for?"

"Why do you think it's him, not me?"

"Because he's the one who lowered the visor to block his face when he pulled in behind me. Ask him to come out and talk to me like a man."

"You got some balls on you, Big Red. That's not the way this is gonna work. You're gonna get out so we can all keep an eye on you and make sure nothing happens other than talking. Go on, get out. And leave your six-shooter on the seat. Yeah, I seen it."

Loq glanced at the man with the deer rifle. He had it shouldered and aimed with nothing between them but the windshield.

As soon as Loq's boots hit the pavement, the man holding the shotgun swung it. The barrel clipped him on the back of his head and dropped him to his knees.

"Go on," shotgun man said. "On your belly, face down. Clasp your hands behind your back."

"The blacktop's a skillet in this heat. It'll burn my face," Loq said.

"Who's gonna notice if your skin gets any redder?" shotgun man snarled. "Go on or I'll fill you full of buckshot. I'm not gonna say it again."

Loq did as he was told, but arched his neck to keep from laying his cheek against the sizzling road surface. The man kept the shotgun on him. Five minutes went by. Loq continued to keep his head up as the cords in his neck grew as taut as a hangman's rope and the bulging trapezius and deltoid muscles made the back of his khaki uniform shirt jump as if a kangaroo rat had gotten trapped beneath it. He'd hold the position as long as it took, not wanting to give the man any satisfaction. He could do it too; he'd set a one-minute record at boot camp by performing 59 pull-ups and another for 67 sit-ups.

The door to the rear pickup finally opened and closed. A pair of dusty boots came into Loq's field of vision.

"That's it. Keep your eyes down and don't turn your head. It's best for everyone," the man wearing the dusty boots said.

"You know about the Washoe ranch hand who died. Tom Piñon." Loq said it, not asked it.

"Whoever told you that was lying."

"If it was an accident, why's everybody treating it like some kind of secret?"

"I'll be doing the asking and you'll be doing the answering," dusty boots said. "You're wearing a fish and duck uniform. Closest refuges are Hart Mountain to the east and Klamath Marsh to the west. You have no official business being here."

"It's my day off."

"What makes you think anybody around here knows anything about a dead Indian and missing children?"

Loq paused as he tightened his stomach muscles to keep his face off the blacktop.

Shotgun man kicked him. His boot tip found the side of the *Maklak's* knee. "Answer the man."

Loq wouldn't give him the satisfaction of seeing him wince. "I found his wife on the side of the road not far from here. She said he got thrown by a horse and died in the Lakeview hospital.

She and her kids went back to their camp and fell asleep. When she woke up, the kids were gone. I told her I'd look into it and that's what I'm doing."

"No one around here ever saw them or knows anything. She's either lying or you are," dusty boots said.

"The thing of it is, she said the rancher her husband worked for took him to the hospital when he got thrown. The rancher's wife came and got her and the kids and drove them to be by his bedside while he lay dying." Loq paused. "That doesn't seem like anybody was trying to hide something. Why's everyone acting so scared now?"

"And I say nobody knows anything," dusty boots said. "Maybe you're making it all up just to get a look into people's houses so you can sneak back in the middle of the night and rob them and rape the women."

Shotgun man kicked Loq in the side of the knee again. "Like I said, with the sheriff so far away, we get real vigilant real quick around here."

"I've given you a pass twice now," Loq said without wincing. "There won't be a third time."

"Listen to him talk," shotgun man taunted. "And what's with that haircut? You fancy yourself some kind of fancy East Coast redskin?"

Loq didn't waste his breath telling him he'd worn a mohawk ever since boot camp when all the Marine recruits had their hair buzzed per regulation. The base barber hee-hawed when Loq sat in his chair. He grabbed a handful of the *Maklak's* shoulder-length hair and held it up for all to see. "You may've been born a brave," he sneered, "but you're not one of the few, the proud, and the brave yet. I don't see you making it through three days of basic before you're squealing for your mama." The barber hee-hawed again. "You're not going to cry like a little girl when I cut off your pigtails, are you?"

Log sprang out of the chair, grabbed the barber's wrist, and wrenched the clipper from his hands. He brandished it at him and then turned to face the mirror and gave himself a buzzcut, leaving a mohawk of half-inch high fuzz. He wore it proudly despite insults from his drill instructor and fellow recruits. Being stronger and faster than anyone else finally earned him their begrudging respect. In Vietnam, he kept the hair style but let the strip of hair grow out while continuing to shave the sides. During his tour, he never got so much as a bullet wound or a scratch by a punji stick even though he led every charge. By the end of the year, the men in his platoon regardless of race, religion, or creed were wearing their hair in a mohawk too.

Dusty boots said, "You need to get back in your rig and drive away. You're scaring women and children and we won't abide by that."

"All I'm doing is the same as anybody would who found a woman whose husband had died and little children were missing," Loq said. "You wouldn't do that?"

"I wouldn't go to a place where I wasn't welcomed, damsel in distress or not. You knock on the wrong door around here, the person behind it is apt to shoot right through it."

Shotgun man chuckled. "And we'd help dig the hole to put you in."

"I've wasted enough time here," dusty boots said. "I'm going to go on about my business. Once I'm down the road, my neighbors will make sure you go back the same way you came. You're not going to drive down to Lakeview and talk to folks down there either. They're busy and don't need to be worrying about someone like you."

Dusty boots walked away. The sound of a door opened and closed, an engine revved, and rear wheels spun smoke as the pickup sped off.

Shotgun man started whistling. It was mostly air and spit,

but Loq recognized the tune. It was "Take Me Out to the Ballgame." He pictured the man hefting the shotgun like a Louisville slugger and taking a few practice swings before readying to hit one out of the park. He also pictured the skinning knife riding in a leather sheath on the man's right hip. Loq's hands were a blur as he whipped his palms to the ground and pushed off the pavement. He was on his feet and knocked the shotgun aside with his arm locked around the man's chest and the skinning knife held at his throat before the sound of the whistle faded away.

"Lay your gun in the bed of my pickup. Now!" Loq ordered the man shouldering the deer rifle.

Deer rifle man hesitated. "Do what he says!" shotgun man cried. "He'll slit my throat for sure." Deer rifle man did as instructed.

"Now walk to your rig and put your palms on the roof of the cab," Loq said.

Again, he complied, although he cried out when his skin touched the blistering metal. Loq walked shotgun man toward their pickup, scooping up the fallen shotgun on the way.

"Hands on the cab. Same as him," he said.

Both men pressed their palms against the roof of their pickup. Loq didn't bother to shoulder the shotgun. He fired it from his hip while holding the skinning knife. He gripped it so rock steady that the barrel didn't jump and the butt didn't recoil. Buckshot obliterated a rear tire. Loq returned to his rig, laid the shotgun and skinning knife on the seat, and continued on his way. He didn't glance at his rearview mirror once.

12

The phone rang the following morning while I was cleaning up after breakfast. Pudge Warbler and Orville Nelson were on a speaker phone.

"Your suspicion about an arsonist on the loose is getting a whole lot more attention as of five minutes ago," the old lawman said. "We got a call from the Bureau of Land Management folks. There was a fire on a section they manage for some professor types who are studying livestock and range conditions. What's to study about a cow preferring alfalfa over sagebrush, I couldn't tell you, but what I do know is by the time a team of BLM fire-fighters got there, the caretaker's trailer was in flames with him trapped inside." He sucked in his breath and let it out slowly. "I hate to think of a man burning alive."

"What makes them suspect arson?"

"Namely a Pepsi bottle full of gasoline with a rag stuck in it like a half-burned wick. They found it when they were putting out a pair of smaller blazes on either side of the big one. This all happened north of Dry Valley."

The name rang a bell. Gemma had mentioned it when we

were flying. She'd said Foster Flat Road linked to a dirt road to Dry Valley.

"We should call Colonel Davies," I said.

"I'm one step ahead of you, son. I already radioed him and he's gonna meet me there. He must've taken a shine to you because he asked if you were gonna be there. I volunteered you would seeing that if this no count sonofabitch set a match to BLM land, his next target could well be one of your refuges."

"I'm on my way."

"Hold your horses for a second. Orville's got some information for you. Word of warning, put on your thinking cap. The college boy has been working overtime on numbers. I'll see you out there."

The sound of Pudge's boots echoing across the linoleum were soon drowned out by the young man's eager voice. "I already gave these to Deputy Warbler. They are addresses for two of the arson suspects. The first is for Judd Hollister whose parents' ranch house burned down. The other is for the dress store owner. His name is Martin St. Claire. He lives on West Adams Street."

"What about the boy Blackpowder suspects torched the schoolhouse ten years ago?"

"He is proving to be more of a challenge because of the lack of surety over his last name. I called the school, but they lost all their records in the fire. The principal has been there for only three years. She does not know Freddie nor do any of the teachers. I also tried to obtain a list of all forwarding addresses provided to the No Mountain post office, but they do not keep records going back more than two years. I will try some other tactics."

"What did Pudge mean about numbers?"

"They have to do with statistics regarding missing American Indian children."

"I take it this is when I put on my thinking cap."

"I must warn you my findings are very discouraging. I spoke with people at the Bureau of Indian Affairs, the state welfare office, and the state attorney general's office. I also came into possession of a draft report that is being prepared for a special US Senate subcommittee. Do not ask me who my source was."

A bullet to the back may have put a hitch in Orville's plans of joining the FBI someday, but it hadn't sapped his appetite for practicing G-man tradecraft. "What did you find out?" I said.

Orville took a deep breath before continuing. "Twenty-five to thirty percent of all American Indian children are forcibly separated from their families and placed in foster homes, adoptive homes, or institutions. In addition, missing person reports are filed on one out of every 130 American Indian children every year."

I sucked my teeth. A century later, Brigadier General Richard Henry Pratt's legacy of cultural genocide was still going strong. "Do both of those statistics hold up here in Oregon—kids who are taken from their family and put in homes and kids who are reported missing?"

"I ran a regressive analysis and isolated the Great Basin," he said. "My findings are still preliminary, but the statistics are consistent with the national average."

"Do the kids reported as missing include runaways and a parent taking off with a kid during a marital spat and the like?"

"They do, but the data indicate missing children in this region are primarily due to nonfamily abduction. The majority disappear without a trace."

"You mean kids who were snatched while walking home from school or were plucked out of their beds at night."

"I have not delved into the data deep enough to put meaningful percentages to the various means."

"What about kidnapping for ransom? Did that stand out?"

"That proved to be statistically insignificant. I would hypoth-esize that since the average American Indian household lives far below the national poverty line, there is insufficient monetary incentive."

I didn't want to ask about child homicides, but I had to. Orville took a couple of deep breaths before replying. "Yes. There are statistics for it. The exact number and ratio will be detailed in my final analysis."

The weight of Orville's information pressed down on my shoulders and soured my stomach. My first instinct was to run outside and jump on the Triumph and race toward the horizon, to push the tachometer past the redline and hold it there until the gas tank ran empty. But the rush of anger and frustration was momentary. I'd never run from a fight yet, and this was certainly no time to start.

"Do you have time to find information on two outfits in Spokane?"

"Of course," he said. "What are they?"

"The first is the church that funds the mobile Indian Services office. It's called New Faith Directions Community Ministry. The second is a clinic called Bright Rivers Behavioral Treatment Center. The couple working out of the Winnebago recommended Wanda Manybaskets go see a psychiatrist there."

"What do you need to know about them?"

"Street addresses for starters. After that, anything you can find. Cameron Parker was loud and clear that if I can't convince Wanda to go to Bright Rivers, he'll have to alert county health that she's a suicide risk. If that happens, the county will commit her for her own safety."

"That was very manipulative of Mr. Parker to put the respon-sibility for her welfare on you. I assume that is why you are suspicious of him."

"And you'd be right. Parker said he and his wife have traveled to a lot of Indian communities throughout the Great Basin over the past couple of years. He's come in contact with lots of Indians, but he seemed overly interested in Wanda once I told him her kids were missing. In practically his next breath, he started talking about getting her out of Harney County and up to the clinic in Spokane. Why would he want to take a mother away from where her missing children might be?"

"That is suspicious. Did Mr. Parker give you the name of the head clinician at Bright Rivers?"

"All he said was he had a reputation for treating American Indians with mental health problems and was writing a book about it."

"More than likely he has written research papers on the subject that have been published in medical journals. That should help identify him. I will get right on it and report back."

I poured what remained of the coffee into a thermos and headed outside. Loq's rig was parked alongside Wanda Manybaskets'. He was using an Oklahoma credit card to siphon gas from his pickup into hers.

"What are you planning on doing with her pickup?" I said.

"Drive it over to the Warblers for her."

"That'll have to wait. There's been a fire. It's out now, but it killed a man."

The *Maklak* grunted. "I heard no thunder last night, saw no lighting. Whoever lit it killed the man, not the fire."

"That's why Pudge asked us to come check it out. We'll take my rig. Grab your guns. I got a feeling it's going to be a long day."

He pointed at my thermos. "Is that coffee for me?"

"I thought you'd want some for the drive."

Loq made a face. "I hope you put sugar in it. Your coffee is bitter. I prefer Gemma's when she's here to make it."

"Me too," I said.

Dry Valley lived up to its name. On the dusty drive to reach the BLM's experimental range-study area, I told Loq what I'd learned from Orville about the number of American Indian kids reported missing every year and forcibly removed from their families. I also told him about Cameron Parker's insistence that Wanda go to Bright Rivers.

Loq didn't comment, but I knew he was filing the information away. He then proceeded to finish his story about what he'd learned in Lakeview. The sheriff there told him that he'd already gotten the call from Pudge and was looking into the situation, but with Wanda Manybaskets having left Lake County and no ransom note or proof that her children were still there, he had little to go on. The hospital didn't provide much help either.

"They gave me the forked tongue runaround." He didn't grin when he said it. "Everybody told me I'd have to ask somebody else. I finally worked my way up to the hospital's chief of staff. I cornered him while he was making rounds. He told me since I wasn't a family member, he was prevented from telling me anything. When I asked if he could at least confirm Tom Piñon had died, he threatened to call security and have me forcibly removed."

"Why do I think the security guards wound up being patients?"

Loq didn't bat an eye. "I left through the hospital's cafeteria. Seeing the doctors and nurses lined up at the cigarette machine gave me an idea. I plugged in two quarters, bought a pack, went outside, and found the place where staffers go for a smoke. I handed out six cigarettes before I found an X-ray technician who remembered a ranch hand that had been thrown from a horse. He recalls there was a woman standing beside his bed, holding his hand and singing a song. The tech said it was the saddest tune he'd ever heard."

"Water carries the boat. Water carries the baby. Swirling, swirling, across the big lake, toward the big mountain," I said. "She told me it's a Washoe lullaby her mother sang to her and she sang to Daisy and Danny. Did he see the rancher who brought Tom Piñon in?"

"No, he didn't. He said it broke him up seeing her singing that song, knowing her husband was never going to wake up. He'd developed the X-rays that showed Tom Piñon's skull had been cracked and his neck broken."

I relayed Wanda's story about the gambler who told him about the job at the ranch. "I don't know if that's something or nothing. Do you think the rancher was the man with the dusty boots who waylaid you?"

Loq finished the coffee. The metal cup clicked when he screwed it tightly back onto the top of the thermos. "When I go back and find him I'll ask."

It didn't surprise me Loq wasn't going to let go of what happened to him there. I wouldn't either.

I recognized the beige International Travelall from my visit to Riddle Mountain. It was parked at the edge of a blackened field next to Pudge Warbler's pickup and a paneled van with the Harney County coroner's shield on the door. A BLM rangeland fire truck was in the next field. Two firefighters were performing mop-up duty. Colonel Marcus Aurelius Davies and the old deputy were huddled with a third BLM firefighter whose yellow helmet was the brightest object in a scene that reminded me of a bomb crater. The stink from burnt aluminum, melted plastic, and something worse was nose-wrinkling.

Pudge made introductions. Colonel Davies wore a half-zipped green bomber jacket with his rank and last name on it. Loq didn't show any reaction when he saw his scars and missing fingers; he saluted rather than shook hands. "At ease, soldier," the colonel said automatically.

"We were about to go over the particulars," Pudge said. "At least three fires were started. Colonel, you want to tell us what you've found so far?"

Davies uh-huhed. "Two of the blazes didn't amount to much

because of a lack of fuel. And, no, I don't mean the gasoline in the bottles that were used as accelerants. Vegetation is fuel to a fire. So is oxygen. The station here is experimenting with different types of forage grown on adjoining plots." He turned to the BLM firefighter. "Is that correct?"

"That's right. The site is used by researchers from Oregon State. They're running a variety of studies. In addition to experimenting with different types of grazing—strip grazing, creep grazing, high intensity, low frequency, Savory, Hohenheim, and so on—they're also growing different types of feed. Some of the legumes here have a high moisture content."

"That makes them less combustible than native forage," the colonel said. "One of the three fires was started on a field of recently irrigated legumes. It smoldered rather than flared."

"Setting a fire's a crime, but murdering a man carries more weight in my book," Pudge grumbled. He jerked his head toward the burned-out remains of a single-wide trailer. "What can you tell us about that?"

"There's some presumption in what I'm about to describe, uh-huh, but I believe the results of a forensic investigation will bear them out."

Without inviting us to follow, he strode toward the murder site. His gait was that of a military officer accustomed to reviewing troops standing in formation. He cocked his elbow and slipped his mutilated right hand inside the unzipped half of the bomber jacket's placket.

"The arsonist had been here before to conduct reconnaissance," Davies said as we hurried to keep up. "Tire tracks bear that out. He knew there were no guards or even watchdogs. He arrived a couple of hours after sunset, parked, and waited, savoring the buildup to what he was about to do, much like a normal person does when getting ready for a date."

"And all I do is change my shirt and splash on some Old Spice," the firefighter muttered.

"He knew exactly where he wanted to start the fires. He knew perfectly well what different plants were growing where. This isn't a burn site, it's a weapons proving ground. He set the devices and returned to his vehicle." The colonel uh-huhed again. "I imagine he had a stopwatch and clipboard and was taking field notes."

"You mean he didn't skedaddle, but stayed and watched which fields burned fastest?" Pudge said.

"The speed, the height of the flames, the heat of the blaze, and the size of the firebrands that were tossed into the sky. All of it. He was comparing one burning field to the next."

"Why would he do that?" the firefighter asked.

"Because he was field testing his arsenal," Colonel Davies said. "He's planning an attack."

"On what?"

The colonel stared straight ahead as if surveying a battle-field. "Only God and him know."

Pudge adjusted the holstered .45 on his hip. "The sono-fabitch watched the caretaker's place go up and didn't do a thing to save him. That's lower than low."

"I believe that was part of his field test too," Colonel Davies said. "Now he knows how much accelerant to use depending on the crop type, whether it's been irrigated or not, how long it takes to reach its objective, how hot it needs to be to ignite a structure with a human occupant, and how long it takes for the occupant to succumb. If it's a wooden building he's targeting and not a metal trailer like this one, he now knows it'll go up that much quicker."

We reached the remains of the trailer. Two men wearing white uniforms streaked with charcoal were zipping up a black body bag. There was no difference between the color of the bag and the charred corpse inside.

"The odds are he never woke up," the colonel said. "From the look of it, the fire was hot and the smoke thick. It takes less than a minute, usually only thirty seconds, to pass out due to the deprivation of oxygen that comes with smoke inhalation. Death could come from either suffocation, poisoning from toxic gases, or heat searing his lungs. That is if he wasn't flash-baked and combusted by the initial burst of flames."

"Who was he?" Loq asked.

"Jerome Baker," the BLM firefighter said. "But everyone called him Hairy Jerry. We all knew him. He was a grad student who never wanted to graduate. Said the lifestyle of being a perpetual student suited him. I think he was a beatnik before he became a full-fledged hippie. You know, tie-dyed shirts and a beard as long as a hermit's. He was a gentle sort, played the flute. Not a silver one but a wooden one. Pretty good at it too."

When the bag's zipper was closed, Colonel Davies approached and bowed his head in prayer. Loq scuffed the ground with the heel of his boot until he uncovered fresh soil. He picked up a handful and joined the colonel. As he held his hand over the body bag and released a steady trickle of dirt, the *Maklak* raised his face to the sky and began to sing. His voice alternated between soprano and tenor, and though I couldn't understand the words, I started seeing a waterfall streaming down a mountainside and birds flying over a verdant valley as animals ran beneath them.

$\sim$

"Where to next?" Loq said as we drove away from the experimental range station.

"Orville gave me addresses of a couple of people who have a history with arson. I thought we could have a talk with them."

"Us, not Pudge and the other deputies?"

"They've got their hands full."

"Is this what the Fish and Wildlife regional director warned about when he hired me?"

"You mean F.D. Powers."

"All I remember is a man in a suit who flew out from Washington DC and told me he was sent by the Great White Father."

"He really said those words?" I shook my head. "When President Nixon came into office, he appointed Powers to oversee the western region of Fish and Wildlife. You probably had senior officers like him in Vietnam. The by-the-book types who were so wrapped up in protocol they never understood Charlie didn't know how to read, much less have money to buy books or a shelf to put them on."

Loq looked down his high cheekbones. "The director said you needed regular reminding you're a wildlife ranger, not a sheriff's deputy."

"You don't strike me as anybody's string around their finger."

"I may have strung up a few of the enemy by their thumbs when I needed intel from them, but *Maklak* think any man who needs babysitting isn't one."

"We need to find who lit the fire that killed poor Hairy Jerry. The day before, it was open scrub the firebug was torching, today a field station, tomorrow could be a neighbor who dies."

"I got no problem chasing down a murderer, but it's not going to help get Daisy and Danny Manybaskets back. I'm not going to let them be forgotten. I don't want this to turn out to be one more time our people get shortchanged because some man in a suit decides something else is more important."

"I'm all for doing both no matter what it takes. And by the way, I don't even own a suit."

"You will someday."

"Not a chance."

"Sure you will. Either the day you walk down the aisle with Gemma Warbler or the day the undertaker lays you in a pine box."

14

The cattle brand of the Hollister family's ranch was the Flying Arrow, but there were no cattle to brand and the pastures had gone to seed. A wooden post sporting an altered Burns city limits sign was planted near the entrance. It read Holli-Wood, Population 1. Blackpowder Smith was right about the ranch house looking like it had been airlifted from Malibu. A wall of windows faced an aquamarine swimming pool. A girl in a pink bikini floated in the middle atop a giant inflatable swan. Led Zeppelin blared from a tower of stereo speakers stacked on the patio.

"What's with that music?" Loq said.

"It's a new British group. The guitarist used to be with the Yardbirds."

Loq's head swiveled as he took it all in, from the metallic green Shelby Mustang GT500 fastback parked in the drive to the girl in the pool to the shirtless young man with a surfer haircut and dark glasses sprawled on a chaise lounge next to a metal horse trough filled with ice and beer.

"You sure we're still in Harney County?" he said.

"That's got to be Judd Hollister. Let's go ask him."

He was either passed out or had blown out his ear drums listening to heavy metal. When he didn't respond to me calling his name, Loq walked around the patio yanking out speaker wires.

Judd sat up with a start. "What the fuh? Ah, dude. Not cool. Who are you?"

I gave him our names. "We're checking on wildfires. Have you had any on your property?"

"Fires? No, dude, not unless you count the one raging in my head right now because you rousted me from bagging some well-deserved z's." His dark glasses focused on my uniform. "Fish and Wildlife? You're in the wrong spot. There's no fish here and the only wildlife is when I throw a kegger." His laugh sounded like he was blowing air out of his nose at the bottom of the deep end.

"Do you have a lot of parties?"

"Life's a nonstop party if you make it one. This place? It's kegger central. All the chicks know where to come to have a righteous time. You know what I mean?" His wink got stuck half way down.

Loq squatted next to the pool, cupped some water, smelled it, and touched his tongue to it. He let it splash back in. "Not cold and fresh like the waterhole where we found Wanda Manybaskets or the spring next to her camp."

Judd's surfer bangs flopped as he cocked his head. "What's he talking about?"

"That's a nice Shelby you have," I said. "Is it the standard 390 V-8?"

"No way, man. I popped for the 428 with a Hurst four-on-the-floor and Hooker headers. That's one cubic inch more than a 'Vette's 427 and makes all the difference. I got more horses under the hood than any ranch around."

"There aren't many roads in Harney County where you can let it rip," I said.

"There are if you know where to look. You street drag?"

"I ride a two-wheeler. A Triumph Bonneville."

"The Desert Sled. Cool. You ever want to, you know, do some side-by-side quarter miles, I know a place. We can keep the bet small seeing you're on the government payroll and probably barely make minimum." He grinned. "I'll even give you odds."

"I'll keep it in mind," I said.

"You thirsty?" Judd reached into the horse trough and fished out a can of beer.

"No, thanks. I'm on duty."

"Bummer." He popped it open. "What about your partner with the mohawk? Hey, where did he go?"

"Hard to say. He wanders off a lot."

"Not cool. He should've asked first." Judd started to push himself out of the chaise to go look for Loq.

I said, "You're lucky your ranch has dodged lightning strikes. Others haven't been so fortunate."

He settled back down. "Lucky in love, lucky in life, what can I say? You see what's floating in my pool, dude? She's fine and not the only one."

"This is some house. It's not what you typically see in Harney County."

"I don't do typical." He swigged the beer.

"Did you design it yourself?"

"I may have had some help, but, yeah, mostly. The sound system's all mine though. Wait a sec, why aren't the speakers pumping? Oh, that's right. I forgot." His grin didn't make him look any brighter.

"All of this must've set you back a fair piece. You're doing pretty good ranching."

"Ranching? No way, man. I don't do cows."

"Don't do cows, don't do typical. What do you do?"

"Enjoy life, what else?" Judd chugged the beer. "Not that it's any of your business, but I inherited this place from my parents. Tragic, sure, but, you know, you got to deal with it. Look the devil in the eye and laugh in his face. That's my motto. You sure you don't want a brew? I got plenty."

Loq reappeared. "We finished?"

"Nice meeting you, Judd." I said.

"Sure, dude. Anytime. Come by and party when you're not on the clock."

Judd was lowering himself back into the chaise lounge as we returned to the pickup and drove away. Loq said, "I did a quick recon of the house and barn."

"What's the inside like?"

"More of the same. Lots of stereo equipment. Shelves of record albums. Psychedelic posters hanging on the wall of movie stars and rockers. Some of them are even framed. Like a DayGlo one of Marilyn Monroe and another of the Beatles. The furniture? Not much. A couple of black leather couches in the living room. A dining table that's made out of glass and chrome. There's a waterbed in the bedroom and a fishbowl on the nightstand filled with tinfoil packets of condoms. All sorts of different brands and styles. Ribbed, magnum."

"Judd thinks a lot of himself. What was in the barn?"

"Not a pickup like the one we saw tossing firebombs. Only a little yellow VW convertible bug. It's registered to the girl in the bikini. At least I think it's hers. I wrote down the name and address. She lives in Burns."

"Are you sure you were a Marine and not Military Police?"

"I spent some time in a few clubs in country on my down days watching the cop shows they played from home. *Mannix*, *Honey West*. The end of my last tour, it was *Mod Squad*. Everyone was in love with Peggy Lipton."

"Is that all you found?"

"That and a 200-gallon fuel tank with a handpump on it next to the barn."

"Those Shelby GT500s are notorious gas hogs," I said.

"And having your own fuel tank is pretty typical for a ranch this far from the nearest gas station," he said.

"It sure is, especially the ones with airstrips. But you know what? Judd told me he doesn't do typical."

Loq adjusted the confiscated skinning knife he now wore strapped to his hip. "You think that lowlife is smart enough to be our arsonist, planning and testing fires like Colonel Davies described?"

"I don't know, but I remember this guy in my platoon from Laguna Beach nicknamed Rip Curl. He moved in slow motion, always listening to the Beach Boys' *Pet Sounds* album. He talked like our friend Judd here. But when the shit really hit the fan, Rip turned into something else. He'd grab the M60 Hog and charge the enemy shouting 'Cowabunga' and firing full-tilt."

"We should go back and string up Judd by his thumbs to see if he's hiding anything."

"Let's do some more digging first."

Loq didn't mask his disappointment. "Where to next?"

"Pudge arrested a dress store owner who burned down a rival's store. He did five years in prison for it."

"A dress salesman? Sure glad I brought my weapons."

"You never know," I said.

Martin St. Claire's house was in a tidy neighborhood and had a green front lawn despite the baking summer heat. The front walk was lined with rose beds that smelled of fresh fertilizer. A wind chime made of seashells hung from an eave on the front porch. The doorbell chimed "Twinkle, Twinkle, Little Star."

The woman who answered was a bottle blonde and wore her hair in a bouffant. She had on turquoise mascara and plenty of red lipstick.

"Are you Mrs. St. Claire?" I said.

"Yes I am." She fluttered her press-on eyelashes as she sized me up. "And who may I ask are you?"

"I'm Nick Drake. He's Loq. We're rangers with Fish and Wildlife."

"Well, aren't you the pair."

"We need to speak to your husband about a matter."

"What do you want him for? Marty doesn't fish or hunt. The closest he gets to the great outdoors is tending to his roses. Now me, on the other hand..." When I didn't respond, her lips curled, which left lipstick on her front teeth. "Oh, I get it. The wildfires. Hey Marty!" she hollered over her shoulder. "A game warden out here thinks you've been a naughty boy again."

She sashayed off. A minute later a man with a noticeable stoop came to the door. He wore rimless glasses and was drying his hands on a dish towel.

"You'll have to excuse my wife," he said in a voice slightly above a whisper. "I've put her through living hell. How can I help you?"

"My partner and I have been asked by Harney County Sheriff's to help out. They gave us your name and address. We need to ask you what you know about the fires."

"Only what I've read in the *Burns Herald*. It says they're from all the dry lightning strikes we've been having. We could use some rain. I've had to water my roses by hand." He pointed the dish towel toward a tin watering can with a big spout.

"Have you been growing flowers long?" I asked.

"It's something I learned in prison. After my first couple of years at the state penitentiary in Salem I was transferred to Mill Creek. That's the minimum-security farm annex. The inmates grow all the food for the main prison. I spoke to the warden and he let me take up raising flowers for use in the prison hospital and chapel."

Loq grunted. "Nice."

"I thought so," St. Claire said. "When I was released and came home, no one wanted to hire an ex-convict. I started growing roses and showed them to a florist in town. He agreed to buy them. It saved him from having to ship flowers in from Portland. Have you ever seen all the gardens there? Portland's not called the City of Roses for nothing. I don't wish to brag, but my little garden here holds its own." He stopped drying his hands and held the dish towel in front of his waist.

"Deputy Warbler told me you were convicted of lighting a store on fire," I said.

"That's true. It's a scarlet letter I'll have to wear for the rest of my life, but I did pay my debt to society. What does that have to do with the wildfires?"

"Not all of them were caused by lightning strikes. Someone has been throwing lit bottles of gasoline out of their vehicle. What kind of pickup do you drive?"

"I don't own a pickup. I don't drive at all. My license expired when I was incarcerated and I never renewed it. Bettina does all the driving. We have an Oldsmobile. A Delta 88."

"Bettina is your wife?" Loq said.

"Yes. I worship the ground she walks on. Not many women would take back a convicted felon." St. Claire smiled wanly. "Is there anything else I can help you with?"

"If you like to grow things, have you ever been out to the experimental range station north of Dry Valley?" I said.

St. Claire paused. "The range station? I don't believe I've ever heard of it. What do they do there?"

"They test different forage. Alfalfa, legumes, wild grasses, you name it."

"Do they cultivate any flowers?"

"The only blooms are on native plants."

"Oh. Well, I suppose that could be interesting. Maybe I'll visit it someday."

"Thanks for your time, Mr. St. Claire."

"Of course. It's the price I have to pay for a moment's indiscretion. Mind you, I don't complain. In fact, I embrace it because it reminds me how painful doing something wrong is and how pleasing it feels to do what's right. Good day, gentlemen."

We were a block away when Loq said, "Who else do we need to talk to?"

"Orville Nelson is still working on IDing a third."

"How's he feeling?"

"Orville? Pretty good, considering. Being in a wheelchair hasn't slowed him down too much and his new calculating machine keeps him busy. He needs to stay busy. He's that kind."

Loq thumped his chest. "Orville's got the heart of a warrior, and I've seen plenty."

"He may have a girlfriend, only he doesn't know it yet," I said.

"Who?"

"Her name's Lucy Lorriaga. Orville met her in rehab. She works there."

"Does he think he can't have a woman because he can't use his legs?"

"That would be my guess."

"I know someone Orville should talk to," Loq said. "His name's KC. He was Delta Force and lost his legs to a mortar. KC barkeeps at the VFW in Burns. Orville should go have a beer with him."

"Orville doesn't drink anything stronger than Shasta Diet Cola," I said.

"They serve soft drinks. KC will tell him the facts of life about how you're still all man when you lose your lower half. It's all in your head, he'll tell him. He met his wife after 'Nam and if you saw them together, well, Orville should go talk to KC."

"I'll let him know."

"Since we don't have anyone else to question, I'm going to go look for Daisy and Danny. Wanda's counting on me."

"You heard what Pudge said about the longer children are missing, the worse the odds are for finding them alive."

"I heard him."

"Be careful, then," I said.

"About what?"

"Letting Wanda get her hopes up. If it comes to the worst, she's likely to lash out at everyone around her."

"Hope is all she's got right now. Besides, I don't plan on disappointing her."

"What are you going to do next?"

"Get on the road and find some answers about why so many native kids get taken away from their parents or go missing. I need to hear people's stories. I'll drive clockwise, starting with the Shoshone and Paiute community at Fort McDermitt and then head east to Duck Valley on the Idaho-Nevada line. I'll go wherever the stories take me."

15

I dropped Loq off at the old lineman's shack. He retrieved from the front seat of his pickup the two woven baby rattles he'd found at the waterhole. "Give these to Wanda Manybaskets," he said and drove away.

I chained Wanda's pickup to the back of my rig and towed it to the Warbler ranch. On the way, I stopped at Blackpowder Smith's. He was in the back room, inventorying stock.

"You were a no show at the volunteer firefighting meeting," he said as he stamped prices on cans of corned-beef hash. "I thought if I could count on anyone, it'd be you. Never took you for one to shirk rolling up a shirtsleeve."

"It's why I'm here," I said. "I wanted to tell you I missed it because I went to lend a hand at the Rocking H. They had a fire."

"You don't say. No one reported it to me like they're supposed to. They lose anything?"

"A field and some fence posts. By the time I got there, they were moving the herd to safety."

"Was it natural or arson?"

"Blaine Harney's convinced it was a lightning strike."

"Or he convinced himself that," the old codger said. "He inherited more than a touch of his pappy's hard-headedness. He's a good rancher, though. Blaine don't miss a trick. How's he taking it now that you and Gemma are dating?"

"They'd split up long before I moved here," I said.

His laugh was a croak. "She did, but Blaine didn't. Count on it."

I filled him in on what Loq and I witnessed at the experimental range station as well as our conversations with Judd Hollister and Martin St. Claire.

"Sounds to me like that young fool is goin' run through his insurance money before the year is out," he said. "If that happens, I don't reckon anyone is goin' bring him home-cooked meals like they done after his folks died."

"Orville is having a hard time tracking down Freddie. Anything on your grapevine about him?"

"Nope. One thing you could do is knock on some doors. There aren't that many ranches a mule ride away. If Freddie's folks were sharecropping, the owner might still live nearby. Ranches in Harney County change hands so seldom Bekins don't even bother to park a truck here."

"It's worth a try."

"Hang on, I did hear something about a missing Paiute kid."

"Daisy and Danny Manybaskets are Washoe, not Paiute," I said.

"This wasn't about them. It's about a Paiute boy over in Malheur County. He disappeared goin' on a couple of months now."

"What happened?"

"Well, the sister of his mother told a fella I know who called me. Seems this husband and wife, the wife being the sister of the woman who told the fella I know who told me, were fighting all the time and their marriage was a demasted ship headed straight for the shoals. The husband takes off one night to cool off after they went at it. He has a reputation of being pretty headstrong. Traces his roots back to a war chief name of Pony Blanket. That's the family last name now. Anyway, when he comes home a couple days later, the wife and son are gone. Only they're not all the way gone. He looks around and sees she's only packed some of her clothes. He figures, okay, they'll come back after she cools off. Being the prideful sort, he doesn't breathe a word about it to nobody."

Blackpowder finished pricing the corned-beef hash and moved on to cans of fruit cocktail in heavy syrup. "Well, a couple days go by, and sure enough, the wife comes back. Only she don't have their son with her. See, she thought he took him when he stormed out. The boy is thirteen, and they call all the neighbors thinking he's bunking with one of his buddies, but nobody knows nothing. Okay, the couple thinks, he's hiding out somewhere because of them fighting. They feel bad that it's all their fault, but believe he'll come back when he gets hungry and misses watching TV. Another day or two go by and he still doesn't show."

He held up a can of fruit cocktail. "The pride they both swallowed right then and there sure didn't taste sweet like this. They go file a report with the Malheur County sheriff. He asks some questions, they answer them the best they can, he tells them he'll look into it, and then—and here's the kicker—they go back home and get a postcard from the boy. He says he's run off and has a new family now and for them to go ahead and get divorced because he's finished with them. Well, that was striking a match to a time-delayed fuse. They blew up blaming each other and wound up driving off in different directions."

"What did the Malheur County sheriff do when he heard about the postcard?"

"Not much he could do because it didn't have a return address and the parents were long gone. He let it drop."

"What makes the mother's sister think something else happened?"

Blackpowder went back to stamping prices on cans. "I was getting to that. A week or so ago, she goes to where the family was living in Malheur County. Town of Vale. She lives over on the other side of Burns in Riley and doesn't drive and had to wait until somebody could give her a lift, why it took her so long. She starts packing up the things her sister left to send to her in California where she's living now. She finds the postcard the boy had sent. Not a single misspelling on it. The handwriting was neat as a pin. Thing of it is, she says the boy's dyslexic. You know what that means? You see your letters all backwards, like a *d* becomes a *b* and so on. Messes up the way you read and write. No way that postcard was written by the boy. The parents were so blind mad at each other, they hadn't even noticed."

Wanda Manybaskets was standing next to the corral watching Wovoka and Sarah when I arrived with her pickup in tow. The pair of cutting horses were agitated. They had moved as far away from her as they could. The buckskin pawed the ground and snorted. He mimicked an oilfield pumpjack as he lowered his head and then tossed it back over and over. The sorrel mare had her teeth bared and her eyes rolled so far back, the whites showed.

"I told them I do not hold it against their kind for my husband's death, but they do not believe me," Wanda said. "Washoe have never been a horse culture like other native people. We paddled boats we made out of reeds on *Dá' ah*."

"You don't know how to ride?" I said.

"I never had to."

"But your husband was willing to learn."

"Tom Piñon tried to do a lot of things that were not the Washoe way. It was because he had grown up being ashamed. He was treated badly when he worked at the casino and was made to believe he was not worth anything."

"I brought your pickup back. I also brought you these." I handed her the baby rattles. "Loq found them next to the water-hole in the grove of old juniper trees."

Wanda held the rattles to her face. She breathed in their smell, sucking it deep into her lungs. "My babies," she sobbed. "Each day they are gone, I lose a piece of me. Soon there will be nothing left."

"Loq also went to Chewaucan and saw your camp alongside the marsh. He spoke with neighboring ranchers, but no one said they knew a Tom Piñon. Why do you think that is?"

"Maybe Loq did not go to the right ranch or they were frightened."

"Of what?"

"You would have to ask them."

"You never told us the name of the ranch or where it is."

"I have never been there. I stayed at our camp with my babies."

"Didn't your husband ever tell you the rancher's name?"

"When he spoke of him, he always called him his boss."

"But his wife gave you a ride to the hospital. Surely, she must have told you her name."

"She probably did, but I do not remember it. I was upset when she told me what happened. It seemed to take forever for her to drive to the hospital."

"If you don't know where the ranch is, how did you get the pickup? Didn't your husband drive it to work the day he got thrown by the horse?"

"Why are you asking me all these questions? You speak like the deputy."

"Information is the only thing we have to work with if we're going to find your children."

"I see." She sniffed the baby rattles again. "Yes, my husband always drove to work."

"But wasn't the pickup still there after he got thrown? How did you get it?"

"The rancher brought it to the hospital. I drove it back to our camp after my husband died. Where is Loq now?"

"He's on his way to the Fort McDermitt Reservation."

"Does he think my babies are there?"

"Maybe someone there knows something that can help us."

"But you did not go with him. Why? Girl Born in Snow said you would never give up looking."

"And I haven't, but I had to do something else. Someone has been lighting fires. One killed a man."

Wanda gripped a rattle in each hand and began to shake them. Dried corn kernels knocked against the insides of the woven willow strips and made a sound like a river washing back and forth on a gravel bar. "Fire is nothing because water can put it out. Water is more powerful."

"Look around. We're in the high desert in the hottest days of summer. The grass is tinder dry. There are lightning strikes nearly every day. A huge swath of Harney County is already ablaze. And now a firebug is starting more. Now that he's killed a person, he's likely to kill more. There's not enough water to stop a really big fire. This ranch, No Mountain, everything around here? It could all burn up. No, water won't stop him."

"But you think you can."

"I have to."

She let the baby rattles fall to her sides. "I have decided I will go to Spokane with Cameron and Arabelle Parker."

I hadn't seen that one coming. "What made you change your mind?"

"They telephoned the ranch this morning and said they could help me find my babies. Since no one here has been able to, I must do whatever it takes. If it means going to Spokane and talking to the doctor, I will."

I wanted to grab her by the shoulders and shake her like the woven baby rattles to snap her out of her melancholy. "Give us more time. We're getting new information every day."

"I can wait no longer. The Parkers are leaving soon and will take me with them."

"At least wait for Loq to get back. Can you do that? I have a feeling he's going to find out something. If you still want to leave after Loq gets back, I'll drive you to Spokane myself. Come on, stay. I want you to. We all do." Wovoka and Sarah drew closer, no doubt calmed by my familiar presence. "See, even the horses want you to."

Wanda finally looked down at the baby rattles. "My great-aunt *Dats'ai lo lee* made these. My mother rattled them when she was a baby and then so did I. I will wait a little longer in hopes that my babies can rattle them again."

16

L ow mesas with black basalt tops and steep faces of cream-colored tuff ran along the sides of a valley southwest of No Mountain. The floor was a checkerboard of dry farms and desert scrub. It showed no recent scarring from fire. Ranch houses were built close to the base of the mesas so as not to sacrifice arable land. I got lucky with the third door I knocked on.

The owners of the Lazy T were two bachelor brothers in their eighties, one tall and lean, the other portly with a double chin. They had a tendency to finish each other's sentences.

"Our family's been working this land since—" the tall one started.

"Statehood. That was in 1859," the portly brother finished.

"You're looking at the end of a dynasty here because—"

"We spent all our time working and not courting like we should've."

"Yep, we don't have any children to pass it on to which means—"

"The government will likely get it when we die."

"But we're not planning to kick the bucket anytime soon even though my brother's eighty-four—"

"And my brother's eighty-six."

"We'll never quit. We'll never sell," they said together.

I asked them if they ever had tenant farmers, and when they said they did, I told them what I knew about Freddie. It was the mule that triggered their memory.

"That was our mule. Old Gus. We—" the tall one started.

"Lent it to the family to go along with the sharecropping bargain we made with them," the portly one finished.

"They used Old Gus for—"

"Plowing a vegetable garden."

"The boy took to the mule. Old Gus was his only friend. The boy didn't have—"

"A dog or a brother to play with."

"One day he rode the mule to school without asking his folks' permission and—"

"They whupped him something fierce, by golly."

"My brother and me felt sorry for him. He was a shy child, but could get ornery—"

"Like most boys do, including my brother did when he was young."

"So did you. Why, you were the most—"

"Smartest and good-looking of the both of us. Still am."

"Pshaw. Anyway, we felt sorry for him and told his parents—"

"It'd be fine if he rode the mule to school. Leave him more time for doing his homework and chores."

"They saw the light and let him. Couple of months go by and—"

"One morning we woke up to find they'd packed up and lit out in the middle of the night."

"Thank goodness they left Old Gus behind. He lived another—"

"Five, six years. Best mule we ever had."

"I don't recollect any mention of the boy and—"

"A fire at the schoolhouse."

"What was the family's last name?" I asked.

The tall one scratched his chin. "Sanders. Or was it—"

"Sanderlin. It was Sanderlin," his portly brother said. "I remember. The father's name was Bill."

"That's right, Bill and Martha Sanderlin. We called the boy—"

"Ready Freddie. Not because he was game but because he had red hair like his mother."

I asked them if they knew where the family went after they left the ranch. "Did you ever hear from them again?"

"Can't say we did. We were too busy picking up—"

"Where they left off with the haying."

"That's the thanks you get," the brothers said at the same time.

On the drive back I radioed the sheriff's office and was patched through to Orville Nelson.

"Freddie is Freddie Sanderlin," I said. "His parents are Bill and Martha. He was an only child." I spelled the last name. "He has red hair."

"I will conduct a search, including military, voter registration, and arrest records," he said.

"Good. Is Pudge in the office?"

"He was as of a couple of minutes ago. I will transfer you."

A few clicks and buzzes later, the old lawman came on the line. I filled him in on what we'd found out about the three arson suspects as well as Blackpowder Smith's report of the missing Paiute boy from Malheur County.

"I'll give the sheriff over in Vale a call and find out what he knows about the boy. I'm surprised he didn't call us first. His office would've gotten the missing person reports for the Manybaskets youngsters," Pudge said. "Maybe he doesn't see any connection between the two. Can't say I do either."

"There's something else," I said. "When I took Wanda Manybaskets to the mobile Indian Services office, Cameron Parker, who runs it with his wife, told me he believes Wanda's unbalanced. He recommended she seek help at a clinic in Spokane that specializes in American Indians with mental illness. On the drive back to your ranch, Wanda told me she'd never go. She said she trusted the Parkers as much as she does a rattlesnake. Now she says she wants to go."

"She does, does she? Why the sudden switch of horses in the stream? Has she talked to the motorhome folks since you took her there?"

"They called her at your place. She told me she's given up on us finding her kids and is willing to try anything."

Pudge's sigh was loud and long. "I feel her pain, but, honestly, I don't know what more we can do. I've been spending all of my time on the phone with the state police and the attorney general's people. I thought maybe they'd have a special task force set up to locate missing Indian kids, seeing what Orville turned up on the numbers. They don't."

He sighed again. "We don't have a lick of evidence on who might've taken them or where they might be. Neither does the sheriff in Lake County. I've been talking to him regular too. No one there has seen hide nor hair of them or recalls ever having seen them. I'm starting to wish they've been taken out of Oregon just so the FBI will get involved, even though that's like hoping for a heart attack when you already got heartburn."

"I asked Orville to look into the clinic. It's called Bright Rivers. He's also looking into the church that funds the Parkers. There's a connection between the two outfits."

"Why, is there something about the Parkers that doesn't seem jake to you?"

"Nothing I can put my finger on, but they sure seem intent on getting Wanda out of here and up there."

"I'll make sure the college boy makes it a top priority. How he finds all the stuff he does without leaving his office is a wonder."

"Has Colonel Davies said anything more about the fire at the range station?"

"I haven't heard from him since we parted ways. He was gonna go back to his mountaintop lair and work with maps. Start laying out all the places there's been fires. See if he can't read something into it. He'll be in touch."

"You'll let me know the moment he does?"

"Goes without saying. You and Loq aren't gonna quit kicking over rocks looking for those kids in favor of finding the firebug, are you?"

"No way."

"That's good because I admit I need the help. If there was a back burner behind the back burner, Bust'em would put the investigation on it. He says the missing kids aren't our business, meaning since Wanda's not registered to vote in Harney County, he doesn't need to care about her. Asking you to work on it is surely gonna earn me another call from your boss chewing me out for shanghaiing you again. Now he's gonna give it to me double believing I shanghaied his newest recruit too."

"Tell Director Powers that stopping a firebug from burning up a refuge is part of Loq's and my job, and searching for missing children is everybody's job. You can also let him know we're not letting up on patrolling our refuges either. I'm on my way to Malheur Lake right now."

～

The Buena Vista Overlook was my favorite perch for getting a 180-degree view of Malheur National Wildlife Refuge. It sat atop a butte above a wide valley of fields and marshland. The Donner und Blitzen River, named by German soldiers in the US Cavalry after they'd been caught in a thunder and lightning storm there, fed ponds that provided year-round water for wildlife. Now, the resident birds were laid low by the stifling heat and smoke. I zoomed my binoculars as I searched through the haze that hung over the valley like early morning mist. I spotted a black-crowned night heron, a pair of great blue herons, and several snowy egrets trying to cool themselves by standing in the shallows.

The refuge had been created by President Teddy Roosevelt in part to stop the wholesale slaughter of the magnificently plumed creatures by feather hunters supplying the women's hat trade. Some sixty years after the preserve's founding, poaching of all kinds was still a problem and one of my duties was to stop it. The oppressive temperature was working in my favor. It had the same wilting effect on an illegal hunter's temptation as it did the energy of the birds.

Commingling with the river, ponds, and marshes were culti-vated hayfields, but no tractors were plowing or combines threshing. Farmers knew the heat from a manifold or a plow's disc hitting a rock would be as disastrous as striking flint with a knife blade. The air pulsed with the crackle of static electrical charges generated by superheated storm clouds overhead and the dirty whirlwinds bouncing and jostling across the high lonesome.

I descended the butte and drove along a canal that had been created to divert water to irrigate fields. I'd driven the route many times and was usually paced by gulps of barn swallows, but not today. It was too hot even for insects to hatch and excite the birds into a feeding frenzy. A cutoff took me away from the canal and between two hayfields. I stopped, got out, and plucked a hay straw.

Standing in the field chewing it, I thought about the farmer who'd grown it. He was an acquaintance. The previous summer —my first in Harney County—he'd invited me to learn about loose haying, a timeless technique that had been passed on from one generation to the next. I viewed the method as a labor of love because it forswore modern threshing and baling machinery.

The farmer cut the grass with a sickle mower and left it where it fell to dry in place. Three days later he returned with a tractor pulling a side delivery rake and putted through the cut hay slowly, turning it into single windrows. After it was turned to his satisfaction, he picked up the loose hay using a buck rake which he'd built out of a one-ton truck frame with the motor and gears turned backwards. The rake tines of his belching, smoking contraption were made of six-foot long logs he'd felled and peeled himself. He scooped up the loose hay and placed it on the flatbed of the truck frame.

When he'd gathered a ton or more, he drove it to the base of a steeply angled ramp he'd constructed from cut timber. It was called a beaverslide. A motorized hoist pulled the loose hay up the ramp by bucket. The bucket was tipped when it reached the top of the beaverslide and the loose hay was dumped over the other side onto a growing pile. The outer layer of the resulting haystack protected the hay inside and would keep it fresh for a couple of years so he could feed his livestock uninterrupted by freeze or drought.

The hay straw I chewed was as brittle as an old chicken bone. I flicked it aside. If the arsonist ever targeted the farmer's field, it would go up as fast as the lineman's shack, taking his hand-built buck rake and beaverslide with it along with all his precious haystacks. I tried to picture the arsonist's expression while he watched his handiwork, but couldn't. I had witnessed plenty of evil in Vietnam, but a man who destroyed lives and livelihood with fire to satisfy his own twisted craving was impossible to fathom.

Back in my pickup, I drove north through the refuge on the Central Patrol Road. I passed a herd of grazing mule deer. I braked when a porcupine slowly lumbered across the road. A great horned owl watched sleepily from a cottonwood tree. All these animals would be at the mercy of fire too. Some, like the owl, would be able to fly away. Maybe if they were fast enough, pronghorn, mule deer, and Rocky Mountain elk might also escape. But the slow-gaited porcupine, along with black bear, badger, raccoon, and other animals—insects, snakes, and lizards included—would surely be caught by the flames and perish.

I couldn't let that happen. Their deaths would stalk my dreams as surely as those of my squad mates who I'd led into a slaughter.

17

I didn't have nightmares about burning animals or dying GIs when I fell asleep in my narrow bunk after reading more of the Edward Abbey book that night, but I did dream about Daisy and Danny Manybaskets. The girl and her little brother had eyes as shiny as buttons and skin the color of a new saddle. Daisy hummed to herself as she played with dolls made of old socks stuffed with straw. Both of Danny's elbows were scabbed and his knees bore fresh scrapes. His hair was home barbered, which left a cowlick in the back. He wielded a broken branch like a sword.

I watched the children from a few yards away as they played at the edge of a marsh. Daisy was arranging her sock dolls around a rock and telling them to hush or she wouldn't serve them frybread dusted with powdered sugar. Danny was sword fighting a leaning cattail, jabbing and hacking at the stalk with his broken branch. The sun was newly risen and its rays bathed the siblings in golden light.

A wisp of smoke from a nearby campfire rose lazily. Wanda Manybaskets stepped out of a wickiup made of cattails. She was carrying a hand-loomed blanket adorned with the scene of a sapphire lake surrounded by snowcapped peaks. As she draped it over a clothesline to air in the morning sun, she sang a lullaby. The click-clacking of dried corn kernels shaken in a woven baby rattle provided tempo to her tune. The carefree scene of innocence and happiness swirled around the family like a boat drifting on a lake. It swirled around me too and I swayed to Wanda's song.

The smoke from the campfire started growing darker, heavier, and I tried to wipe the stinging from my eyes. Then a flash bloomed red as the wickiup erupted in flames. Wanda shrieked and grabbed the beautiful blanket from the clothesline and attempted to smother the fire engulfing their home. I started to run to help her, but my feet wouldn't move. I looked down and saw I was sinking in mud as the marsh's waters rose. I tried to lift each leg, straining as I did, but I could not free myself from the quickening mire.

"Save my babies!" Wanda screamed at me. I turned to where the children were playing. The waters of the marsh rolled forward like waves, one after another, surging around their knees, the crests lapping at their hips. Daisy hugged her sock dolls to her chest and cried, "Mama, Mama!" Danny thrust his make-believe sword in the faces of the swells. "Take that!" he shouted. "Take that!"

I twisted my hips and pumped my arms, trying to gain leverage and break free. "Run, Daisy. Run, Danny. Run!" I shouted as the water grew higher and reached my waist and then my chest.

But it was too late and the children were gone. Wanda's eyes became two burning bonfires as she glared at me. "My babies!" she roared, flames leaping from her throat. "My babies! You let them die."

～

I woke in a feverish sweat. The sheets of the narrow bunk were twisted around my neck. I clawed free. First light glowed on the horizon. I shook off the nightmare, threw on my clothes, and ran outside. The Triumph started on the second kick and leapt forward as I twisted the throttle wide open and hung on. I redlined it all the way to Judd Hollister's.

When I reached the beach house that had been plopped in the middle of cattle country, I braked, shifted into neutral, and revved the 650cc engine. The spitfire whine did nothing to bring anyone out. I clamped the front wheel brake tight, shifted into first, and spun a donut in place. The whirling rear wheel spit gravel like a .50-caliber machine gun chucking brass from the open bay of a Huey.

That finally did the trick. Judd stumbled out the front door. He was wearing cutoffs and a sleeveless white undershirt adorned with a likeness of the cartoon character Rat Fink.

"What the fuh, bro? Stop it before you ding my ride."

"Hundred bucks says I leave you in the dust on a quarter mile," I said.

He raked his fingers through his hair. "What's up with you, dude? It's way too early for serious."

"A hundred," I said. "You game or chicken?"

"Aw, man. Now you went and said it. Okay, give me a minute while I grab my keys and tell the chick under my sheets I'll be back before she knows I'm gone."

When Judd returned, he was wearing a pair of blue Keds low tops to go along with the cutoffs and undershirt. He was shaking his head as he got in the metallic green Shelby and fired it up. The rumble of the big block engine amplified by the chrome headers drowned out the sound of my bike. He pulled away from the house and didn't mash the pedal until he was a hundred yards out. I followed but stayed clear of his dusty wake.

When we reached the two-lane blacktop, he sped up to 85

miles per hour and held it there until we reached a turnoff to a wide-open salt flat. The sun filtering through the smoky haze hit the alkaline crystals covering the ancient lake bed and made them dazzle. Tire tracks crisscrossing the pan told me it was not Judd's first visit. He pulled to a stop at a wavery black horizontal stripe that had been spray painted on the ground. His window was rolled down when I drew alongside.

"You want, you can hand over the hundy now and save yourself the wear and tear on your bike," he sneered.

"We'll see who's handing over what," I said.

"You got, what, seventy-five horses max? This baby cranks out three-fifty-five. It's no contest."

I wiped my finger across my goggles. "Do you want to count one, two, three or call ready, set, go?"

"Aw, dude. Really? Okay, if you insist. See those wooden stakes with orange ribbons planted down there? That's our finish line." He hunched over his steering wheel. "Call it, sucker."

I depressed the clutch lever with my left and gripped the throttle with my right. "Ready, set, go!" I shouted. And hit it.

I slammed my chest onto the gas tank and laid my forehead onto the handlebars as the bike reared and shot forward, getting as low as I could to reduce drag. I didn't need to see where I was going on a straightaway. I never let up on the gas as I clutched, shifted, clutched, shifted. The toe of my left boot was working in harmony with my hands as I climbed through the gears. The Triumph couldn't compete with the much more powerful muscle car in a race any longer than a quarter mile, but in that distance, weight to power ratio gave me a chance. Not much of one, but just enough if my reflexes were faster than Judd's.

Sand stung my shins and the motor between my legs screamed as it hit 6,700 RPMs and kept climbing. I didn't let up. I could feel the presence of the looming Mustang fastback inches away on my right side. If Judd didn't hold his steering wheel tight, a quarter-inch drift to the left would send the bike and me somersaulting into oblivion.

I kept count of the seconds. One one hundred. Two one hundred. Three one hundred. I'd calculated it would take me a tick over twelve seconds to travel a quarter of a mile. At ten one hundred, I snuck a glance. The front bumper of the metallic green Shelby was at my hip. Eleven one hundred. It was even with my shoulder. I eased back on the throttle ever so slightly. Twelve one hundred. It reached my front wheel. Thirteen one hundred. It was in front. The orange ribbons whipped from our exhaust as we roared past. Judd smacked his horn in victory and cut right to make figure eights.

I throttled down and the RPMs fell away. It took another quarter of a mile to slow down enough for me to sit upright without being hurled backward out of the saddle. I savored my own victory in having figured out a way to get close to Judd without raising suspicion. By the time I circled back to the finish line, he was out of his car whooping and hollering and stomping his blue Keds.

"Dude, that was a righteous race. I mean, I beat you and all, but wow. Far out. Hey, let's go back to my place and celebrate. You and me, we got some shit we can talk about."

"Cool," I said, claiming the trophy I'd been after all along.

18

J udd led the way. The interior of his house was as Loq had described, sparse on furniture and heavy on wall hangings and stereo equipment. The owner pointed to a black leather couch. "Make yourself comfortable, dude, while I go fetch some brewskis."

"I'm good with water," I said.

"Don't give me that you're on duty crap. We're partying here."

"Fine, but I don't drink."

Judd screwed up his face as if trying to solve a calculus equation. "Like, not even beer? What are you, a Jesus Freak or something? Don't tell me you're straight."

I turned the insides of my arms toward him so he could see the scars that dotted my veins. "Does that look straight to you?"

"Whoa, dude. You're into shooting the heavy stuff, huh? What, speed, coke, smack? I got some weed, but nothing stronger. I can roll you a joint."

"Water's fine," I said.

"Okay, one glass of water coming up. All right if I put an ice cube in it?" He snickered and headed toward the kitchen.

While he was gone, I checked out the art. The paintings in

frames and the lithographs under glass bore signatures. I was no expert, but since Pop Art was being used to sell everything from rock albums to canned soup, I knew who Andy Warhol was.

A girl who looked about seventeen glided into the room. Her bangs were cut straight across the top of her eyes and she wore a short silk robe with a tropical flower print.

"Are you here to fix the pool? There's too much bleach. It's turning my hair green."

"Maybe you should wear a swim cap," I said.

She giggled. "You're funny. What's your name?"

"Nick Drake. And yours?"

"Chrissy, but Judd calls me Barbie. He calls all the girls Barbie. He thinks he's being cute." She put the tip of her pinkie finger to her lips. "You're pretty cute too."

I wondered if Chrissy had been the girl in the pink bikini floating on the inflatable swan. I asked if she drove a yellow VW convertible.

"Boring," she said with a roll of her eyes. "Ask me something more interesting."

"Like what?"

"Like if I skinny dip." Chrissy giggled again. "I do, you know." She skipped away.

Judd returned. He was carrying a glass of water and two opened bottles of beer. "Don't worry, they're both for me." He handed over the water and plopped on the couch. It caused the beers to fizz. He tried stanching the eruption of suds by clamping his lips on both bottles at once. It only made matters worse and a yellow waterfall dripped off his chin and ran down the middle of Rat Fink.

"You have quite an art collection," I said.

"You dig them? Check out the one of Mick Jagger in those leather pants. I swear he's packing it, know what I mean?"

I pointed the water glass at the signed Marilyn Monroe lithograph. "Is that a real Andy Warhol?"

Judd nodded. "You like him?"

"I'd never heard of Warhol until he was shot last year."

"The chick who did it was crazy. She, like, fired three times but only hit him once. Then she tried to shoot his manager in the head, but her gun jammed. What a loser. She did manage to pop some other chick who was there. Warhol getting shot made that piece worth a whole lot more. When he dies?" Judd raised a beer bottle toward the ceiling and made a rocket launch noise.

"Is the one with DayGlo colors and the big letters spelling out LOVE a real Peter Max?"

"That's his signature at the bottom, dude. I mean, he hasn't been popped like Warhol so it's nowhere near as valuable. The most pricey piece I got? Check out that big cartoon-like one with the chick holding a rifle that has *Pop! Crack!* lettered on it. It's like the *Batman* series on TV, the one starring Adam West. When Robin and him were fighting the Joker or Penguin, these colorful graphics popped up while the music played. *Pow! Wham!* It was, like, hilarious, dude, but they canceled it last year. You ever watch it?"

"No."

"How come?"

"I was in Vietnam."

"Really? That's, like, heavy. Anyway, that piece there, you know who painted it?"

"I'm guessing someone who illustrates comic books."

"That's a Roy Lichtenstein. He's, like, the man."

I thought about the Frederic Remington paintings and bronzes in the study at the Rocking H. As the crow flew, Blaine Harney's ranch wasn't that far away, but the art there was worlds apart from the style on display here.

Judd sucked down some more beer. "I like the Lichtenstein

the best because she's popping off a round. The Warhol's my second favorite because he took a round. They brighten up the place, sure, but mostly I like them because they have something to say."

"Such as?"

"Up Yours! Know what I mean?" Judd drained one bottle and drank from the next.

Any poster that was thumbtacked to the wall wasn't original or even a limited edition. They weren't worth the paper they were printed on, but a signed and framed lithograph had to cost a lot more than a rancher got for raising and selling a calf.

"Where do you buy a signed Andy Warhol in Harney County?" I said.

"Nowhere, that's where." He laughed. "I know a guy who's a dealer in New York. These are investments, like a bond or a stock certificate, only groovier to look at."

Judd blew on his beer bottle and made it whistle. "You're not wearing your uniform and gun like you were before. You ever have to pop off a round at something other than a bear charging you or a coyote foaming with rabies? Like, pop a person. A poacher or someone?"

"Why do you want to know that?"

"Because the only place you see that is on TV. How about it? Have you ever fired your gun at someone? Hit them?" His eyes narrowed. "Kill someone?"

"I served three years of combat duty leading long recon patrols. What do you think?"

Judd sank back into the black leather couch "Man, you must have seen and done some real heavy shit. Am I right? I mean, you know, from what I heard and all. I didn't go overseas. I tried. I even went and talked to a recruiter in Burns, but he said seeing I'd been orphaned, they couldn't take me. Some kind of law." He polished off the second beer. "Three years, huh? Is that where you got into shooting smack?"

I stood and reached for my wallet and fished out four twenties and two tens. I put them on the glass coffee table. "Thanks for the race, Judd."

"You're leaving already? We're just getting started."

"I got to go. You have a fine machine out there."

"Sure, dude, thanks. I mean, you don't have to pay me the hundy. I got plenty."

"You won it. It's yours."

He scrambled to his feet. "Your ride is pretty fine too. I've never been a two-wheeler, but if you ever want to sell it, I'd be open to buying it."

"It's not for sale," I said.

"Okay, sure. I mean, yeah, I can dig it." He paused. "Got to go punch the clock, huh? Hey, you know, if you ever find yourself short cash wise, I could hook you up with the odd job here and there." Judd focused on the crooks of my arms. "You know, help you pay expenses." He grinned.

"Doing what, cleaning your pool? Chrissy told me it's got too much chlorine in it."

"That Barbie? I meant other sorts of jobs. The kind that pay pretty good. Well, they pay real good, if you know what I mean. And it's all off the books."

"What kind of jobs?"

Judd glanced at his art collection. When he turned back to me, he wore a sly grin. "I told you, I don't do ranching and I don't do typical. I do business deals here and there. Sometimes I need help with security. Seeing that you're not so straight after all, something comes along I think is up your alley, like driving fast and handling a gun, I'll get in touch. You could do it in your spare time, put some extra coin in your pocket to feed that habit of yours. How's that sound?"

I gave it a ten count before answering. "That'd be cool, Judd. Real cool. Give me a call."

"Far out. Will do."

Pudge Warbler's rig wasn't in the sheriff's department parking lot when I pulled in on my Triumph. I went looking for Orville Nelson to see if he knew where the old lawman was. I found him at his desk. He'd scooted his wheelchair a half turn so his back was to the door. He was hunched over as if in pain.

"Are you feeling all right?" I said.

Startled, he jerked his head, but didn't turn around. "I did not hear you enter," he said over his shoulder. "Please give me a moment. I am in the process of urinating."

"Sorry," I said and quickly backpedaled.

"You do not need to leave. And, please, do not be embarrassed. If you are, then I shall be too. Urination is only a bodily function. I must utilize a collection system similar to what Armstrong, Aldrin, and Collins used when they flew to the moon."

"Knowing you're a *Star Trek* fan, that's good company."

"Capturing bodily fluids has always been one of the space program's greatest challenges. Alan Shepard had to urinate in his space suit. I feel fortunate that the only barrier for me is I have to urinate at my desk because the door to the men's room is not wide enough to accommodate my wheelchair."

"Somebody needs to fix that and fast," I muttered, thinking if Sheriff Burton was too cheap to authorize the money to pay for it, I'd bring over a sledgehammer and do it myself.

When he was finished, Orville shoved something into a bin and then wiped his hands with a towel and stashed that in the bin too. He turned his wheelchair back around.

"I was still in the hospital during the lunar landing," he said. "My room had a television and I never took my eyes off it, from the countdown to the *Eagle* landing to the splashdown." Orville fixed his gaze on the clunky scientific calculator on his desk. "The entire time I was watching, I imagined myself flying with them. In zero gravity, I could float and not be restrained by these." He patted the top of his thighs. "For me, space does not represent the final frontier. It embodies freedom."

I fought to keep my emotions in check. Orville wasn't asking for sympathy, only understanding.

He looked up. "I have not been able to locate the whereabouts of Freddie Sanderlin and I am still working on profiling the two organizations in Spokane."

"Actually, I stopped by to tell Pudge about something else. His pickup's not in the lot. Do you know where he went?"

"He is having a private meeting with the editor and publisher of the *Burns Herald*."

"Bonnie LaRue? What made him go see her?"

"She invited him. My guess is she is considering endorsing him for sheriff."

"Only if there's something in it for her." I knew firsthand how the newspaperwoman operated. She'd tried to use me on more than one occasion to get a story. Since taking over publication following her husband's death, Bonnie LaRue had proven time and time again that anyone who underestimated her did so at their own peril.

"I grant you, Mrs. LaRue can certainly be intimidating, but the paper's endorsement would go a long way to securing a victory come election night," Orville said.

"I don't see Pudge groveling for it. Maybe he's turning on the old charm like he did when they were dating."

Orville blushed. "I am not at all comfortable talking about my superior's personal life."

"Trust me, neither am I, especially when it comes to Pudge and romance. Look, I'm on my way to have a talk with the Parkers, but I wanted to tell him about Judd Hollister. I saw him this morning. Pudge will find it interesting."

"If you would like, I can pass on the information."

I filled him in. "Judd's up to something because there can't be anything left of the insurance settlement after five years that allows him to buy Warhols and other pieces of Pop Art. What sealed the deal was when he asked me whether I'd shot anyone and if I'd help him on a job."

Orville fixed his gaze on the clunky scientific calculator on his desk. "That was either very reckless or he holds himself in such high regard that he considers himself invincible. Both traits are disturbing."

"I gave him the impression I was still using heroin."

"That was a very clever subterfuge. Now he will think he has something over on you. I will certainly relay this to Deputy Warbler. I will also dig deeper into Judd Hollister's background. All I have been able to ascertain so far is his address and that he has no criminal convictions."

"I know you're busy, but could you also find any information about Pop Art transactions?"

"Certainly. Current prices and recent purchases should be readily available with a phone call to the major art dealers in New York."

"While you're at it, see if there's anything about stolen Warhols, Roy Lichtensteins, or Peter Maxes. Judd says he got them from a dealer, but who knows if that person is legitimate or not."

"Do you believe the dealer is a fence?"

"It's worth looking into. Can you do all that while not letting up on researching missing children and the church and mental health clinic in Spokane?"

"I will not let it become a Hobson's choice."

"I told Loq about what you found on missing Indian kids. He's going from reservation to reservation asking question. Maybe he'll turn up something. Don't forget to tell Pudge about Judd Hollister. I'm off to talk to the Parkers."

The Winnebago with "Indian Services" lettered on the awning was not parked next to the county health building. I drove around the block and then widened my search until I'd covered all of the downtown area. I returned to the county health building and asked staffers there if anybody knew anything about Cameron and Arabelle Parker's whereabouts.

"I talked to them this morning," a receptionist told me. "We let them fill up their water jugs here and use the restrooms. They're very nice people. Not many would do what they're doing. It's long hours, no pay, and no thanks."

"Do you know if they left for Spokane already?" I said.

"Arabelle told me they were driving over to Harney Valley this morning to talk to some of the Paiutes who live there. Where, exactly, I wouldn't know, but I imagine they'll be back before dark. They sleep in their motorhome and being under a streetlight close to the sheriff's office has to be a comfort."

I thanked her and rode back to the lineman's shack and exchanged the motorcycle for my pickup. The road east took me to Harney Valley. I crossed over both forks of the Silvies River that drained into Malheur Lake. Much of the valley had once been the Malheur Indian Reservation, but after the Bannock War of 1878, the federal government had deauthorized it. Parcels within the old boundaries had recently been reestablished as reservation land for the Paiute. Not many roads bisected the valley and I covered the main ones without spotting the white Winnebago with the brown *W* and matching stripe.

After a couple of hours, I gave up searching. The Parkers could've circled back on another road to their parking spot next to the health building. With the day growing late, I decided to return home and start fresh in the morning.

I had only driven a few miles when I spotted a man walking up ahead. Even though he had his back to me, I recognized him from the white hair that reached the top of his shoulders and held in place by a red bandana worn as a headband. A bundle hung over his shoulder and he gripped a walking stick made of gnarled juniper. It was Tuhudda Will, a Paiute elder who'd been born in the same snow storm as November.

As I pulled alongside, he glanced over. "Nick Drake. I knew you were coming before you left. This is so," he said in his slow, deliberate manner.

"Hello, my old friend. Can I offer you a ride?"

"If it pleases you, though my own two feet can take me."

Tuhudda opened the door, laid the bundle on the seat, and scooted in next to it. He held the walking stick upright.

"Your camp is behind us," I said. "Where are you going?"

"To do what I have been asked to do by the old ones, *Nuwuddu* and *Numu* both. They spoke to me in a dream."

"What do the first and second people want you to do?"

"To ask the clouds to give up their rain. This is so."

19

We passed by the lineman's shack as I drove straight to Pudge Warbler's house. Tuhudda Will said he needed to pick up something there.

"The *kida*," I said before he could tell me. "To carry *paa'a*."

His red headband rose and fell. "You are getting to know our ways better each day."

"November told me about the water basket. I saw her making it."

"Girl Born in Snow is as good a teacher as she is a healer. This is so."

I didn't ask him how he knew she'd been making a *kida*. I no longer questioned how the two Paiute elders were able to communicate so freely. There were no telephone lines stretching out to the Will camp in Harney Valley. The single-wide trailers and wooden shanties that housed his extended family had no electricity either.

We found November in the kitchen. She was bent over the stove, pulling a tray of biscuits from the oven. "You will eat supper before you go," she said, showing no surprise that

Tuhudda had arrived. "I will pack some food for you to take along with the *kida*."

"If it pleases you, then I will," Tuhudda said.

"Sit and I will bring you supper."

"Pudge and Gemma aren't home?" I said.

"He is spending the night in Burns and Gemma is still flying like *Kwe'na'a*. She will return when she returns."

Tuhudda and I had no sooner sat down then Wanda Many-baskets joined us. I introduced them.

Wanda studied the old man closely. "Are you here to help find my babies?"

"No. I have been asked to perform the rainmaking ceremony. This is so," he said.

November came in from the kitchen. She spoke to Tuhudda in rapid-fire *Numu*. I couldn't keep up, but I recognized the Washoe words she'd said the first time she met Wanda, *we muhu*. Tuhudda reacted visibly to it and replied quickly. He said *paa'a*, which I knew meant water, and *oha'a*, which meant baby, but he ran the two words together. She uttered the two words the same way when she answered him.

When they finished speaking, Tuhudda turned to Wanda and bowed. "May your journey be rewarded," he said.

"And yours, old one," she replied. "Do *Numu* use tobacco smoke and sacred plants for your rainmaking ceremony like *Washeshu* do?"

He gave her an appreciative nod. "You are knowledgeable about such things."

"And do you carry pipes and bowls once used by your ancestors?"

"They are in my bundle."

"May I see them?"

November interrupted. "We must eat first, *lebík'iyi*."

After we finished, Tuhudda set his bundle on the table and

opened it to show Wanda the contents. He pulled out a pair of conical pieces of soapstone fitted with mouthpieces made of hollowed bird bone.

"The smoking pipes," he said.

Next he withdrew a trio of small bowls. They were made of soapstone too. He added to the growing collection a chunk of rose-colored quartz, a geode whose crystalline center sparkled beneath the overhead light, a fish vertebra as white as snow, and five pieces of shiny black obsidian that resembled figures: wolf, deer, coyote, man, and woman. Three pouches made of tanned animal hide were the last to come out. Their tops were tied closed with leather thongs.

Tuhudda held the pouches up one by one. "This is tobacco, this is sage, and this is dried wada root and grass seeds."

"The third is the traditional food of our people," November said. "We grind them and pat them into cakes."

"This is so," Tuhudda said. "Other *Numu* offer the foods they are known by."

I ran through the names of a few of the dozen different bands of Paiute as I looked at the pouches. There were *Kamö-dokadö*, the hare eaters, *Kidütökadö*, the yellow-bellied marmot eaters, and *Kutsavidökadö*, the brine-fly eaters.

Tuhudda pulled out a square block that was wrapped in dried fish skin that had the look of wax paper. He gently unfolded it to expose a cake of pemmican. "This is dried buffalo meat that my own hands pounded into powder and mixed with hot fat and dried berries," he said. "*Bagootsoo* once thundered across this land, but no more. The pemmican will remind the clouds of what once was and what could be with their help."

"May I add something to your bundle?" Wanda said.

"If it pleases you."

The Washoe woman reached into her pocket and then held out her palm to show a freshwater clamshell no bigger than her fingernail. "This is from *Dá' ah*, the lake sacred to all *Washeshu*. It will help bring the rain."

"Thank you for your gift," he said with a bow.

I don't know what surprised me more, the fact that Wanda was now saying *Washeshu* instead of Washoe, or that she had an object from home other than the two woven baby rattles. I wanted to ask her if she had anything else that might prove useful in locating her children, but before I could, Tuhudda announced it was time to go. He wrapped the tiny clamshell in a strip of soft hide and placed it along with the rest of objects in his bundle.

"Nick Drake will take you," November said.

"If it pleases him," Tuhudda said

Somewhere along the line, I don't remember exactly when or where—it could've been a high school science class or maybe during the two years I put in at community college before enlisting in the Army—I'd learned there were three distinct parts of a shadow: umbra, the blackest part where the light source is completely blocked; penumbra, a dark gray region where only a portion of the light source is obscured; and antumbra, the region from which the obstructing body appears entirely within the disc of light.

I used this information whenever a cherry was assigned to my squad. "If we ever have to fall back in a firefight," I explained, "go for the umbra so the enemy can't see you. Penumbra is likely to draw fire." If the cherry still didn't understand about using shadows for cover, DJ, my radio operator, would set them straight. "Sarge is into big words, dig? But all you got to remember is 'Black is beautiful.'" And he gave them the clenched-fist salute.

As I drove Tuhudda Will up the steep and rocky road that climbed the western flank of Steens Mountain, the peak was already umbra and the silhouetting sky penumbra.

"How far up do you have to go?" I asked him.

"To where the clouds live."

"The very top," I said. "I should've known that."

The peak was nearly 10,000 feet above sea level, the highest point in all of Harney County. The road was mostly switchbacks and then ran along a knife edge between two deep gorges, Little Blitzen and Big Indian. A blowout or a wrong turn to either the left or right would send us careening off the edge and plummeting to the bottom two thousand feet below.

"It takes me three days to walk here from my camp," Tuhudda said. "Longer if the snow is deep. I came here one spring to hunt for bear. I wanted to give my wife's family a wedding present."

"Did you find one?"

"He found me. I made camp and fell asleep without hanging my food from a tree. He was eating it when I woke up."

"What happened?"

"The bear told me I needed to grow smarter. Today it was someone stealing my food. Tomorrow it could be someone stealing my wife."

"What did you do?"

"I thanked the bear for the lesson and walked back down the mountain. I got married and no one ever stole my wife."

"Smart bear," I said.

"On the walk home, I realized it was not a bear. It was Coyote. He is always tricking *Nuwuddu* and *Numu* to get what he wants, but that time I tricked him."

"How so?"

"I would have given him some food if he had asked. Something that is always shared can never be stolen."

The headlights reflected off the white bark of aspen trees that grew at higher elevation. I'd seen them in autumn when their leaves had turned the color of flames. I opened the window and cold air blew in, making it difficult to imagine the wildfires burning in the valleys below. The arsonist was a thief too. He was robbing people and animals of their food, their homes, and their sense of well-being. By murdering Hairy Jerry, he had also stolen a life. The agencies who'd removed Indian kids against their parents' will were also thieves. Not only had they stolen children, they'd robbed parents of their hopes and dreams and a people of their dignity and traditions.

We passed through the grove of aspens. "There is the trail to the East Rim," Tuhudda said. "I must walk the rest of the way."

I parked and got out as Tuhudda gathered his bundle, slung it over his shoulder, and gripped the walking stick in one hand and the *kida* in the other. "Thank you, Nick Drake."

"You don't have a blanket or a jacket. It's likely to get cold up here tonight."

"I will make camp and build a fire."

"I always carry a box of emergency supplies," I said. "There's a blanket in it. You can have it. I've also got tea, pilot bread crackers, and some jerky too. You go ahead. I'll collect some wood and bring it up along with the blanket and other things."

"You know our custom. If you give me a gift, I must give you one in exchange, but I have nothing to give right now."

"You make it rain, Tuhudda, and we'll call it square."

20

Tuhudda Will arranged rocks into a circle and built a small fire within it using dry sticks of aspen. I decided to keep him company. The campfire cast an eerie glow as night fell. We were high above the haze of smoke that continued to cloak Harney County, and while the clarity of stars overhead was a welcome sight, the fiery fragments from a meteor shower streaking past were a reminder that even the lives of suns and planets were finite.

We sipped hot tea from mugs that I also kept in my emergency box. I asked him when he would begin the rainmaking ceremony.

"Tomorrow. If the signs allow," he said

"What kind of signs?"

"There are different ones for different places and different times," he explained slowly, emphasizing some words, swallowing others. "Here? I think it will be if the wind comes from the east. Also if the vultures circle left not right when they ride the hot air rising from the brown world."

"Can you do it if there are no clouds?"

"If the clouds are not here, then I will sing to them. If my song is pleasing, they will gather and come closer to hear it better."

I gripped the mug with both hands and inhaled the scent of lemongrass. "Can you tell me how you use the smoke and the different plants or is that part of the ceremony sacred?"

"I will tell you, Nick Drake, because Girl Born in Snow wishes you to learn these things. She told me she is teaching you our ways so that when she makes the journey to the spirit world, you will be able to keep watch over Gemma for her. This is so."

The Paiute elder added a stick to the fire. "I put the tobacco and sage in pipes and blow the smoke so the clouds can see it. The smoke tells the clouds that *Numu* can make clouds also and we are their brothers and sisters. This is so. I pour water from the *kida* in a circle and place the gifts of stones and food inside the circle. If the clouds accept the gifts, they may gift rain in exchange. It is up to the clouds."

Tuhudda sipped some tea and then chewed on a piece of jerky. It brought a smile to the old man's lips. "I like jerky. It lets me know I still have teeth."

The fire popped and crackled. A rockfall clattered down the East Rim that towered above the Alvord Desert. It was probably set off by a bighorn sheep or a mountain goat settling down on a ledge for the night.

"Can I ask you a question about Wanda Manybaskets?" I said.

"The *Washeshu* woman. You can ask, but I do not know if I know the answer."

"November calls her *lebík'iyi*. I'm assuming that's a Washoe word. What does it mean?"

"Sister's granddaughter."

"Grandniece, because *Dats'ai lo lee* is Wanda's great-aunt. There's another Washoe word I don't understand. *We muhu.*

November said it and then it seemed like she was translating it to you in *Numu* as *paa'a o'haa*. Water baby."

"This is so."

"What's a water baby?"

"Many people have stories about them. Shoshone, Serrano, Yokuts. I can only tell you what *Numu* believe. *Paa'a o'haa* are powerful spirits who live in springs and ponds and lakes. They take the form of second people babies."

Little people, I thought. Lots of cultures had variations of the same. The Irish had their leprechauns, the Hawaiians *menehune*. When I was in Vietnam, I'd heard legends about a figure whose name translated to "Marsh Boy."

"Why do the spirits appear as young children?" I said.

Tuhudda took another bite of jerky, chewed it carefully, and washed it down with tea. He looked overhead and watched as another shooting star zoomed by. I thought he was avoiding answering me, but then he stared into the fire and began to speak.

"It is said that in the old days when our ancestors walked this land, there was a time when no food could be found. Not a squirrel to be caught, not a seed to gather. The people of the brown world were starving. It is said that during this time when babies were born, their mothers' milk would not flow. The mothers loved their babies so much that they could not bear to see them suffer. They took their babies to the water and placed them in it so they would suffer no more forever. Water babies are their souls."

I could hear Wanda's lullaby among the crackle and hiss of the fire. *Water carries the baby, swirling, swirling, across the lake to the big mountain.*

Tuhudda said, "Some people believe this is so. Others do not because they cannot believe someone would do that to their own flesh and blood." He fed another stick to the fire. "I say, who are we to know what the world was like before our time and what our ancestors had to do? Who are we to say we would not have done the same if our babies were suffering? And who are we to say that a mother's love is not the hardest love of all to bear?"

I finished my tea. "Are water babies good or evil spirits?"

"*Paa'a o'haa* can be dangerous and cause sickness and death, but they can also choose to be good. Healers seek their help and bring offerings to renew their powers."

"I heard November tell Wanda Manybaskets that she can talk to *we muhu*."

He shrugged. "Girl Born in Snow has always been a powerful healer. This is so."

"Why does November think water babies have anything to do with Wanda Manybaskets?"

"You must ask Girl Born in Snow for that is her story to tell, not mine."

Not wishing to offend him, I deliberated before asking, but curiosity won out. "Have you ever seen one?"

"I have heard the sound of a baby's cry along the shore of Malheur Lake that is close to my family's camp," he said. "Was it a water baby calling or was it a loon? I do not know because I did not go down to see."

"Why not?"

"If it was a water baby, how was I to know if it would be angry with me or not?"

I had lived with Paiute neighbors nowhere near long enough to know all of their traditions and beliefs, and I knew next to nothing about the Washoe's. But I did know enough never to be skeptical. I felt a chill, and it wasn't just because the temperature on top of the mountain was starting to drop. I hadn't brought a jacket and so I draped the blanket over Tuhudda's shoulders and bid the old man good night.

"How long will you stay here?" I said before walking back down the trail.

"That is up to the clouds."

"When the rain starts to fall, I'll come get you and spare you the long walk home."

"If it pleases you, so be it."

Driving down the curving, narrow mountain road in darkness was even trickier than driving up. I stayed in first and second gear to save my brakes, but even then I had to use them so often the brake pads smoked and a smell like burning human hair filled the cab. When I finally reached the two-lane blacktop and turned north for home, I floored it to blow the stench out the driver's side window.

I had the road to myself, which wasn't all that unusual even in broad daylight, given the scarcity of people living in Harney County. My thoughts bounced back and forth between what I knew and didn't about the missing Manybaskets children and the arson fires. The list of unknowns for both was long and lean. Pudge Warbler's network of other county sheriff's departments and state police might turn up a lead. So might Orville Nelson or Loq, wherever he was. Until that happened, I was left with two options: Wait and see what might develop or go make something happen. They were the same choices I often had to decide between when leading patrols in country.

The problem with stirring up a hornet nest was having to rely on making assumptions. From what I'd seen, that had been the Achilles heel of the Vietnam War. Politicians had assumed the tiny country was the only thing standing between communism and Main Street. The jumps to conclusion kept growing from there. The North Vietnamese army wouldn't put up much resistance. South Vietnam would welcome America with open arms. The war wouldn't spread to Cambodia and Laos. The people back home would always support it.

I'd been guilty of jumping to conclusions both on and off the battlefield. Since being back in the real world, I promised myself never to fall victim to the practice again. But there I was talking myself into poking Judd Hollister with a stick on the notion he was crooked. He didn't have a job but lived in a fancy house filled with art and had an expensive car parked out front. He'd surely burned down his parents' house with them trapped inside to get the insurance money, and when it began to run out, he turned to crime to pay for his lifestyle. Now he was setting fires in Harney County as practice for doing something bigger. Understanding why he was lighting them wasn't as important as stopping him cold.

As I began mulling over a plan to poke Judd hard enough to see what buzzed out, headlights shined on a long straightaway that ran parallel to an irrigation canal bordering a hayfield. I flicked off my high beams as I grew closer. When the distance between us didn't shorten as fast as I thought it should, considering my speed, I realized the vehicle was parked on the shoulder. Its hazard lights began flashing. The function had only become standard on cars three years prior, but I was already conditioned to play Good Samaritan. When I saw the idled vehicle was a dark-colored pickup, I pulled to a stop in my lane but kept a car length's distance away.

"Engine trouble?" I called to the driver through my open window.

"No, I hit a deer," a woman's voice replied. "It ran right in front of me. I feel awful. Can you see if the poor thing is down there?"

I relaxed my guard at the sound of her voice. "Hang on a second, I'll use my spot light."

As I swiveled the side-mounted spot toward the shoulder of the road, the Latin descriptions of a shadow began echoing in my ears. The silhouette of a bouffant hairdo was turning from umbra to penumbra. Something was flickering inside her cab. Something yellow and something orange. The dark-colored pickup suddenly shot forward, bringing our open windows side-by-side. I ducked as a burning bottle sailed through mine. Glass shattered when it hit the metal frame of the passenger door. Flames erupted.

The dark pickup kept going, gaining speed. I shouldered open my door and rolled out, landing in the middle of the black-top. I leapt up, drew my revolver, and began firing at the fleeing arsonist, using the taillights as a target. As I got off the sixth and final round, I realized my clothes were on fire. I dove into the irrigation canal as the flames from the Molotov cocktail reached the fuel line. The gas tank exploded and my pickup blew up as if I had run over a landmine.

21

Dawn was nibbling the horizon when I finally flagged down an oncoming pickup. It was pulling a horse trailer. The driver wore a slouched cowboy hat and eyed the blackened hulk of my rig still smoldering on the side of the road.

"Drop a cigarette on your lap, didja, or was ya striked by lightning?" he drawled.

"Fuel leak," I said. "Can I get a lift to No Mountain?"

"Sure thing, partner, but there ain't no hospital there. I'm on my way to Prineville. I can drop ya off at the one in Burns."

"No Mountain's fine," I said. "I live there."

"If ya don' mind me sayin', ya look and smell like burnt toast and need a doctor as sure as a rooster needs sunup, but a man's choice is a man's choice. Hop in, I'll git ya home."

His radio was tuned to a country-western channel and he hummed along to the likes of Buck Owens and Loretta Lynn. When Johnny Cash launched into "Folsom Prison Blues," the cowboy sang the words. "That tune there is the story of my life," he said when the song ended. "I ain't never spent a day in jail, but my marriage sure feels like one sometimes."

A familiar red Jeep Wagoneer was parked in front of the old railroad lineman's shack when he let me off.

"Butter 'n' toothpaste," he said. "Slather those burns with 'em. That'll cure ya." He tapped the horn as a farewell and drove away.

When I opened the door to the darkened shack, Gemma Warbler sat up in the narrow bunk. "Where have you been?" she said with a yawn. I turned on the light. She gasped. "What happened?"

"The firebug torched my pickup."

She threw off the sheet and leapt out of bed. "We have to get you to the hospital."

"It looks worse than it is."

Her white camisole and underwear were a stark contrast to my blackened and tattered shirt and jeans. "Get out of those rags while I run get my medicine kit from the Jeep. If I find a burn that's more than second degree, I'm taking you straight to the hospital, no argument."

I sat on the edge of the bunk to pull off my boots. I got one off before growing lightheaded. I laid down. The next thing I knew, Gemma was tugging at the other boot. As it plopped to the floor, she took a pair of silver surgical scissors to my clothes. She didn't have to snip much to peel them away.

"The boots protected the feet and ankles," she said in a clinical tone as she conducted a visual that reminded me of a corpsman performing triage on the battlefield. "There are second-degree burns on the right calf. The right forearm also has a second degree. Both extremities must have been closest to the flames. There are heat rashes and first-degree burns on the right hip and right side of the torso. The right cheekbone has a first-degree burn bordering on second degree. The stubble of whiskers on the right side of the face show singeing. So does the right eyebrow." She cupped my chin and stared into my eyes. "You didn't put anything on these did you?"

"Only water. I jumped in a canal to put the flames out."

"As long as it was clean, that helped. Application of cold water is good for minor burns. These need ointment and you need antibiotics. You'll also need something for the pain."

"I don't feel any."

"You will once the shock wears off. And when I debride the second-degree burns, you'll feel it a lot more." Gemma frowned and her manner softened. "I came over after I landed like I said I would. I have to admit I was annoyed at you for not being here. I got into bed to wait and fell asleep. I didn't know you were out there fighting for your life. You could've died."

I reached out and squeezed her wrist. "But I didn't."

"But you could've."

"But I didn't."

She waved the silver surgical scissors. "Don't you get it? You can't die. I don't want you to."

"That makes two of us."

"I'm being serious." Her eyes starting watering.

"I know you are."

"This thing between us has thrown me off. I'm worried."

"In the plane, you told me nothing scares you. Remember?"

"And nothing does when I'm flying, but this—"

"This what?"

"This thing. This feeling. You. Me. Us. When liking someone turns into something more. A lot more. I did that once before and got married. It didn't turn out so well." Gemma sighed. "Oh Nick, what am I going to do with you?"

"Smear butter on the burns, for starters. That's what the cowboy who gave me a lift said."

"What?" The sparkle slowly returned to her eyes. She

wrested her wrist from my grip and put her hands on her hips. "Butter's for bread. Leave the doctoring to me."

Gemma cleaned the wounds with water and antiseptic that I knew was labeled for use on livestock only. She removed pieces of fabric that were stuck to the burns and popped blisters. Instead of gritting my teeth or biting on a piece of wood, I hummed a Johnny Cash tune. Not the one about prison, but about falling into a burning ring of fire and the flames going higher and higher. I didn't listen to a lot of country-western music, but as I watched Gemma work, I knew what kind of fire Johnny was singing about. He was right. Love could be a burning thing.

I dozed off while Gemma coated the wounds with antibiotic cream and wrapped my forearm and calf with white gauze. When I woke, I had a sheet pulled up to my chin. Something sticky was on my right check. It was first aid cream that smelled like curdled vanilla ice cream. The horse doctor was sitting at the rickety wooden table near the unlit stove. Her father sat across from her. They were drinking coffee.

The old lawman noticed I was awake. "I got a radio call from a state trooper who found your rig. Or what's left of it. You're lucky you weren't near it when it exploded. The boy in blue says the flames set off the ammo in your Winchester and shotgun. Or what's left of them. Looks like someone took a machine gun to the cab. Did you get a good look at him, the firebug?"

"Her," I said.

"What the Sam Hill are you talking about?"

"A woman was driving the pickup I stopped to help." I told him about the hazard lights and the story of hitting a deer.

"Well, if that isn't cagey," Pudge said. "What did she look like?"

"I only saw her silhouette. She wore her hair high. That much I did see."

"What did she sound like?"

"Ordinary. No accent. Neither young nor old."

Gemma scoffed. "As far as you know, it could've been a man with long hair and a high voice."

"Or it could have been a man wearing a wig and masquerading as a woman," I said. "A disguise goes along with lying about hitting a deer. Of course, it might not have been a disguise at all. Maybe it was a man who likes to dress up like a woman."

Pudge whistled. "Well, wouldn't that beat all. We need to find that pickup. A dark color, you say? You mean black, blue, or what?"

"Either one. If it's blue, it's midnight blue. It could also be dark green, like a paint color popular on sportscars called British Racing Green."

"Do you think whoever threw it targeted you specifically, or were you just in the wrong place at the wrong time?"

"I've been asking around about the fires, including questioning Martin St. Claire and Judd Hollister. Maybe someone was tailing me when I took Tuhudda Will to Steens Mountain to make rain. But they didn't follow me up there. I didn't spot any headlights behind me."

"They wouldn't've needed to. What goes up, must come down," the deputy said. "This firebug's not only loco, but devious, setting up an ambush like that. Did you say old Tuhudda is gonna do a rain dance? Hope it works."

I swung my legs out of bed and grimaced. Gemma had been right about pain following right on the heels of the shock wearing off. When I stood, flames shot up my leg.

"Hurts, doesn't it?" she said. "I told you so."

"Do you have any aspirin?"

"I'll bring it to you. Lay back down and prop that burned leg up on a pillow."

I shook my head. "The firebug killed Hairy Jerry and now tried to kill me. He or she is going to kill somebody if they're not stopped."

Gemma turned to her father. "Come on, Pudge. Tell Nick to give it a rest. Those second-degree burns are likely to become infected if he doesn't keep still. The cure for gangrene is amputation."

"I would if I thought it wasn't a waste a breath," Pudge said. "You know who it is you set your cap at. Tell you what I will do. Now that Drake doesn't got a rig of his own, I'll drive him myself so I can keep an eye on him. His leg turns black and starts stinking, I'll arrest him for resisting good sense and take him to the hospital myself."

Gemma crossed her arms and harrumphed. "Make sure you throw away the key."

~

A long-sleeved shirt and new pair of jeans covered the gauze on my limbs. There was nothing I could do about the singed eyebrow, but I did wipe off the stinky ointment Gemma had smeared on my cheek. When I checked the mirror, it looked like someone had given me a hard slap.

Pudge drove us to Burns. On the way there, I cleaned my .357 Magnum with a rag and oiled it with Hoppe's. I hadn't dropped the revolver when I jumped in the canal. At basic training, my DI would order us to stand in formation for hours in the pouring rain while we held our M16s above our heads. Punishment for letting go was a lot more painful than sore arms.

"You sure about this?" I said as Pudge turned down West Adams Street. "Just because Martin St. Claire once owned a dress store and now grows flowers doesn't make him a cross dresser."

"Son, I may have grown up in little old Harney County, but that doesn't mean it was under a rock. You wear a star as long as I have, you've seen it all. Burns has a private gentlemen's club where all the members are, well, gentlemen, if you catch my drift. The Bar C Ranch is owned by two sisters, only they're not sisters. Nobody faults those gals, nobody shies away from them at church either. Their life is their life, and it isn't no business of mine. Same with St. Claire. What he likes to wear is no business of mine either, but his record of burning down a building by chucking a brick and lighting a wad of kerosene-soaked news-paper is. If he's doing it again wearing a three-piece suit or a frilly dress, it's striking the match that's gonna send him back to the pen, not his wardrobe."

The deputy parked in front of the house with the tidy lawn and rows of roses bordering the front walk. I spun the newly oiled cylinder of my service weapon, checking to make sure the chambers were dry, and then loaded them with fresh rounds before following Pudge to the front door.

Surprise bloomed on the flower grower's face when he answered the old lawman's knock. "Why, Sheriff Warbler, it's been a long time."

"Long enough I reckon that you don't recall it's Deputy Warbler now. How's it going Martin? Those are some mighty fine roses. I'm surprised they don't wilt in this heat."

"It takes extra care and watering, but I do what I can because roses are my livelihood now."

"I believe you met Ranger Drake from previously."

St. Claire issued a weak smile in my direction. "I did. How can I help you?"

"Can we come in?" Pudge said. "It's awful hot out here and at my age I don't do nearly as good in it as your flowers do."

"Is this an official visit, Sheriff, I mean, Deputy? Should I be concerned?"

"Not unless you got something to be concerned about."

"Don't you need a warrant to come inside?"

"Only if you're not gonna invite us in for what I call a neighborly visit. It's not like I'm searching for anything, or arresting anyone, only having a chat."

"I see. Of course, please, come in."

St. Claire led us into the living room. The wall-to-wall shag carpeting was gold and went with the sofa and matching recliners. They bore clear plastic slipcovers. The folding doors of a dark-brown stereo console were open, revealing a newish Magnavox color television. The picture was on. It was tuned to a hospital soap opera. St. Claire turned off the set and gestured for us to sit. Pudge did so on the couch and fanned himself with his short-brim Stetson. I sat on one of the recliners. It was hard to gain purchase on the clear protective slipcover so I dug in my boot heels to keep from sliding off.

"May I offer you something to drink?" St. Claire asked.

"Ice tea, if it's already made. Otherwise, water'll do the trick."

"And you, Ranger Drake?"

"Either one. Thanks."

Before St. Claire could leave, Pudge said, "Say, is that pretty wife of yours home?"

"She was a moment ago."

"I wouldn't mind saying hello to her, seeing I'm here."

Consternation crossed St. Claire's face, but quickly disappeared. "I'll see if Bettina's available."

When he left, Pudge whispered, "He means decent. She was probably watching TV in her unmentionables doing her nails when we knocked, why it smells like lacquer thinner in here."

Fingernail polish made me think of Bonnie LaRue. The newspaper woman was known for her stylish flair and Fifth Avenue fashions. "Orville told me you met with Mrs. LaRue. Is the *Burns Herald* going to endorse you?"

"That college boy knows everything. How, I don't know how. She's considering it, but it remains to be seen if she does."

"Do you have to persuade her, like take her to San Francisco to see the opera? She once told me you promised to do that, but stood her up instead."

Pudge's cheeks puffed and he exhaled loudly. "That woman, she doesn't keep anything secret unless it helps her sell more newspapers. For your information, and by that I mean Gemma and November's information, no we are not resuming anything other than business. Bonnie's endorsement won't be based on what I say or do. She knows me well enough to know this old dog isn't about to play new tricks. It'll be what Bust'em agrees to say and do."

"That's not going to change either. Sheriff Burton will give her whatever she wants as long as it earns him a prominent place in an article," I said.

"He always has, that's for sure, but I got the impression from Bonnie, Bust'em is starting to get a little too big for his britches."

St. Claire returned with a tray bearing a pitcher and four glasses. As he was setting it down, Bettina made a grand entrance. She was wearing a tight sweater, capris, high heels, and carrying a clutch purse made out of alligator skin. Her hairdo was the size of a tumbleweed and held in place with jasmine-scented hairspray. Fresh mascara and eyeliner accented her eyes. The eyebrows were plucked and penciled into arches.

Pudge scrambled off the plastic slipcovered couch. Pain shot up my leg as I stood too. "Ma'am," he said, holding his hat to his chest.

"Deputy Warbler. What a surprise." She fluttered her press-on eyelashes. "And if it isn't the handsome game warden. You look even more rugged than I remember. To what do we owe this pleasure?"

"We need help doing our jobs is what," Pudge said.

"Please, sit. Marty, where are your manners? Pour our guests some refreshments." Bettina sat on the couch and when Pudge did too, she scooted next to him. When everyone had a glass, she raised hers. "To old friends and new, my favorite toast: Bottoms up!"

St. Claire held his glass awkwardly. "Go on, Marty, sit down," she said sharply.

He eyed a spot on the couch next to her and then the empty recliner next to me. He chose the recliner.

Pudge said, "As much I'd enjoy spending the day chitchatting with you folks rather than being outside in the heat and smoke, there's no dancing around this, so I'm gonna go ahead and get right to it. The department has its hands full trying to solve two crimes at once. One has to do with missing children and the other with fires. More to the point, fires lit on purpose."

"And, naturally, you think Marty has something to do with the fires." Bettina jabbed her glass at her husband. The kiss of her red lipstick marred the rim. "I told you when I took you back it meant me having to wear the ball and stripe for the rest of my life."

"Now, Bettina, I'm only doing my duty checking off the people who've got priors with arson," Pudge said. "How about it, Martin? I know Drake here already asked you, but what can you tell me? You know I was always straight with you when I arrested you. I even put in a good word to the judge, why you got five years instead of seven."

St. Claire pursed his lips as he gathered his thoughts. "Deputy Warbler, I swear on a stack of Bibles I know nothing about any of the recent fires, nor did I have anything to do with them. I understand why you suspect me, but your suspicions are baseless. I would do nothing that would ever put my roses in jeopardy. They depend on me, and I will never betray them by breaking the law and risking incarceration."

Pudge betrayed no emotion. "Drake here nearly got killed last night. He stopped to help a motorist and got a Molotov cocktail throwed at him for his efforts. You can't see 'em, but his legs and arms are trussed up like a turkey."

Bettina eyed me. "And here he is, still standing. My, oh my."

"I got to ask the both of you, where were you last night around, when was it, Drake, eleven pm, midnight?"

"About then," I said.

"Right here. Asleep," St. Claire said. "Tell him Bettina. Tell the deputy we'd gone to bed. We'd watched the ten o'clock news like we do every night and then turned in right afterward."

"That right, Bettina?" Pudge said.

She swallowed a sip of ice tea and then took out a tissue that was tucked in the sleeve of her tight sweater and patted her lips. That prompted her to take a compact and tube of lipstick from the alligator clutch and reapply a fresh coat. She was examining herself in the tiny mirror when she said, "Marty's not telling the whole truth."

"What?" St. Claire sputtered.

Bettina snapped the compact shut and smiled at Pudge. "He goes to bed every night at the same time. I stay up and watch Johnny Carson. I love the way he gets the stars to reveal their dirty laundry. Zsa Zsa Gabor. Joey Bishop."

"If I was to check the records, what are the chances I'd turn up a registration of a late model pickup in your names?"

"I already told the ranger we don't own a truck," St. Claire said. "We have an Oldsmobile. I don't even drive."

"You mean you don't have a license to drive," I said.

Bettina's penciled eyebrows arched even higher at me. "Why, aren't you the clever one, Ranger Drake." She patted Pudge's knee. "Marty's telling the truth. We were both here and we don't own a truck. And the only cocktails we know how to mix are Old

Fashioneds and Bloody Marys. Is there anything else we can help you with?"

"That's all for now, thank you." Pudge stood. I took my cue. As we started to file out, the old deputy turned and, still clutching his hat, said, "You know, Bettina, and I say this with all due respect to you and your husband, you remind me of my late wife. She had a real flair about her too. The way she dressed, her makeup, everything."

Bettina cocked her head like models did when being photographed. "Why thank you, Deputy. That's quite a compliment."

"Yep, even when my wife got the cancer, she still kept up her looks. It wasn't vanity, mind you, it was, well, it was her way of saying she was still alive, still fighting. You know what I mean?"

"I do."

"When the treatments took all her hair from her, she didn't give up on herself, no ma'am. I drove her to Portland and we got the most expensive wig money could buy. Spent a couple of weeks pay on it, but it was worth every penny. Helped her face her last days on this God-given earth, it did. Didn't dim her beauty in my eyes one bit."

He paused as if picturing her. "My late wife, well, she styled that wig a lot like yours." Pudge kept staring at her, but not hearing a denial, finally put his hat back on. "Bettina, Martin, thank you for the ice tea."

22

Pudge wanted to drive straight to Judd Hollister's and question him too. I told him about my last encounter with Judd, how once he took me for a drug addict, offered to use me on a job. "Let's wait and see if he contacts me first."

"That's too risky," the old lawman said. "We don't know what he's up to."

"And the fastest way to find out is if he tips his hand."

Pudge rubbed his jaw. "All right, I suppose it makes sense not to spook him, but once you find out what he's planning, call me before you do something that's likely to get yourself killed."

We headed back to his ranch. I wanted to ask Wanda Many-baskets if I could borrow her pickup until I put in a requisition for a replacement. I wasn't looking forward to the conversation I'd need to have with Director F.D. Powers to explain what happened to my government-issued vehicle.

"Good eye about Bettina wearing a wig," I said. "I couldn't tell it was fake hair."

"You don't watch the *Porter Wagoner Show* or *Glen Campbell Goodtime Hour* do you, son?"

"What's that got to do with it?"

"Dolly Parton. Tammy Wynette. Most of those stars with big hair wear wigs. They got to because of all the traveling they do. If they didn't don a wig, they'd be so busy shampooing their own and sitting under a hairdryer they wouldn't have time to get up on stage and sing."

"I can't see Bettina lighting and throwing a Molotov cocktail with those long red fingernails, and I don't even want to picture Martin wearing her wig."

Pudge chuckled. "Reminds me of a time a bunch of us boots from Camp Pendleton walked into a joint. It was our last leave before shipping out to the Pacific and some of the boys were determined to get a smile put on their face no matter how much it cost. Well, this place had all these B-girls. You know, girls paid to keep us buying watered-down drinks. They were something, all dolled up." He wolf-whistled.

"Anyway, this lanky kid from Kansas, couldn't've been more than eighteen if he was a day, asks one to dance. Everything was going hunky-dory when the jukebox was playing 'Boogie Woogie Bugle Boy' and the like, but then some joker dropped in a nickel and put on 'We'll Meet Again.' Vera Lynn's singing those sad lyrics and the music's slow and the Kansas kid starts hanging onto the B-girl like he's been shot down over water and she's a life jacket. All of a sudden he breaks off and tells her he's real sorry. Then he comes back to us and whispers, 'Don't get fresh with the girls if you know what's good for you. The one I danced with has a blackjack hidden in her nether regions. I felt it.'"

When we neared No Mountain, Pudge said, "I got a confession to make. I lied."

"That was you on the dance floor?"

"No, I lied to Bettina back there to get her to confirm she's wearing a wig. There's not a thing about her that reminds me of my late wife. Mine was a natural beauty and didn't need all that warpaint to make her shine. When she lost her hair because of the cancer, she didn't want to wear a wig. Said it was a waste of good money. Wore a scarf instead." The old lawman chewed his bottom lip. "Prettiest scarf you ever saw. I keep it folded in the top drawer of my dresser. Not a day goes by I don't take a look at it."

He made the turn and we clattered over the cattle guard. The twin to my white Ford pickup with the Fish and Wildlife emblem on the door was parked in front of the ranch house. Loq was back. We found the Klamath in the kitchen with November and Wanda Manybaskets. He held a mug and tilted his head at November. "Her coffee tastes better than yours too."

"So does everything she makes, especially her frybread," I said. "Find anything out on your trip?"

"Wait a sec," Pudge interrupted. "Where have you been?"

"Fort McDermitt. Duck Valley. Skull Valley. Walker River. Pyramid Lake," Loq said.

"Those are all Indian reservations."

"I don't like that word. I like land or nation."

Pudge blew out some air. "Okay, land it is. What did you find out?"

"That Orville Nelson is smart. They all had stories about children being taken away from them and put in year-round boarding schools or foster homes or orphanages. They also had stories about kids who disappeared."

Wanda grabbed his arm. "Did anyone see my Daisy and Danny?"

Loq said no. November said, "Do not give up hope, *lebík'iyi*. As long as these men keep looking, they will find the children."

Wanda shrugged away from the old healer. "The parents of other lost children, what are they doing?"

"The ones whose kids were taken away by the government

complained, but the authorities who took them waved papers saying they had the power to do it. They even said some of the parents had agreed to it and showed them papers with their signatures on it. The parents said they never would've signed away their children. Some said they couldn't have signed because they didn't know how to read."

Loq drank some more coffee before continuing. "The parents belonging to tribes with their own police force are working with them. The others have asked their local sheriffs for help."

Pudge said, "Any of those departments been able to find out anything or have they been as confounded as Lake County and us?"

"Nothing that's anything."

"Who else did you visit?" I asked. Loq looked down at his coffee mug. It was only for a second, but I caught his hesitation. I spoke up before he could answer. "Pudge and I have something to show you about the fires. Come on, it's in his office."

I led the way and once we were inside, I closed the door behind me. "Okay, what is it you didn't want to say in front of Wanda?"

The *Maklak* didn't reply right away. He walked over to the bookshelf and tilted his head to read the titles on the spines. They were mostly classics and military histories, but a fair number were books about the Paiute. Loq grunted his approval.

Finally, he turned around. "The lands I visited are home to Paiute, Shoshone, and Goshute. At every one, I was told over the past couple of years, they've been visited by a white couple driving a motorhome who talked to them about what to eat and what not to drink and helped them fill out government forms."

"The Parkers," I said. "Cameron and Arabelle. He was always working on forms when I saw him. Maybe he got parents to sign away their kids without them knowing it. Did anyone mention the Parkers by name? Say anything that incriminates them?"

"Mostly they remembered the name of the motorhome," Loq said. "No one thought it was funny."

"I don't follow."

"Winnebago are a tribe. They were nearly wiped out by smallpox and lost their homeland in Wisconsin when they signed a bad treaty. The government kept relocating them, first to Iowa then Minnesota then South Dakota then Nebraska." His eyes became slits above his high cheekbones. "Winnebago are people, not a house on wheels."

"I surely doubt there's much we can do to change the name of that vehicle," Pudge said. "Let's concentrate on what we can do, namely linking that pair to the youngsters who were either forcibly removed or up and disappeared."

"I asked the people that, but they said their children were usually taken away a month or two after the Parkers had left."

"By government agencies," I said. "Bureaucracy runs on paperwork. There's got to be a trail." I looked at Pudge. "What do you think?"

"I think it's not much to go on, but it's all we got."

"There's something else," Loq said.

"What?" Pudge said.

"When I left Walker River, I stopped at the Reno-Sparks Indian Colony. It's on the way to Pyramid Lake. I asked about Wanda Manybaskets."

"What did you find out?" I said.

"Not to ask about her."

Loq told us the story. He'd arrived in Reno in the early evening. He was weary after consecutive days and nights of long drives across the Great Basin. He planned to eat dinner and then sack out in the back of his pickup. In the morning he would make a few inquiries about missing children before continuing to the reservation at Pyramid Lake. A cafe's neon sign at East Second Street led him to turn off Highway 395. The intersection was the center of the Reno-Sparks Indian Colony.

Loq entered the cafe. Two stools, side-by-side, were still unoccupied at the busy counter. He sat on the one closest to the door. Most of his fellow diners were American Indian. So was the waitress serving the tables as well as another tending to the customers at the counter. The bus boy clearing dirty dishes and setting out clean ones had a single braid and wore a beaded wrist band.

"Tonight's special is rainbow trout," the waitress said as she filled his water glass.

"Is it fresh or store bought?" Loq asked.

"It was swimming in the Truckee River this morning."

"Sounds good."

"It is. You also have a choice of mashed potatoes or fries, green beans or squash."

"Potatoes and squash. Can I get a cup of coffee?"

"You don't want to wait and have it with dessert? We have homemade pies baked fresh this morning. Apple, peach, and blackberry. You can have a slice a la mode if you want. Ice cream is store bought though."

"I'll have the coffee now."

She poured him a cup and went off to place his order with the short-order cook. The door behind him opened and closed. A man took the stool to his right. He was wearing an Indian Colony Tribal Police uniform. He took off his peaked cap and placed it on his lap. He had a crew cut and flat nose.

Loq acknowledged him with a nod. "Evening, brother."

The policeman took in Loq's Fish and Wildlife uniform and

badge. "You too. That must be your rig with the government plates in the lot."

"It is."

"You patrol the Fallon and Stillwater refuges?"

"No, I work in Oregon."

"You're far from home." The cop squinted at him. "I'm Washoe. Who are your people?"

"I'm *Maklak*," Loq said. "The Klamath Nation."

"Nation, huh? I like the sound of that. We're called a Colony, but sometimes tourists come here because they think we're part of England. One asked me why we don't wear kilts. Another wondered where he could find a pub." He chuckled.

The waitress brought Loq his meal. The trout had been lightly floured before cooking, which gave the crisp skin a golden hue. When he was a boy, he and his father would fish for suckerfish in Upper Klamath Lake using nets made out of woven iris grass. A two-foot-long suckerfish could feed the family for days.

"What brings you to Reno?" the tribal cop said. "Don't tell me it's to try your luck at the casinos. Everyone here knows the dice are loaded."

"I've been visiting the lands from Fort McDermitt to Skull Valley and now here. The people tell the same story. One out of four children have been taken from the family and put in government-run care. Schools, foster homes, adoption, and the like. Other kids have disappeared."

"That's a journey of a thousand tears," the Washoe cop said. "The same is true here. The BIA pushes us aside and says a single mom or dad on hard times can't take care of their kids so the children are removed. They say it's for the best."

"Is that what you say?" Loq said.

"I say it depends. Sometimes, yes, it's necessary. A parent gets into alcohol, drugs? Those things are smallpox to us. But most times the rest of the community will pick up the slack and help out a family in need. No one's going to let somebody else go hungry because they could be that somebody someday."

The waitress brought the tribal policeman coffee. He stirred in two packets of sugar. "What made you take this journey of yours, brother?"

"Another ranger and I found a woman during a wildfire on a refuge we patrol," Loq said. "She told us her two children disappeared. She's from here."

The cop threw back his head. "When you say here, do you mean the Colony?"

"That's what she said. She's Washoe, but she wasn't living here when her children went missing. She was in Oregon."

"What's her name?"

Loq put down his fork. "Wanda Manybaskets. She was married to Tom Piñon."

"Was?"

"He was thrown by a horse and broke his neck."

"I know Tom Piñon. He doesn't know how to ride."

"Maybe that's why he didn't stay on when the horse began to buck."

The policeman pondered that for a bit. "Yes, he shouldn't've gotten on if he didn't know how to get off."

"Do you know Wanda Manybaskets too?"

"Let's go outside," the cop said.

"Why?"

"Because it's better these things are spoken about while under the sky instead of a roof."

Loq drained the rest of his coffee, put some bills on the counter, and followed him. The cop's patrol car was parked next to his rig. Loq leaned against his pickup. Guarding his back had always come instinctively. It came even more so now after how the men at Chewaucan Marsh had reacted.

The tribal cop put his peaked cap back on and adjusted his gun belt. "You shouldn't believe everything Wanda told you."

"You do know her."

"I've known her since she was young. I'm ten years older, but she lived down the street."

"Why shouldn't I believe her?" Loq said.

"Wanda moved to the Colony when she was little. She came from Lake Tahoe and acted like she was better than everyone else. She told tales and got other children into trouble because of them."

"Including you?"

"Not me. I wasn't in school with her. But I heard the stories about what she was saying and doing. When she went to high school, she treated the teachers with disrespect. She said she knew all she needed to know already." He scowled. "Education's important, but so is never forgetting who we are and what our ancestors taught us. Our culture is our salvation."

"Lot of kids act up in school," Loq said, recalling his own days in the cramped one-room schoolhouse in Chiloquin.

"Yes, but Wanda, well, everyone knew she was bright. She could get one hundred percent on a test without ever studying or doing her homework. People starting talking about her."

"What did they say?"

"The old ones said she had very strong *wegeléyu*. That's Washoe for special power. I know the word in Paiute is *puha*, but I don't what it is in the Klamath tongue. I'm sure you got something like it. It's what the old ones believe the land, animals, and some people have."

"What about the not so old ones like you? Do you believe Wanda Manybaskets has power?"

"I'm a policeman. I believe in law and order, right and wrong. But I'm also Washoe. Of course, I believe there is *wegeléyu*. Who has it or what has it, and what they can do with it, I don't know. I do know Wanda got in trouble though."

"You mean, she broke the law. Was she put in jail?"

"She got suspended from school more than once and had run-ins with tribal police over petty stuff. Breaking curfew. Being at a party that served alcohol. Things like that. But that's not the kind of trouble I'm talking about. It was the kind teenage girls in high school get in." He used his hands to mime a pregnant stomach.

"Daisy and Danny," Loq said.

"Who are you talking about?" the cop with the flat nose said.

"Her twins who are missing. They're six years old now."

The tribal cop looked down at the ground for at least a minute. When he looked back up, he said, "This is why we're talking about this under the sky so the words won't get trapped in a room for others to hear after they've been said."

"Then say them, brother," Loq said.

"When Wanda got pregnant in her junior year and it began to show, her parents demanded to know who the father was. Wanda insisted she'd never laid with a man. She said a spirit had made her pregnant. She told everyone that. Kids in school. Teachers too. No boy or man stepped forward to say otherwise.

"Her parents loved their daughter, but they were upset with her for telling them that the father wasn't a person. How would they be able to share their joy and share the baby if there was no other family to share it with? Seeking guidance, they took Wanda back to Lake Tahoe to ask the help of a shaman they knew. The shaman drew his power from Standing Gray Rock. It's one of our people's most sacred places and has much *wegeléyu*. Part of the power comes from *we muhu* who live in a cave there. You know about *we muhu*, water babies? Do Klamath have them?"

Loq nodded.

The tribal cop ran his finger down his flat nose. "I don't know if they exist or not, but years ago when the highway department blasted tunnels through Standing Gray Rock to build a road around Lake Tahoe, nearby Carson Valley flooded. Some say *we muhu* were angry and caused it."

"What did the shaman tell Wanda's parents?" Loq asked.

"They brought him gifts to show respect and the shaman invited them to stay with him. They did so for three days and three nights. During this time, the shaman sang and chanted and performed rituals that only the old ones know about. On the third night, Wanda felt a great pain and became very sick. She was in such pain, so sick, that she collapsed and her eyes rolled back and her breathing slowed. Her mother thought she was dying and pleaded with the shaman to do something. He performed more rituals. In the middle of the night, Wanda started screaming. Her baby was being born even though not all the months had passed that needed to pass. The shaman and her mother helped her give birth. It wasn't one baby that came into this world, but two. First a girl and then a boy."

"Daisy and Danny," Loq said.

"The babies were very small and very weak. Wanda fell asleep again. Her mother wrapped the infants in a blanket and put them on her daughter's breast, but the babies wouldn't nurse and they died. When Wanda woke again, she called for them. Her mother tried to comfort her, her father too, but he was so heartbroken he was made speechless and only walked in circles slapping himself on the side of his head. When her mother told her the babies were in the spirit world, Wanda grew so upset, she threatened to end her own life. Her mother pleaded with the shaman to do something.

"The shaman said there was only one thing to do. And that was to take the babies to the *we muhu* who lived in the cave and ask for their help. The cave was connected to the lake. They took the babies to the water's edge and the shaman called for the *we muhu* to show themselves. They did. Wanda's parents were very much afraid, but not Wanda. She told the *we muhu* she had much *wegeléyu* and would do whatever they asked if only they would bring her babies back to life.

"The *we muhu* said the only way the babies could live was to become *we muhu* too. If you agree to give them to us, they said to Wanda, we'll give you a gift. You'll always be able to hear them, no matter how old you grow, how far away you go. Wanda agreed and gave the *we muhu* her two babies."

"What did Wanda and her parents tell people when they returned to Reno," Loq asked.

"Her mother said the babies had been born prematurely and died in childbirth, but eventually the story burned a hole in her heart and she had to tell someone. That person couldn't hold the story in their heart either and told another person. Some of the old ones said the shaman must've turned Wanda into a witch. They said she'd cast a spell on Tom Piñon."

"You said I shouldn't believe everything Wanda says, but you tell her story like you believe it. Do you?" Loq said.

"Some parts, yes. Other parts?" The Washoe policeman shrugged. "I think believing in spirits is better than not believing in anything at all."

A car pulled into the parking lot. As a couple got out of the front seat, two children clambered out of the back seat. The kids laughed and shouted as they raced ahead to the front door of the cafe.

"Careful," their father said. "Don't trip and hurt yourself."

The parents began walking faster to catch up.

"Wait for us," the mother called to her children. "Don't open the door before we get there."

Loq and the tribal cop watched the family disappear inside. The Washoe said, "Reminds me of my two kids. They're always in such a hurry to grow up. They don't realize in doing so, it means my wife and I will near our ends in this world that much sooner." He sighed. "Do you have any children?"

"No," Loq said.

"When you do, you'll know what I mean."

23

Pudge Warbler's face reddened as if he were standing in direct sunlight. "Are you saying this is all a snipe hunt? We're spending money and manpower, not to mention heartache, looking for ghosts?"

"I'm telling you what the tribal policeman told me," Loq said.

Pudge blew air. "Well, I certainly don't believe in ghosts. Now, the way I see it, one of two things happened. Either the babies were stillborn or the parents gave them to someone else to raise. Either way, it wouldn't be the first time a teenage girl got pregnant and her folks concocted some kind of fairy tale to tell her where the babies went to keep her from being sad. There's a lot of orphanages and adoption agencies in the business of taking care of fairy tales."

I asked Loq if the X-ray tech at the Lakeview Hospital he spoke to mentioned seeing little kids when he saw Wanda singing the lullaby beside Tom Piñon's deathbed.

"No. He said he only stuck his head in the room."

"Kids play under beds," I said, more for myself than anyone

else. I decided not to mention having seen Daisy and Danny in a dream. I turned to Pudge. "What about the pair of woven baby rattles along with the four bowls and spoons Loq saw in the wickiup beside the marsh?"

"They're no proof those children are alive," Pudge said. "Look, I don't want to sound like I don't respect Wanda's people's beliefs. If you pressed me on it, I'd say those babies surely died right then and there given she was months early and how rough the circumstances were. And I'm not about to question what kind of funeral her parents conducted on the spot, be it burial, cremation, or committed to the deep of the lake. As a parent myself, I surely do understand that whatever they told Wanda to help dry her tears came from the heart. But I do need to decide if hunting for those children is all for naught. I got to ask Wanda directly."

"Let's talk to November first and see what she thinks," I said.

Pudge slapped the star on his chest. "She can say whatever she wants, but this here says it's my responsibility to pull the cord on the search for kids and kidnappers."

"No argument there," I said. "But November might know something that can help your decision-making easier."

The old lawman hemmed and hawed before saying, "All right, go fetch her. I got to return a phone call anyway. But make sure not to bring the Manybaskets woman back with you. I need to hear it from November on her own."

Loq followed me out of Pudge's office. He headed toward the guest bedroom while I went to the kitchen. November was alone kneading dough.

"Pudge needs some help," I said.

"I am busy making bread," she said.

"It's about Wanda."

She tsked. "Why are you men busy talking instead of busy looking?"

"This is part of it."

"Bread is not like the sun. It will not rise on its own."

"For Wanda's sake," I said.

November muttered and then went to the sink to wash her hands. "Go," she said. "I do not need you to lead me. I am not blind."

I returned to Pudge's office. He was still on the phone. "Right," he said into the mouthpiece. "Fax it on over, Orville." He listened some more and then said, "Yep, Drake's here now. We'll reconnoiter with you after we take a looksee. Good work."

When he hung up, I said, "November's on her way. What was that about?"

"Arson. Sounds like our firebug has been at it again. A dairy farm over in Sage Hen Valley lit up."

"How bad?"

"As of a minute ago, they'd lost a couple of buildings. The volunteer fire departments from Hines and Riley are there fighting it now. Orville said he's got some pretty darn good information about our suspects too."

Before I could ask him what it was, November joined us.

Pudge went right at it. "It appears our houseguest hasn't been straight about her children. I figure she's told you everything and so I need you to tell me what the heck she's up to."

"Eyes find lost ones, not wagging tongues," the old healer said.

"Ah, for crying out loud. Have you known all along her two babies died in childbirth and she believes they got turned into some kind of spirits that only she can see and hear?"

I spoke up. "Loq met a tribal policeman in Reno who knows her. He told him about Wanda's pregnancy in high school and a visit to a shaman, that she believes her twins became water babies, or as you call them, *paa'a o'haa*."

"You may know how to say the words, but that is not the

same as knowing what they are," the Paiute elder said with a glare.

"Then help me understand. Help Pudge too. Otherwise there's nothing more he can do but call off the search."

The Paiute elder mumbled. "I must sit. My old feet have been standing in the kitchen while I made bread." She plopped on the couch and folded her gnarled hands on her lap. Minutes passed without her saying a word.

Pudge drummed his fingers. "I don't have time to spend on a wild goose chase."

"You are always in such a hurry to hear a story," she finally said. "It is the same when you tell one. You even take letters out of your words so you can say them faster."

"Then tell it to me anyway you want. I'm all ears, but I got to know if I can take looking for her missing youngsters off my honey-do list so I can concentrate on catching whoever's lighting fires. Those crimes are real."

"Wanda is not a criminal."

"Lying to a peace officer is. Come on, November. Does Wanda have children who are lost or not?"

"Perhaps they are only waiting to be found."

"What's that supposed to mean?"

She tsked. "If you are not looking for something, then there is nothing for you to find."

"I don't have time for riddles."

The old woman closed her eyes. Her head began to bob. It made the gray hairs as fine as spider webs that streaked her black braids dance. "When Wanda Manybaskets was very young, she could hear her ancestors talking to her. *Dats'ai lo lee*, Young Willow, most of all. They told her about the way things used to be for *Washeshu*, and how those days were lost when the people forgot the old ways.

"As she grew older, Wanda felt different than the other children who lived in the Reno Colony because of what the old ones told her. She was angered by this and did things to try and win their friendship, but they were frightened by her and did not want to be her friend. Wanda told her parents, but they were so busy working to pay the rent and put food on the table, they could not hear her. One night when Wanda was home alone, a large woman appeared at the foot of her bed. The woman's voice was the same that Wanda had heard before, but now she could see who it belonged to. It was Young Willow. She told Wanda that one day she would have children, and although children should always listen to their parents, Wanda must listen to them instead.

"One month passed, and then another. Wanda was with child. How that came to be, she did not know. When she gave birth early and the shaman told her the only way to save her babies was to give them to the *we muhu*, she did not forget what her great-aunt had told her, and so she agreed. From that moment on, she listened to her children instead of the other way around. The last time they talked to her, they told her to come find them wherever they might be because children need to be found and not lost."

Pudge groaned. "I still don't get it. How's that supposed to help me figure out what's what?"

November unclasped her hands and stood. "Wanda Manybaskets can hear her babies and go to the place where lost children can be found. I am going back to the kitchen to put my dough in the oven for it has risen and needs to become bread."

Pudge continued to scowl after the old woman left. "I'll be damned if I'm gonna go chase ghosts."

Loq returned. "Wanda's gone."

"What do you mean *gone*?" Pudge said.

"I checked her bedroom. She's not there. Nor are the baby rattles. I looked in the stable. I looked out front. Her pickup's gone too."

Pudge swore. "November! That old woman was stalling me so Wanda could vamoose. Now I'm gonna have to go after her."

"I'll go get her," I said.

The old lawman squinted. "Why, what makes you think you can find her better than me?"

"She already said where she'd go. The clinic in Spokane. She either went to find the Parkers to get a ride or she's driving there herself."

"I was going to put the Parkers on a list of people of interest who need questioning based on what Loq learned at the reservations," Pudge said. "If Wanda's with them and they're guilty of something, you interfering might create some kind of legal loophole for them to squirm through."

"The Parkers have already left Harney County," I said. "They weren't parked next to the public health building when I went looking for them yesterday and they weren't driving around Harney Valley like they told people they were going to do."

"Oh Lord, son, why does everything have to get so complicated whenever you stick your nose in? The thing is, I can't spare you right now. There's that arson fire going on in Sage Hen Valley right now and what Orville turned up about the suspects. Judd Hollister's involved and that involves you too."

"I'll go," Loq grunted.

"You?" Pudge said.

"Nick can help stop the arsonist and I'll find Wanda Manybaskets and stop the Parkers. Two birds, two stones."

Pudge puffed his cheeks and blew out air. "All right. You go track the Manybaskets woman and find out where's she at. But that's it. Locate her and report back pronto. Don't do nothing else that could spook the Parkers. You find, you see, you call."

The *Maklak* turned to me. "What happened to *I came, I saw, I conquered*?"

"Ask Julius Caesar," I said.

24

Pudge and I made fast tracks to Sage Hen Valley. On the way there, he told me what Orville Nelson had discovered.

"That college boy, he's better than a bird dog during quail season. Guess what he sniffed out? He's got all those searches going on and he takes the time to double back on Judd Hollister and turns up an old speeding ticket. Says he got the idea when Bust'em sent me out to Drewsey to serve a warrant for a traffic violation."

"I'm surprised Judd's only gotten one, given the way he races his muscle car."

"A state trooper pulled him over for doing ninety-five on the Frenchglen Highway. According to the trooper's notes, Judd didn't seem perturbed by the fact it was gonna cost him a pretty penny. As a matter of fact, he thanked the boy in blue for confirming his Shelby's speedometer was slow by five miles per hour. As the trooper was writing him up, Judd's passenger—did I say he wasn't riding alone? Well he wasn't—started oinking."

"Everywhere there's lots of piggies living piggy lives," I said.

"What's that supposed to mean?"

"It's a Beatles song from the *White Album* released last year."

"Well, I don't like it. Not one bit. No lawman should be called that."

"What did the state trooper do?"

"He told the passenger to hand over his ID. The passenger argued that he wasn't driving, but the boy in blue said you can either give it to me or the desk sergeant at county lockup. Judd told the passenger to do it. The trooper wrote down his name and driver's license number in case Judd decided to contest the speeding ticket in court and the passenger would serve as a hostile witness."

"I'm impressed Orville was able to obtain all that," I said. "What's the passenger's name?"

"You're not gonna let me finish the story, are you? And right after November gave me the business for taking shortcuts." He reached into his top pocket and extracted a folded sheet of facsimile paper. "Read it yourself."

The trooper had written down Frederick J. Sanderlin. "Ready Freddie," I said.

"I thought that might make your day."

"How old is the ticket?"

"About a year."

"Harney is one of the least populated counties in the entire country, yet two men who were suspected of arson as boys wind up in the same car. What are the odds?"

"I'd ask the college boy to figure it out on that newfangled calculating machine, but I don't want to distract him from hunting down all the other things I need."

I glanced at the fax. "It doesn't list Freddie's address."

"Guess the trooper forgot that part, but he did put down the driver's license number. Orville's working on getting a last known right now."

"He should also run car registrations. We'd hit the jackpot if Freddie is the owner of a dark pickup."

A column of smoke was visible ahead. "That has to be the farm," Pudge said.

Colonel Davies had beaten us there. Pudge parked next to the colonel's beige Travelall. Two fire engines were stationed on either side of a barn engulfed in flames. Fire fighters were training their hoses on it. The water sizzled when it hit the burning structure. Across the yard, wisps of smoke rose from the smoldering ruins of what was once a corral.

The colonel was standing next to a man with a soot-stained face and bib overalls peppered with fresh burn marks that looked like he'd been jabbed by a lit cigarette over and over.

"I had ten Holsteins in there," the farmer said. "I tried to get them to come out, but they were too scared to run through the flames. I got heat blisters on my palms from trying to hold the door open for them."

"Sorry for your loss," Pudge said.

The farmer eyed the deputy's badge. "I don't care if it means breaking the law, I catch the dirty SOB who done this, I'm gonna light him up."

"What makes you think it was a someone and not a milk cow kicking over a lantern that started it?" Pudge asked.

"'Cause I saw him, that's why."

"When?"

"I was working around back when I heard a car drive up. I didn't pay it no mind, figuring it was a door-to-door salesman of some kind. Being close to the main road, we get more than our share."

"Look out!" a fire fighter shouted. "She's coming down."

The ground shook as what remained of the barn's roof collapsed into the center of the inferno. The added fuel sent the flames and smoke billowing like a mushroom cloud.

"Dirty SOB," the farmer swore.

"You were saying you heard a car pull up. When did you finally come around to see who it was?" Pudge said.

"When I heard the gunshots, that's when."

Pudge's gun hand automatically went to the butt of his .45. "He discharged a weapon? At what?"

"Sophie, I expect."

"Who's Sophie?"

"My herd leader. It's probably why the rest of the cows wouldn't come out when I called. They only follow Sophie. Dirty SOB, he walks into my barn as pretty as you please, plugs my best milker, torches my hay, and walks out the same way as he walked in."

"What did he look like?"

"All I remember is the uniform."

"What kind of uniform?"

"Blue with a Smokey the Bear hat pulled down low. He was a state trooper. Or at least dressed like one."

"You didn't go after him?"

"Hell no, but I would've if I'd been holding a gun like he was."

"What kind of gun?"

"He had a pistol. Not a revolver. A semi-automatic. A loud one."

"What did he do then?"

"Drove off as pretty as you please."

"In a trooper's patrol car?"

"Nope. A pickup. Dark blue. I didn't look at the license plate, I was too busy running for the barn to get my cows out. I used to have a dog did that, but she died last spring. Belle and Sophie worked together like hand and glove. Now they're both gone."

The farmer sniffed and ambled away. I told Colonel Davies about my encounter with Judd Hollister and the arsonist throwing a fuel bomb at me. Pudge told him about questioning Martin St. Claire and the fact that Judd and Freddie Sanderlin knew each other.

The colonel uh-huhed. "While you've been doing that, I've been analyzing the field of play and have identified key terrain. I brought a map. Care to have a look?"

"You bet," Pudge said.

The hood of the colonel's Travelall proved to be more than ample to accommodate the map he unfurled. I picked up some rocks and used them to hold down the corners. They may not have been expensive works of art like the Remington bronzes Blaine Harney used as paperweights, but they did the job just as well.

I'd looked at plenty of maps with battle plans drawn on them when I was in country. The one Colonel Davies had drawn up was equally detailed with notes, directional arrows, and times. He pointed out landmarks with his mutilated hand to orient us. "Here we are in Sage Hen Valley. There's Burns to the east, No Mountain down here, Jackass Mountain further south, and Foster Flat to the west of it."

The map had shaded places marked with letters. "The key is pretty straightforward," he said with an uh-huh. "LF stands for lightning fire, CUF for cause unknown fire, CAF for confirmed arson fire, and SAF for suspected arson fire." His mood turned somber. "KBF is killed by fire."

We gave a moment of silence for Hairy Jerry. The colonel continued. "The shadings are self-explanatory. Black means scorched. Red means burned to the dirt."

"What are we supposed to be seeing here that you see we don't?" Pudge said.

"Most of the intentionally lit fires reveal a pattern based on habitat type, use, and location. Grassland versus desert. Occupied versus unoccupied. In town versus remote. These fires were planned in advance, executed according to a schedule, and the variables and outcomes documented."

"Field testing," I said. "That's what you called them when we were at the BLM experimental range station."

"Uh-huh, Sergeant. I'm still convinced they're proving grounds for weaponizing fire."

"You said 'most of the intentionally lit' fires. What about the other ones?" Pudge said.

"Those were random acts of violence," the colonel said. "Like most pyromaniacs, the perpetrator of those was driven to start them to achieve some form of psychosexual release. They're the work of someone who's unable to control themself as opposed to the planned ones that are the work of someone who adheres to a strict regimen."

"Beauty and the Beast," Pudge said. "Jekyll and Hyde. Sounds like our arsonist has got himself a split personality."

"I don't think so," the colonel said. "I believe the fires aren't the work of a single arsonist, but a pair. One is the brains, the other the instrument."

"Judd and Freddie would be my guess," I said. "Which one's the brains, I couldn't tell you."

"That's why we need to catch them in the act," Pudge said. "Which is gonna be tough given how big Harney County is."

Colonel Davies nodded. "I believe I can narrow the key terrain in the field of play for us considerably. With the purposeful fires, the enemy has a strong motivation for what they're doing. The act itself is criminal and most criminals have a common denominator which is—"

"Money," Pudge said. "Stealing it, swindling it, or counter-feiting it."

"Uh-huh. If obtaining money illicitly is the enemy's objec-tive, we can eliminate large portions of the field of play. Here, let me show you on the map."

He pointed to the areas labeled CAF and SAF. "First, we can rule out the places we know or suspect the arsonists have already torched because there's little left there to burn. We can also eliminate salt flats, lakes, old lava flows, and marshland too. Those habitats can't be burned. Large portions of the county are uninhabited and undeveloped. Since there's nothing of monetary value to be obtained there, we can eliminate those too."

The colonel took a marker from his pocket with his left hand and began circling places on the map. "You're both combat veterans. You'll recognize this. It's the same as planning for a bombing run or an airborne invasion. Where in the county is target-rich? Here." He circled Burns and the neighboring town of Hines. The two comprised the largest population center in the county. "The next are here, here, and here." He circled the tiny towns of Riley, Drewsey, Crane, Frenchglen, and No Mountain "And then there are these." Again he made circles, this time around the ranches big enough to warrant names on the map. Circle R, Double O, Roaring Springs, Whitehorse, and Rocking H.

Pudge eyed the circles. "Ranches as potential targets is a stretch unless this is a new angle on rustling cows. Even when we take the ranches off the map, there's still too much key terrain for the sheriff's department to keep eyeballs on if we're gonna catch these pyros red-handed. If it's money they're after, it's probably a bank or a jewelry store they're planning to knock off. It'll be Bust'em's call, but I bet those will be the places he's gonna deploy deputies and any Burns city cops and state troopers he can enlist. Protecting the entire county won't be easy."

"War never is," Colonel Marcus Aurelius Davies said as he rolled up his map. "But neither is keeping the peace."

25

W e left the farm. Pudge decided to head straight to Burns. He wanted to see if Orville had turned up an address for Freddie Sanderlin as well as to brief Sheriff Burton and the other deputies about arson targets.

"Let's stop in Riley on the way," I said.

"What for?"

"Remember what Blackpowder heard on his grapevine about a dyslexic Paiute boy who went missing in Malheur County about two months ago? The boy's aunt who put two and two together about the postcard he supposedly wrote lives there. Maybe there's a connection with the missing kids from the reservations. Arabelle Parker told me they're at the end of a two-month rotation in the Great Basin. Maybe they drove through Malheur County."

"Sounds like a longshot, but since it's nearby, okay. We can't stay more than a couple of minutes though."

The deputy plucked his radio's microphone from the cradle and was patched through to Blackpowder Smith, who gave his old friend an earful for being absent at the last meeting of No Mountain's volunteer fire department.

"Ever since you started wearing a star, I've been waiting to give you orders," the crusty barkeep said. "I can't wait to hear you say 'Yes, boss.'"

"You know the only thing you and me are good for is the bucket brigade. Neither one of us is about to climb up a ladder and risk breaking a hip," Pudge said. "I got Drake here with me. We want to know the address of the woman in Riley whose nephew went missing in Malheur."

"It's about time you asked for it. Word gets around that anything anyone tells me doesn't get acted upon is goin' make my grapevine wither and die. Her name is Charity Liveslong. Paiute on her daddy's side, Quaker on her momma's. The nephew's name is Charley Pony Blanket."

The address was for a white cottage on the banks of Silver Creek that ran past Riley, a town thirty miles west of Burns. Mrs. Liveslong perked right up when she answered the door and Pudge asked for a moment of her time to talk about her nephew. "Did you hear from Charley too?" she said.

"Does that mean you did, ma'am?" Pudge said. "When was that?"

"He called last night. Please, come in."

The inside of the cottage was plain, the furniture simple. Nothing hung on the walls. We sat at a kitchen table in wooden chairs with straight backs and hard seats. I could tell Pudge was trying not to tip his.

"Is your nephew back home, that why he called?" he said.

"No, he's not. He wants to go home. Very much so. But that's impossible because his parents have separated. His mother, my sister, lives in California now. I don't know where Charley's father is."

"Where's the boy at?"

"He's not exactly sure of the name of the town. He called me after he tried his home number, but it's been disconnected. He said he's somewhere in Washington because he remembers seeing the welcome sign when the bus crossed the Columbia River."

"He took a bus by himself? How old is Charley Pony Blanket?"

"Thirteen."

"That's pretty adventuresome, plus he would've had to have money for the fare. Who's he staying with?"

"He said his foster parents. That's what Charley called them. He said it was against house rules to use the phone. He snuck downstairs to call. He was whispering. We didn't speak long because he said someone was coming. I didn't get a callback number before he hung up."

"Did he happen to call collect?" I asked.

"Yes. I accepted the charges, of course."

"The phone company should have a record," I said to Pudge.

"Another job for Orville," he said.

"When Blackpowder told me the story, he didn't say anything about the boy being in foster care. He made it sound like he'd run off when his parents were yelling at each other."

"Charley would always go outside so he wouldn't have to hear my sister and her husband argue," Charity Liveslong said. "Our mother was Quaker, but my sister forgot her teachings."

Pudge asked her where the boy would go when the parents fought.

"I imagine he had a secret place like most children do. I doubt it was very far from the house. They lived on the outskirts of Vale."

"Did you call the Malheur sheriff after you heard from Charley?" Pudge asked.

"Right away. I spoke to the deputy on duty. He said there wasn't much they could do without a phone number or an address."

The old lawman turned to me. "I wonder how he got hooked up with foster care? It's not like you can knock on a door and say 'Would you be my foster parents?'"

"Maybe it's not as regulated as we're led to believe. There could be something about that in the Senate report Orville got his hands on about Indian kids being taken from their parents."

The lawman clicked the inside of his cheeks and turned back to Mrs. Liveslong. "Had your nephew ever been put in someone's care before? Did a social services agency ever step in because of his parents' fighting?"

"The only officials my sister ever met with were school ones. The teachers thought Charley was slow because he couldn't read or write. They held him back a couple of times. For a while they even thought he was going blind. It wasn't until a school nurse read about a special program for children with dyslexia that he was tested for it. Once he was diagnosed, there wasn't much the school could do for him. They didn't have any teachers with special training."

"Do you have a photograph of your nephew?"

"I do." She went to get it. When she returned, she showed us a snapshot of a boy with shaggy hair and a pug nose. He was grinning at the camera. He had a large gap between his two front teeth.

"He has my sister's nose. Well, actually, our mother's nose. She was originally from Pennsylvania. You can keep the photograph."

Pudge took it and gave her his card. "We'll try and track down an address through the phone company. In the meantime, if your nephew calls again, ask him where he's at and who helped him get there. Call me straight away. You live in Harney County and that makes you my responsibility, not the Malheur County sheriff's."

"Thank you," she said. "Peace be with you."

We pulled out of her driveway. Pudge glanced at his fuel gauge. "I better fill up here in Riley or we'll be pushing this rig the last few miles."

The gas station was cloaked in a mirage-like haze caused by fumes from leaking oil and spilled gasoline rising from the hot pavement. Pudge pulled alongside the pump. A teenager came to the driver's side window.

"Fill her up with ethyl," Pudge said. "You might need a chisel to scrape some of those bigger bugs off the windshield. They're likely baked on."

As the pump jockey went to work, Pudge asked me if I wanted a soda. "They got a machine next to the lifts. My treat."

He got out and walked around the side of the gas station where the mechanic bays were. I thought about Charity Liveslong's nephew. Plenty of thirteen-year-old kids ran away from home. Most either came back when they got scared and hungry or were picked up by truancy officers. Then there were the unlucky ones, boys and girls alike, who fell victim to predators. Most of those were never seen again. That Charley Pony Blanket had gotten on a bus and wound up in a house in the same state where Wanda Manybaskets was going was probably a coincidence. But soldiering had taught me that *probably* was nothing to stake a life on.

The pump jockey finished squeegeeing the windshield, topped off the tank, and screwed the gas cap back on. "There weren't but a quart of gas left in the tank. Took the full seventeen gallons. At thirty-seven cents per, that'll be six dollars and twenty-nine cents. Are you paying or should I wait for the deputy?"

Even at Pudge's slow gait, I realized he'd been gone a long time for only getting a soda. "Anybody here besides you?" I asked.

"The regular mechanic and a customer. Why?"

"Who's the customer?"

"Some guy whose pickup was overheating. No surprise given how hot it is. You going to pay?"

"What color's the pickup?"

"Dark blue."

"The deputy will pay. I'll go get him." I got out, reached behind the front seat and slid Pudge's 12-gauge shotgun from the rack. "Stay here. Keep behind the pickup."

I pumped a shell from the magazine into the firing chamber and made for the outer wall of the gas station. I couldn't hear anything coming from the service bay on the other side. I led with the shotgun as I neared the corner. I still couldn't hear anything. I turned and swept the open bay with the barrel.

A dark blue pickup with its hood up was parked over the hydraulic lift, but the wheels were still on the ground. Pudge was standing in front of two men. Greasy coveralls told me which one was the mechanic. The other man was in his early twenties and wearing jeans and a black untucked short-sleeve sport shirt. His black hair was slicked back with something like Vitalis or Brylcreem.

"Gus Bishop, that's your name?" Pudge was saying to him, reading from a driver's license he held in his left hand while his right gripped the butt of his holstered .45.

"What my folks named me," he said.

"And is this address correct? You live in Redmond."

"Home sweet home."

The mechanic noticed me and the shotgun. "Hey, what is this?"

The man named Gus Bishop glanced over. He didn't show any surprise or alarm.

"Everything okay?" I said.

"Just having a chat," Pudge said without taking his eyes off the two men. "Gus here had a little radiator problem. That right?" he said to the mechanic. The mechanic nodded vigorously.

I pointed the barrel of the shotgun toward the floor, but kept my finger alongside the trigger guard.

"What brings you this way?" Pudge asked the younger man.

"What business is it of yours?" Gus answered.

"Sheriff's business. You didn't answer my question. What brings you down here?"

"It's personal."

"Nothing's personal when the law's doing the asking," Pudge said.

"All right, I'm visiting a lady friend. She lives in Burns. I drive over every chance I get."

"She must be a pretty special gal for you to spend two and half hours behind the wheel each way plus gas money. Not to mention it being a work day. You do work, don't you?"

"Of course I got a job. What do you take me for?"

"What kind of job?"

"The paying kind. What other kind is there?"

"Who pays you and what do you do?"

"I work construction. Whoever is building something pays me."

"Hours must be flexible, it being a work day and you down here paying a social call. What's your lady friend's name?"

Gus stuck out his chin. "I don't have to tell you."

"Yep, you do."

"Well, I don't want to give you her name."

I walked over to the pickup and looked into the bed. It was clean. I glanced in the window. A suitcase was on the front seat. The door to the glovebox was shut. Gus followed me with his eyes.

Pudge noticed them, but didn't turn around. "What do you got?" he called to me.

"A suitcase in the cab. No visible weapon. It could be under the front seat or in the glovebox."

"Hold on," Gus said. "I'm not packing a gun. Go ahead and check if you want."

"Tell me your lady friend's name," Pudge said.

"Aw, man. I don't want to because, well, she's married, is because why. Her husband treats her pretty mean."

"And how do you think he'd treat you if he found out you were her backdoor man?"

"I'm nobody's backdoor man. I walk through the front door wherever I please. What me and her got is different. She's going to leave him. First chance she gets. She told me so. We're going to get married. Well, as soon as her divorce comes through."

"I look in your suitcase, what am I gonna find? A gun?"

"No, I swear. I don't even own one. A change of clothes is all. I usually spend the night."

"Meaning her husband travels on business. Why you're able to use the front door instead of slinking in through the back. What line of work is her husband in?"

Gus started to answer and then caught himself. "I'm not going to say. I'm not going to tell you who he is either. My lady friend's got her good name to protect."

Pudge handed him back the driver's license. "I don't care how bad a man her husband is. You going behind his back with the missus doesn't make you any better."

The old deputy spun on his heel and marched out. I memorized the license plate on the back of the blue pickup before following.

26

As soon as we pulled out of the gas station, Pudge picked up the mike and radioed Orville Nelson. "I need you to run an ID for me and I needed it fifteen minutes ago. Name is Gus Bishop. Address on his DL is in Redmond." He recited the driver's license number and street address from memory. "Drives a dark blue Dodge Power Wagon four-by. Oregon tags."

I chimed in with the pickup's license plate number.

Pudge cradled the mike. "Memorized the tags, did you?"

"Like you did with everything else. You didn't write it down to make him think it wasn't a big deal."

"You never tip your hand in a poker game either."

"What made you think he might be Freddie Sanderlin besides the color of the pickup and still being in the neighborhood of a fire?"

"This." The old deputy patted his paunch. "For a man who says he works construction, he doesn't have a black fingernail on him. And then there was his story about his lady friend. It's the rare man who'll admit right up front that he's seeing a married woman. A few don't because they want to protect her reputation, but most won't because of their own reputation. They don't want to be known for playing second fiddle." He was driving slowly, hunched over the steering wheel while glancing at the sideview mirrors. "Then there was the matter of him saying he didn't own a gun. What kind of man living east of the Cascade Mountains doesn't own a gun? What tipped you?"

"His name."

"What about it?"

"The brothers who owned the ranch where Freddie's parents were sharecropping lent him a mule to ride to school. They said it was the boy's only friend. The mule's name was Old Gus."

Pudge snorted. "Well, I'll be. I used to get a real chuckle out of these movies they made about a talking Army mule named Francis. Starred Donald O'Connor. He didn't play the mule. A real mule played the mule. Chill Wills was the mule's voice. Had this western twang. The things that mule said. Funny, yep, but more often than not spoke the truth about the way life really is."

"If you thought Gus Bishop is Freddie Sanderlin, why didn't you arrest him on the spot? I was backing your play."

"I know you were, but I could've been wrong, talking mule or no talking mule. Plus he didn't have red hair. At least not any longer. Probably dyes it along with all that goop he uses to slick it back. But mostly because I don't got a lick of evidence linking him to any crime. If Gus is Freddie, then I got a bead on him now and can use it to my advantage. Playing along like I did makes him think he got away with it. Like I always say, a criminal's worst enemy is himself when he believes he pulled something over on the law. Makes them get sloppy."

"Why don't we go back and follow him and see where he goes?"

"Wouldn't do no good. He's seen my rig and would spot it from a mile away. If he really is going to Burns and sees us tailing him, he'll drive real slow and pick a house at random to stop in front of. He'll pretend to be waiting there to make it look like that's where his cheating heart lives. After a while, he'll drive away as if he realized her husband hadn't gone on a business trip after all. He'll head straight back to Redmond, obeying the speed limit the whole way, knowing as soon as he crosses the Harney County line, I'll have to give it up and he'll be scot-free."

"We should stake out Judd Hollister's place to see if he goes there."

"That's what I aim to do. But there's no we in it. You need to sit tight until Judd calls you. If Gus is Freddie, you can't show up wherever Judd asks you to meet him. Freddie's likely to be there too. He'll blow your cover and you to kingdom come."

Pudge clicked the inside of his cheeks again. "What you need to do is string Judd along on the phone. Make him think you're raring to help him out for a cut of the take to pay for dope. Get all the info you can and then call me straight away. That way me and the other deputies can lay a trap and come down on Judd and Freddie like a rock falling off the top of Steens Mountain."

"I should've opened the suitcase," I said. "It was right there on the seat of his pickup."

"I thought about that too, but even if you'd found an Oregon State Police uniform in there and a semi-automatic with a smoking barrel, any two-bit lawyer would make them inadmissible in a trial. No warrant. No probable cause. The shyster would have Freddie kicked loose faster than Francis the Talking Mule kicking a bad guy in the seat of the britches."

Orville reached us on the radio as we were pulling up to the pink-walled sheriff's office on North Court Avenue. "I have it," he shouted, his excitement filling the cab.

"Hang on to whatever it is. We're here now," Pudge said.

By the time we opened the front door, Orville had propelled himself down the hall from his file room office. He was careening into the lobby, his wheelchair almost tipping over as we entered. I caught him by the shoulder and kept him upright.

"The driver's license is a counterfeit," he said breathlessly. "It is a complete false identity. The address in Redmond is a hamburger stand. The license plate is registered to a 1965 Chevrolet Nova." Orville gulped air. "Gus Bishop is Freddie Sanderlin. Am I right?"

"Looks like it," Pudge said.

"What a break, sir. I have more. The State Prison Bureau sent a fax in response to the inquiry I submitted earlier trying to collect information on Sanderlin's whereabouts. He has an arrest record. He served three years in the state penitentiary in Salem for his part in a breaking and entering robbery. He was paroled last summer, but has never checked in with his parole officer."

"That explains how he got himself that fake ID. Got all the information he needed while on the inside about people on the outside who could forge documents," Pudge said.

"I checked the dates. Three days after his release, Freddie was in the car when Judd Hollister was ticketed for speeding. He probably got the fake driver's license after having been ordered to give his real ID to the state trooper."

"Judd giving Freddie a ride means they had to have known each other from before," I said. "Maybe their friendship dates back to when the Hollister family house went up in smoke. Remember Colonel Davies' theory. One's the brains, the other's the instrument."

Pudge scowled. "If Judd and Freddie did that crime together, then the only way to prove it is to get one of those boys to sell out the other."

"Judd would be the first to crack if faced with a murder charge," I said. "He'll say Freddie did it all on his own, that he didn't even know about it until Freddie showed up and threatened him unless he handed over part of the insurance money. Judd won't let anyone forget Freddie's already done a stint in prison."

"And he'd get away with it too. Sell one of those fancy paintings to buy himself a first-class lawyer." Pudge gave a look of disgust. "Either way, if Freddie did it on his own or schemed with Judd, he's got to know Judd would rat him out to save his own hide. We got to be careful. If Freddie thinks we're closing in on them, he's likely to shut Judd up for good."

"About Judd's art collection, I have information on that too," Orville said.

"Don't you ever get any shuteye?" the old deputy said.

"I sleep four hours a night."

"Only four?"

"It is more than sufficient. Thomas Edison slept three hours. He called sleep a heritage from our caveman days."

"Well, Orville, you're wearing me plum out. Okay, let's hear it. What about Judd's paintings?"

"Technically, none are paintings," the FBI hopeful said. "The pieces Ranger Drake described are limited-edition lithographic prints signed by the artist. Their value depends on the artist, the subject, their condition, and their provenance."

"Sounds Biblical," Pudge said.

"In this instance, provenance refers to a traceable chain of ownership from when it left the artist's studio."

"You don't say."

"Judd told me he acquired them through a dealer in New York," I said. "Did you get a chance to ask about prices and stolen art?"

Orville said he did. "That is where I learned about provenance and limited-edition lithographic prints. There are many printing techniques, but stone-plate lithographic prints that are hand-pulled by the artist in limited numbers are the most valuable." He paused to catch his breath. "A dealer I spoke to said it is impossible to put a price tag on a piece without a physical inspection. A trained expert must verify the signature, the printing technique, and the number on the print signifying what place it had in the order of the limited edition. A lower number tends to command a higher price."

"Did he mention any recent art heists?"

"The robberies that earn front-page headlines typically involve very famous paintings from major art museums in Europe. The most recent was in 1966 when paintings by Rembrandt and Rubens were stolen from a London gallery."

"Do they ever get recovered?" Pudge asked.

"Yes, because most are held for ransom, like a kidnapping. Insurance companies are likely to pay off because the paintings are irreplaceable."

"That it?"

"There has also been a recent rash of robberies of private collections of provenanced art here in the US. The victims were owners of large country estates, namely around Dallas, Phoenix, and Las Vegas."

"What about the kind of art Judd owns, the lithographs?" I said.

"The dealer told me the primary crime for that medium is forgery," Orville said. "It takes experience and expertise to distinguish an authentic piece from a counterfeit. They test the paper and ink for manufacturing age, origin, and chemical composition. They are like fingerprints."

"If Judd and Freddie are trafficking in forged art, fire's not a friend. It's their worst enemy," Pudge said. "Why would they be playing with matches that could turn the loot into ash? No, we got to ask ourselves, how's fire a help? It doesn't when robbing a bank. The money inside is likely to burn right up. A jewelry store? Same thing. They'd have to sift through burning embers to find whatever diamonds fell out of the melted gold." The lawman's short-brim Stetson waggled. "It's got to be something else."

"What about a diversion?" I said. "The Viet Cong were always doing that to send us in the wrong direction. Say Judd and Freddie started multiple fires on F Street. Burning houses would draw every cop and fireman in town, leaving the other side of Burns wide open."

"Where there's a bank on Broadway," Pudge said. "Even if the teller hit the panic button while they're sticking it up, the bank robbers would have plenty of time to make a getaway before anybody putting out a fire on F Street could respond. I think you're on to something, son. That still leaves figuring out what target they got in mind. Banks aren't the only places that keep cash on hand. The mill in Hines still pays hourly workers in greenbacks every Friday at quitting time. There's more than one store in town that sells jewels and watches. Why, even that new grocery warehouse store opened on Highway 20 is cash and carry."

Sheriff Burton yanked open the door to his private office. "What's all the commotion out here? I was on the phone to the attorney general and couldn't hear myself think."

"Well, Bust'em, we got us some hard information about the arson fires and some likely suspects," Pudge said. "We think they're planning a robbery."

"Of what?"

"That's still an open question. Maybe if you rounded up all the deputies, we could sort it out and come up with a plan."

The sheriff hesitated. "Who knows about this?"

"Just us for now."

"You haven't spoken to anybody? Not the mayor or the *Burns Herald*?"

"Why would I do that? There's nothing to report yet."

Burton brushed his perfectly trimmed mustache with his fingernails. "Come into my office and we can talk about it. Just you. Drake isn't even supposed to be here. I already warned him. Orville, go back to filing papers. That's an order."

The sheriff returned to his inner sanctum. Pudge said, "I expect it's gonna take a while to get Bust'em to see the light of day. Since I'm your ride home, you'll either have to wait for me or make other arrangements."

"I'll figure something out," I said.

The old deputy ambled into Burton's office. I could hear the sheriff order him to shut the door. Orville spun his wheelchair around and raced back to his cubicle. I followed.

"Sheriff Burton is going to make sure he receives all the credit for this just in time for the election," Orville said.

"Only if a bust goes down. If it doesn't, he'll pin the blame squarely on his opponent."

Orville wheeled closer to his desk and reached toward his calculating machine. "I need to spend more time on my voter database."

"Before you do, can you get ahold of the phone company and track down an address in Washington? The Paiute boy who went missing in Malheur County called his aunt collect last night. Her name is Charity Liveslong. Here's her phone number and address in Riley. Her nephew, Charley Pony Blanket, said he was somewhere in Washington living at a foster home."

"I will get right on it."

"Before you do, let's radio Loq and tell him about it. He's probably in Washington by now."

Orville tried raising Loq, but got no response. "He must be away from his pickup or out of range. I will keep trying and give him the message."

I used Orville's phone to call the Warbler ranch. Gemma

picked up on the fourth ring. "Want to have an early dinner in Burns tonight?" I said.

"You're asking me out on a date?"

"I am."

"You mean, Pudge got busy and can't give you a ride back home."

"How about The Pine Room? I'll walk over. Let's meet in thirty minutes."

"Make it an hour. I need to freshen up. I've had a busy day. First there was this pigheaded burn victim I had to tend to and then it was a real pig. Well, thirteen actually. A sow had a late-season litter and the piglets all came down with greasy pig."

"I don't want to ask what that is."

"Exudative dermatitis. It's a staph infection that causes skin lesions."

"That settles it," I said. "I'm ordering steak."

27

The Pine Room provided a welcome respite from the smoke and heat. The ceiling fans were turned on high and the downdraft was strong enough to ruffle the heavy cloth napkins set on the tables.

The hostess waited as I settled into a booth. "Your waitress will be right with you, hon. Can I get you started with a cocktail?"

"I'll take water and my dinner companion will have a glass of red wine. She'll be along any minute."

"She being Gemma Warbler." The hostess winked. "Oh, don't look so surprised, hon. Messes with that strong, silent-type look you got going there. There are no secrets in Burns. Pudge is a regular here at the Pine. That means anybody dating his daughter gets sized up. If we hadn't already given you our stamp of approval, you'd be standing outside looking in the window instead of sitting here about to eat the best meal of your life."

I didn't have to wait long before the horse doctor arrived. Gemma wore silver and turquoise earrings and had pinned her ponytail up, but not all of it stayed pinned. The escaped strands made her look even more beautiful. She'd traded her usual denim pearl-snap shirt for a pocketless white one with black piping at the yoke. In place of jeans she wore a long linen skirt the color of sagebrush. I even detected a hint of makeup. Not much, just right.

"You put your time to good use," I said.

"How's that?" she said as she sat down.

"It takes a half hour to drive here and that only left you thirty minutes to get all that done."

"All what done?"

"Look like that."

"And what's *that*?"

"You're really making me work here, aren't you?"

Gemma laughed. "Next time, all you have to say is you look gorgeous."

"Well, you do."

"You're not so bad looking yourself despite that burn on your cheek. And I'm the only one here who knows what you got underneath those clothes."

I glanced around to see if anybody listening looked shocked.

"I was referring to the bandages, hotshot," she grinned.

The waitress brought Gemma a glass of wine. She ordered a filet and I got the cowboy steak. As we waited for our meals, Gemma refrained from asking what her father and I'd been doing all day and I didn't volunteer any information either. I told her about Tuhudda Will and how he'd go about asking the clouds to gift their rain. She told me about the piggery she'd visited and the couple who owned it.

"They're Basque and have six children with a seventh on the way," she said.

"Orville Nelson is living at a boarding house owned by a Basque woman," I said.

"What's her name?"

"I only know her last name. Lorriaga. She has a daughter named Lucy."

"I know Lucy. Before she began training as a physical therapist, she considered veterinary school. She came to talk to me and asked what it was like. I took her on a couple of ranch calls to show her. In the end, she said she'd rather help people than animals. Lucy made the right call. She's a born people person."

"I think Orville's starting to understand that too. Lucy was his physical therapist when he was in rehab. He's clearly fond of her, but swears it's only platonic. He thinks his disability makes her off limits."

"Orville's whip smart, but that's the stupidest thing I've ever heard. If Lucy's fond of him as much as he's of her, she won't let a wheelchair get in the way. The heart wants what the heart wants."

The food came. The bone in my cowboy steak was the size of a tomahawk and stretched over both sides of the plate. The waitress handed us steak knives. They reminded me of the skinning knife Loq had taken from the vigilante at Chewaucan Marsh.

"Loq said I should introduce Orville to a veteran who works at the VFW. He lost his legs in 'Nam," I said.

"KC," Gemma said. "I know his wife."

"Is there anybody you don't know?"

"Burns is a small town and Harney County's even smaller."

"So the hostess told me."

More hair loosened from the pin. "You still think living in your shack in No Mountain allows you to play ostrich." She took a bite of her filet and followed it with a sip of wine. "Does Loq think Orville seeing KC and his wife together will convince him he has a shot with Lucy?"

"It's hard to know what Loq is thinking at any given time, but, yes, that'd be my guess."

"Orville doesn't need advice from KC or Loq. You either. He only needs to tell Lucy how he feels."

"I'd hate to see the kid get his heart broken," I said.

"Orville's a man, not a kid, and the only way he's going to get hurt is if he hurts himself by not telling Lucy how he feels to find out how she feels about him."

"What makes you so sure his disability won't be a big deal for her?"

"Look at me. I fell for you, didn't I? When we first met, you were, well, you know how you were. Having flashbacks left and right, blaming yourself for the men in your squad who got killed, and putting pebbles in a tin can every morning and every night to mark the days you'd gone without using heroin. You were always rattling that can at yourself whenever you got a craving. Everything you looked at was through the lens of war, though I suspect it still is."

I eyed her glass of wine and knew if I took a sip, just one, it wouldn't be long before I was rummaging through the medicine kit in the back of her red Jeep Wagoneer for pain meds, even if they were horse tranquilizers.

"I'll never forget my men or the war," I said. "And, sure, the flashbacks have been retreating in the rearview mirror some, but I can never be sure they won't come roaring back. Addiction? That's always going to be a day-to-day fight. Always."

"I know that, and it doesn't turn me off either. In fact, I find the courage and imagination it takes to try and put your life back together after what you went through kind of sexy."

I clinked her wine glass with my water glass. "Not as much as I find what you're wearing."

"We'll see about that." Her eyes sparkled.

We took our time finishing dinner. The restaurant felt like a million miles away from a world scorching under a relentless sun and at the mercy of wildfires and heartless firebugs. I almost forgot thinking about missing children, but almost was a far cry from completely. And though I didn't voice it out loud, I wondered how Loq was getting on tracking down Wanda Many-baskets and what he'd do when he finally caught up to Cameron and Arabelle Parker. Pudge was mistaken if he thought Loq would only go, see, and call.

It was still daylight, or what passed for it in the smoke-filled gloom, when we left The Pine Room. Gemma drove like she flew —fast, relaxed, but sure-handed. A couple of miles out of No Mountain, the haze began to lift, revealing a reef of clouds circling the peak of Steens Mountain like an atoll. As colorful as coral, they reflected the sun setting to the west. The changing light also shined down on the hayfields and desert scrub below, tinging them with splashes of orange, red, and purple. Here and there, lights began twinkling on the high lonesome from distant cattle ranches.

Gemma gave a contented sigh. "I never tire of this scenery. It's reassuring and breathtaking all at the same time. When I lost my mom, the sky and land told me everything would be okay because they would always be here for me, and as I've grown up, they always have been. I'm the luckiest girl in the whole world because I get to work outside with all this beauty around me. That, out there, what we're looking at? Well, I'd say it's a whole lot prettier than any canvas painted by Frederic Remington because it's real, alive, and always changing. You can't put a price on it."

And with those words, I finally saw it. I saw the whole thing. Colonel Davies had circled it on the map himself. The Rocking H. It was target rich because of its art collection, not its cows.

"That's it!" I said. "You got it. They're going to hit Blaine's."

"What are you talking about? Who's going to hit him and how come?"

"The firebugs. They're going to create a diversion to draw

everyone away from the Rocking H, leaving them free to waltz in and steal the Harney's Remingtons. Every last one of them, the oil paintings and the bronze statues. They're worth a fortune. Maybe they're the same gang that's been robbing the mansions down south. They've been testing fire to get the right combination for all the different types of vegetation around the ranch house. Irrigated pastures. Dry hayfields. Orchards. All of them. The buildings too. They want to avoid lighting the house up because that's where the art is."

Gemma gasped. "We need to tell Pudge right away." She slowed to make a U-turn as we entered the outskirts of No Mountain.

"Too late," I said. "You need to drop me off." And I pointed to the old lineman's shack up ahead.

"Why?"

"See that green Mustang parked in front? It's Judd Hollister's. Let me out and then go straight home and call Pudge. Tell him it's the Rocking H and to call Blaine. If he can't reach him, that could mean they've already cut the phone lines and jammed the ranch's shortwave antenna. The robbery could be going down tonight. Tell Pudge to alert the fire department too because they might also be lighting fires in Burns to keep the law bottled up."

"What are you going to do?"

"Play along with Judd. He thinks I'm in it for the money. Go on, pull in front and as soon as I'm out of the Jeep, drive away, but not too fast. We don't want to make him suspicious."

"No way! Don't be a fool. You can't go alone. As far as you know, Judd could be the one in the wig who threw the firebomb at you. Come home with me and wait for Pudge and the other deputies."

"You know I can't do that. Besides, if the robbery is tonight, Judd will go without me. Blaine and everyone living at the

Rocking H is in danger. I can slow Judd and Freddie down until your father gets there. Go on and call him. I'll be okay."

Gemma set her jaw and white-knuckled the steering wheel. "Well, you need to be a whole lot better than okay," she said fiercely. "You need to be damn well perfect if you're going up against thieves and murderers alone."

$\sim$

Judd Hollister was sitting in the ladder-back chair on my front porch as he watched me get out of the Jeep and Gemma drive away. "Dude, who's the Barbie? She looks fine."

"A neighbor friend is all. She was giving me a lift."

"What's wrong with your ride?"

I was betting my life that it was Freddie Sanderlin wearing the wig who threw the Molotov cocktail at me in another one of his psychosexual random acts of violence and he wouldn't have told Judd about it.

"Long story, but my pickup's out of commission," I said.

"And you couldn't ride your bike?" He pointed at the Triumph parked beneath the overhang next to a 16-foot skiff on a trailer.

I stepped up on the porch and towered over him. "I've never been much for playing Twenty Questions."

"Whoa, dude. No reason to get uptight. It's cool. I told you I'd give you a call if I ever had a job for you. You never gave me your phone number. I had to ask around to find out where you live."

"What's it pay?"

"I like that, yeah. Most people ask what do they got to do before asking what's it going to pay." Judd smirked. "A fair chunk of bread, man. More than you make in a month. You ready to hear what you got to do to earn it?"

"Does it matter?"

His head went up and down again. "Righteous, man. That's the perfect thing to say. It's all about the bread so you can buy another ride on the dragon, isn't it?" He grinned some more. "Seriously, dude, the job's easy. All I need you to do is drive something with four wheels instead of two. Think you can handle it?"

"If you're talking about your Shelby, yes, I can do that. I'd love to see what it tops out at on something longer than a quarter mile."

"I've buried the speedometer more than once," he bragged. "Hundred thirty-five easy."

"We'll see what it can do with me behind the wheel."

"Hold on, man. We need to go over a couple of things first."

"Like what?"

"Like, the job's tonight."

I didn't show any surprise. "Good. The sooner, the better. I'm not big on being patient."

He grinned. "Another thing. Do you have a problem doing something that's more illegal than using heroin?"

"I already assumed that since you said it pays good."

Judd laughed. "It does. After it's done, there's no talking about it to anyone. Ever. If something was ever said and it came back that you said it, well, that wouldn't be good. I got partners who wouldn't like it. Not one bit. They're not what you call the understanding types."

"And I wouldn't want them to talk about me either." I jutted my chin. "That definitely wouldn't be good for them."

"A tough guy, huh? I like it. One final thing. You got to bring your gun. I got this job planned perfectly, so you shouldn't have to use it, but just in case."

I glanced down at the holster on my hip. "Mind if I take it off for a minute while I change out of my uniform?"

He laughed. "Whatever floats your boat, dude."

I went inside and swapped shirts and grabbed a black wool watch cap and tied a blue bandana loosely around my neck. When I walked back outside, Judd got up from the ladder-back chair. He eyed the gun and nodded his approval.

"Giddyap," he said. "Let's ride."

28

J udd drove. "You'll take the wheel later. We're going to stop at my pad first."

He punched an eight-track tape into the deck and cranked up the volume. "Born To Be Wild" howled from the speakers. I should've guessed he was a Steppenwolf fan. As soon as we were clear of No Mountain, he mashed the gas pedal and speed-shifted through the gears, making the chrome headers thunder. The speedometer hovered at 100.

"Let me know if I'm driving too fast for you," Judd taunted.

"Don't you ever worry about speed traps?"

"Not tonight. The state troopers got their hands full."

That confirmed diversion fires would be lit in Burns to keep all the branches of law enforcement busy.

The sunset faded to black. Darkness settled over the high desert. Even the silhouettes of the basalt-capped buttes disappeared while waiting for the moon to rise. The headlights of the muscle car stabbed holes in the inky night, but when we turned off to Judd's, a white dome glowed at the end of the road. Every light in the multi-windowed house was shining. A dozen or more cars and pickups were parked in front. I spotted the yellow VW bug. Its ragtop was down.

Judd switched off the ignition, but music still blared. It was coming from the towers of speakers by the pool. A hot summer night party was in full swing. Girls in bikinis and boys in swim trunks splashed in and out of the water. A few people were dancing. A group of boys—some looked to be teens, the others no older than their early twenties—were huddled around a keg passing a joint and taking turns lapping suds straight from the faucet.

"I told you my place is kegger central," Judd said as he got out.

"What about the job?" I said.

"We'll get there. Cool your jets while I make the scene."

He was establishing an alibi. Everybody there would remember the party, the good time they had, how only Judd knew how to make life in boring old Harney County a blast. No one would notice when he slipped away for an hour or so to rob the largest ranch in the county.

I went to the edge of the patio and scanned the crowd for Gus Bishop—Freddie Sanderlin. I was in luck. There was no sign of him. The smell of pot wafted through the air. I watched as Judd went from person to person, punching the boys in the shoulder, patting the girls on the ass, acting like the BMOC. Everyone cheered when they saw him.

Chrissy was among them. She was wearing a pink bikini. "Well, if it isn't the cute pool guy who doesn't clean pools," she said, making goo goo eyes at me from behind her bangs. "Want to rub suntan lotion on my back?"

"It's nighttime," I said. "Shouldn't your parents have already given you a glass of milk and tucked you into bed?"

"Don't be such a downer." Chrissy giggled, reached behind her back, and pulled the strings. Her top fell to the ground. "I told you I like to skinny dip." She started tugging at the bottoms. I sidestepped her and kept walking.

Judd reached the far end of the patio and turned to survey the crowd. When he spotted me, he motioned to join him. "Some very fine Barbies here, but as much as I'd like to stay and lay, duty calls."

We cut through the house. I eyed the Warhols, Peter Maxes, and the cartoonish Roy Lichtenstein with the girl firing a rifle and *Pop! Crack!* emblazoned on it. Judd had told me they were investments. Now I realized that behind his cover as a laidback, devil-may-care party boy lurked a shrewd operator who'd devised a scheme to launder the profits from stolen art by acquiring provenanced lithographs that he could trade like stock certificates and bonds.

We got back in the Shelby Mustang with Judd behind the wheel. He drove over to the 200-gallon fuel tank next to the barn and asked me to get out and top off the muscle car.

"The gas cap is behind the rear license plate," he said. "It's on a spring hinge. Just pull it toward you."

When it was full, I climbed back in and we sped toward the Rocking H. Judd didn't turn on the car's stereo. "I'm going to be straight up with you," he said, his words suddenly clipped and hard-edged so I wouldn't miss the threat that came with them. "This job, tonight? It's a big one. A lot of planning went into it. A lot of people are counting on it coming off without a hitch. I prefer to work far from home, but the prize here was too good to pass up."

He glanced over. "Are you listening?"

"There's nothing wrong with my hearing," I said.

"Then hear this. I don't take risks, but I had to take one asking you along because I'm a man short. This is a test. A big one. You pass, there'll be more jobs like it. You'll be earning more money than you ever dreamed of. But if you screw up, don't follow my directions, don't protect me when I tell you to, turn chicken and run, or tell anybody about this, you fail. Simple as that. And in this business, the only room for failure is a hole dug way out in the desert. Got it?"

"When do you get to the part when you tell me something I don't already know?"

"I hope you're as tough as you talk," he said. "For your sake and mine."

Judd slowed and turned onto a gravel road. It led to the Rocking H. We continued for a couple of miles. He slowed again. The headlights of the Shelby Mustang reflected off a chrome bumper up ahead. A pickup was parked in a turnout. A dark blue Dodge Power Wagon. I slipped on the black watch cap and pulled up the bandana to cover my face.

"You don't need to do that," he said. "This isn't the job. This is where we switch places and you take over driving. Those are my guys."

"Like I said, I won't say anything about this afterward and I don't want anybody saying anything about me. This makes sure they won't."

Judd pulled to a stop. Gus Bishop—Freddie Sanderlin—and another man were standing by the Dodge four-by. Freddie was dressed in an Oregon State Trooper's blue uniform, but without the hat. His slicked back, dyed black hair gleamed in the Mustang's headlights. A leather duty belt held a holstered semi-automatic. The other man was strapped too.

Judd took the key out of the ignition and handed it to me. "Come on, let's get this party started."

When I got out of the car, Freddie and the other man eyed me suspiciously. "Who's he?" Freddie said.

"My new driver," Judd said. "Do I have to remind you what happened to Phil?"

Freddie shrugged. "Hope he works out better than old Philly. Rest in peace."

"Update me," Judd said, his tone growing even more clipped and hard-edged.

"Everything's in place." Freddie checked his wristwatch. "There's a hot time in the old town tonight. The courthouse. A block of shops downtown. Cops and firemen are running back and forth with their tails cut off trying to figure out what to put out first."

"And here?"

"Oops, someone flicked lit cigarettes in a field of dry haystacks a couple of miles from the ranch. Pastures of green alfalfa in the opposite direction had gallons of gas spilled on them. They're smoldering something fierce. A fence rider's hut surrounded by sagebrush is in the path of burning tumbleweeds being blown by the wind." Freddie spit when he laughed.

"And the people at the ranch?" Judd said.

"The cowboys took off to put out all the fires. They headed in different directions. Some in their pickups, others on horseback. They're dumber than the cows they herd."

"What about our guys?"

"They're stationed where they're supposed to be and waiting for the go sign."

"Any of the six not show?"

"I made sure they all did," the other man said.

"Good. They're your responsibility. Make sure they do their jobs. If any cowboys return early or a nosy neighbor shows up, your team is the welcoming committee. Understand?"

The man slapped his sidearm. "We all got rifles too. No one's gonna get close."

"Let's go over the plan one last time." Judd pointed at Freddie. "Now that the fires are lit in Burns and here, you're going in first to see if anyone stayed home. You knock on the door. If anybody answers, you're the concerned state trooper telling them you spotted a fire. You ask if anyone else is home. You round up whoever's there and lock them in a closet."

"And if there's no lock on the closet?" Freddie failed to suppress a grin.

"Do whatever you need to," Judd said.

Freddie gave a spitting laugh again.

I thought of the pretty young woman with raven hair I'd seen preparing food in Blaine's kitchen. She would've stayed behind to have a meal ready for the hungry ranch hands when they returned from fighting fires. Waving a spatula at Freddie like she had at me wouldn't save her.

Judd turned to me. "You're my wheel man. You stay with the Shelby. Keep the engine running when I go inside and your gun ready just in case I need you. I know what I'm after and I know where it is." He gestured at Freddie. "He'll help me load the goods into the back of the car and then you'll drive me back to the party. When we get there, it's like we were never gone."

"When do we get our share?" I grunted through the bandana.

"It's always about the bread for you, isn't it? Don't worry, you'll get paid the same time as everyone else does after I fence the goods. It won't take long. We'll meet up and split the take. I'll let everybody know the when and the where."

"What about the house after we're done?" Freddie said impatiently.

Judd took his sweet time before answering. It was as if he got some kind of kick out of making Freddie squirm. "Once I'm gone, do your thing. Make sure no one will ever know something was taken."

Freddie clapped his hands and danced a jig. "Whoosh! Old Mr. and Mrs. House will light up the horizon for miles. Brother Barn and Sister Stable too. Moo, cow. Neigh, horsey. Nighty night anyone shut in the closet." Spit sprayed my bandana as he giggled.

Judd squinted at us. "Any other questions?"

"One last thing," Freddie said, his thin lips tightening into a sneer as he turned it on me. "How come he gets to wear a mask?"

"He's shy," Judd said.

"What's his name?"

I didn't make so much as a twitch waiting for Judd to answer. I couldn't recall if Pudge had called me by name when we'd encountered Freddie at the gas station.

Judd said, "Don't worry about it. He doesn't know your name either. It's better this way."

Freddie scowled before shrugging. "Okay," he said. Then quick as Wanda's imitation of a rattlesnake, his fingers shot out and yanked my bandana down before I could slap his hands away.

"You were with that fat deputy!" he shrieked and reached for his semi-automatic.

By the time he pulled it, my boot was already arcing up from the ground. The toe caught his wrist and sent the gun flying. The third man drew his gun, but I drew faster and shot him where he stood. He tumbled backward. Judd dove for cover while Freddie scrambled around on the ground searching for his gun.

I could've taken them right then and there and held them at gunpoint until I found something to tie them up with, but I had no way of knowing if the armed men hiding by the ranch house heard the gunshot and what they'd do if they had. Would they come rushing here or would they rush the house and kill anyone still inside? I leapt in the Shelby and inserted the key. The ignition fired instantly and I stomped the pedal.

Freddie found his gun and came up shooting.

"Stop!" Judd screamed at him. "You'll hit my car!"

But Freddie didn't listen and kept firing. I fishtailed onto the road and speed-shifted even faster than Judd had. Headlights in the side mirror showed the men had regrouped and begun pursuit in the Power Wagon. The Shelby's souped-up V-8 roared. The speedometer's red needle climbed. The muscle car's wide tires shot twin rooster tails of gravel. I was hoping the armed men up ahead would hesitate when they recognized the familiar car hurtling toward them, but the Dodge pickup chasing behind was also familiar and the gunfire coming from it quickly erased anyone's doubts. I saw flashes of rifle fire as I ran the gauntlet. The windshield spidered. The right headlight shattered.

The long driveway to the ranch came up fast. I downshifted and put the car into a four-wheel drift to make the 90-degree turn and passed cleanly between the pair of upright timbers that marked the entrance. I sped up and laid on the horn. That's when the metallic green fastback rocketed over a hump protecting an irrigation pipe and went airborne. All I could do was hold onto the wheel. The Shelby smacked down like an F-4 Phantom landing on the deck of the USS *Kitty Hawk*. I slammed on the brakes and skidded to a stop.

Blaine Harney kicked open the front door of the ranch house and sighted through the scope of a bolt-action .30-06.

"It's Nick Drake," I shouted as I scrambled out of the car. "They're coming to rob you."

"How do I know you're not one of them?" the big rancher growled.

"Because you know Gemma would never love a thief."

There was no way of taking it back or knowing how her ex-husband would react. I gritted my teeth and watched as the knuckle on Blaine's trigger finger whitened. The rifle cracked.

29

The bullet whistled over my head and metal clanged behind me. Blaine pulled the bolt back to chamber another round. The blue Power Wagon screeched to a stop and the driver jammed the gears into reverse. Blaine sighted and fired again. More metal clanged when he hit the pickup's grill. The four-by's engine screamed as it raced backward up the drive.

"Sonofabitch tries coming onto my property—" Bullets thudding into the ranch's walls cut him off.

"Inside, quick!" I shouted. "There's eight, nine gunmen."

The big rancher continued to shoot at the retreating four-by as he backed up. More return fire came as I stayed low and sprinted toward the door. He kicked it shut as soon as we were inside.

"I thought something was wrong when the phone went out and the shortwave too," he said. "When a fence rider rode in hellbent for leather shouting about multiple fires, I remembered what you said about arsonists."

"They're after your Remingtons," I said.

"Well, I'll be. And you said something about them being better off in a bank vault too."

I peeked out the front window. The Dodge pickup had disappeared from view, but I knew it wasn't gone for good. Judd and Freddie weren't about to call it quits now. Not as long as I was alive to ID them.

"Who else is here?" I said.

"Elena. She does the cooking and so on. Rafael too. He's a stable hand. I had him stay behind to prepare fresh mounts in case any of my men needed one. Some horses get real jumpy around fire, even when you blindfold them. They can smell and hear it."

"Where are they now?"

"I'm here," a woman called from the darkened hallway that led to the kitchen.

"Elena!" Blaine said. "Are you all right?"

"I'm a little scared." The young woman with skin the color of polished mahogany and dark eyes that matched her thick hair stepped closer.

"I won't let anything happen to you."

"Is Rafael with you?" I asked.

"My cousin, he must still be in the stable."

"Aw, hell," the rancher said. "I can't leave him out there."

"Hold on. First things first," I said. "We need to make a stand here. They've lit fires in Burns too. We're on our own."

"When my men hear gunshots, they'll come running."

"And they'll be riding straight into an ambush," I said. "Are they armed?"

"Of course they are. They're cowboys."

"We can't wait for them. We need to get all your guns and ammo ready fast. We'll take the high ground upstairs. Station the rifles around the rooms so we can move quickly from one gun to the next, window to window. We can catch them in the open, but sooner or later they're going to use fire to try and force us to give up. They'll start with the outbuildings."

"The stable!" Elena cried.

"I haven't forgotten about Rafael," I said. "I'll get him while you two get ready here. Kill the lights. Barricade the front door with furniture. The backdoor too as soon as I slip out."

"How will you get back in if I do that?" Blaine said.

"Don't worry about how. Just don't shoot me when I do."

Blaine and I hurried to the study. We took the paintings off the wall and stacked them on the floor away from the windows. We pulled the long guns from the cabinet and laid them on the big table between the Remington bronze statues. The rancher extracted boxes of cartridges from a drawer and matched the calibers to the rifles. I selected the .30-caliber pump. It was fifty years old, but I figured it was the closest in weight to my Winchester .30-30.

"They won't leave any witnesses behind," I said as I loaded the rifle and crammed extra cartridges in my pockets. "Once they get the art, they'll burn the ranch to the ground."

Blaine didn't look up from loading rifles. "They can try, but the family's stood firm on this spot for four generations. I don't aim to be the first who wilts."

"I'll go for Rafael," I said. "Once I'm out the backdoor and you've barricaded it, head upstairs and lay down cover fire for me."

"With pleasure," he said between gritted teeth.

I turned to Elena. "Do you have a pet name for your cousin, call him anything special?"

"Yes, Raffi. Why?"

"No reason."

I eased the backdoor open. Something scraped and bumped behind me when I closed it. I pictured the big rancher wrestling the refrigerator against the door. I gave it a ten count. Gunfire erupted from an upstairs window at the front of the house. It attracted noisy return fire, but I still ran close to the rear wall. Flowerbeds had been planted along the house's perimeter and the turned soil muffled the sound of my footsteps. When I reached the end, I made a dash across the open yard and ducked behind a cottonwood.

The moon was finally up, but the haze had returned and the pale light cast short-lived shadows. I could make out the outlines of the bunkhouse, barn, and stable on the far side of a wide clearing—a clearing I knew lay in full view of the riflemen stationed at the ranch's entrance to my left. I assumed others were hiding to my right. To assume otherwise was to make a cherry's mistake. I picked out a relay course between patches of umbra and mapped my race accordingly. It felt like weeks since I'd said "Ready, Set, Go" to Judd Hollister on the salt flat. I muttered it to myself now and took off.

I made it to the safety of the first black patch without drawing a shot. I took a deep breath and ran across the exposed field to the next. I was right about not being alone. A gunman popped up from a low spot on the right and fired. I slid into the oncoming shadow like it was home base and fired back. The gunman had never served with a soldier like DJ telling him how to survive a firefight. He chose to hide in the gray. He chose wrong.

I didn't dwell on having shot him. I had shot the man standing with Judd and Freddie in the shoulder on purpose, but there was no time for tricks or mercy now that innocent lives were at stake. There would be time to wrestle with demons later. That is, if I was lucky enough for there to be a later.

Without knowing if Rafael was alone or a gunman was inside holding him as a shield, I passed up the front door of the stable and shimmied between the rails of the corral attached to the side of the building. A pair of horses snorted and nickered at me. I put a hand on the first one's muzzle. "Shh," I whispered. "Attagirl."

Orders were being shouted near the ranch's entrance. Judd was yelling for someone to get a move on and outflank whoever was down by the outbuildings and trading shots with one of his men.

"Attagirl," I whispered again and urged both horses to show me the way to the side door. They snorted again. A hoof rubbed my boot. A tail flicked my shoulder. I walked with them until they nosed against a wooden rolling door that had been left ajar a couple of inches.

I crouched and listened at the door's gap. Nothing. I got on my stomach and stuck the rifle barrel in the gap and used it to ease the rolling door open a little wider. Metal wheels rubbing on a metal track squeaked. Wood groaned. A barn owl hooted. I stopped and waited and then slithered through the opening.

Half way through, a glimpse of the moon appeared again and a sliver of silver shone through the gap and illuminated me. I slithered faster, clutched the rifle to my chest, and rolled to the left to get out of the light. Footsteps thudded and a man holding a pitchfork rushed toward me as I lay on my back. I pushed the rifle straight up to block the tines plunging toward my chest.

"Raffi!" I hissed. "Raffi! Elena sent me."

The teenager hesitated. "Elena?"

"She's in the house with Blaine. I came to get you."

The tines stopped pushing my rifle. The pitchfork retracted. Rafael was the stable hand who'd led Blaine and Gemma's horses away, the teen with the green ball cap with a farm-supply logo on it. "Who's shooting at us?" he said.

"Robbers."

"But the cattle are far away."

"We need to get out of the stable. Now."

As soon as I said it, a new round of gunfire started. This one was more furious than the last. The fusillade was directed at the top floor of the house. It came from all sides.

"They're going to hit Elena and Mr. Harney!" Rafael said.

"It's cover fire. They're forcing eyes away from the windows so the leader can close in."

"Why?"

"Come on, we got to get you out of here. Do you know where the cowboys went, the nearest ones?"

"There's a fire in the south pasture."

"I'm guessing you know how to ride."

"Since I was three."

"Bareback? There's no time to saddle. Grab a halter. Let's go. Quietly."

I led him into the corral. Flames from the barn were already licking the night sky. Oily smoke billowed from the windows of the bunk house.

"Which horse is the fastest?" I whispered.

"Maggie. The bay."

"Halter her and get on. Get down as low as you can. Bury your face in her neck. I'll open the rear gate and give her a slap. Don't use the driveway or the roads. Cut across the fields. Ride as fast as you can to the nearest cowboys. Tell them what's happening."

Rafael hesitated. "But the men out there will shoot me."

I put my hand on his shoulder. I hadn't talked to a teenager about to face gunfire since I'd left 'Nam. Three years there and it never got easy. It was just as hard now, but I didn't have a choice. There was no returning to the house. We'd be cut down before we got there. We couldn't stay in the stable. It was next on Freddie's list to torch and he was on his way.

"You'll be okay," I said. "They'll be too busy returning my fire. You ride. Ride as fast as you can. Don't look back. No matter what. If Maggie stumbles and goes down, get up and run. Run and hide."

Rafael slipped the halter on Maggie, grabbed a handful of her mane, and swung aboard. He dug his knees in and clamped his elbows on either side of the bay's neck. "I'm ready."

I slid the barrel bolt fastening the gate, pushed it open, and slapped Maggie hard on the rear. She took off. The other horse followed instinctively. I shouldered the rifle, aimed at where I thought Freddie was, and pulled the trigger. I pumped in another cartridge and pulled it again.

I remembered what Colonel Davies said about fighting a pyromaniac. "You're going to burn, Freddie!" I shouted. "And I'll be the one striking the match!"

As I pumped another round, I glanced over. The horses were running shoulder to shoulder, egging each other on as if in a stakes race, the finish line somewhere in the dark ahead. Guns blasted, but not at them. They blasted at me.

30

I kissed the ground as waves of lead splintered the corral's posts and rails. Piles of road apples provided little cover. It was time to fight fire with fire. I propped on my elbows and sighted down the Remington's barrel. It didn't have a mounted scope, only a bead front, rear open sight, but my target would be hard to miss.

I aimed at the metallic green Shelby Mustang in the front yard, zeroing in on the trunk where the gas tank I'd filled earlier was mounted. I pumped three rounds into it. The fat rear wheels lifted off the ground as the sparks from the bullets penetrating the metal ignited the gasoline. The tank detonated.

"My car! My righteous car!" Judd's angry cry was nearly as loud as the explosion.

He had snuck into the fruit tree orchard during the fusillade and was hiding near the house. Now he ran toward the flaming Shelby while firing a semi-automatic wildly. My third shot had emptied the Remington's magazine. As I pulled cartridges from my pockets to reload, a rifle shot sounded and Judd's legs went out from under him. He plopped on his butt with his weapon continuing to fire. A flash came from a broken window on the top floor of the house as another round cracked. Judd fell backward.

As he lay in the light of the moon that dodged between the drifts of stinking smoke from his burning car, I wondered if Judd had mistaken the sounds from Blaine Harney's .30-06 as the *Pop! Crack!* lettered on the Roy Lichtenstein lithograph and if he finally knew how Andy Warhol had felt when he'd been popped. The difference was the mop-haired artist had survived his wounds and Judd would not.

Engines roared and vehicles that had been stashed on the road took off. Some of the hired guns who witnessed their would-be paychecks go up in flames when Judd went down decided against working for free. I knew Freddie Sanderlin wouldn't be among them. Without Judd acting as a governor on his pyromania, he would now be free to rage at will. He'd light up the house even though the valuable art was inside and damn whoever was with it. It was never about stealing paintings for Freddie. It was about stealing people's sense of normalcy and fanning their worst fears to try and give himself power over his own twisted nightmares.

I smeared muck on my face and hands for camouflage, grabbed a tin pail hanging from a hook used to hold curry combs, and slipped out of the corral. It was a quick run over to the dirt airstrip where Gemma and I'd taken off. I filled the pail from the tank of airplane fuel Blaine kept for passing pilots and ran back to the house. Halfway there, I turned and pumped a couple of rounds into the metal fuel tank. The explosion dwarfed the one made by the Shelby and launched a red ball of flames hundreds of feet into the night. It would be hard to miss by the Rocking H cowboys and surely send them racing home where they'd run into the fleeing gunmen. My money was on the cowboys winning a shootout.

I fast-stepped between the burning barn and bunkhouse

without encountering anyone. I reached the clearing where I'd crossed earlier and halted in a patch of umbra. Muffled voices came from the dark somewhere up ahead. Before I could pinpoint them, the front door of the house opened and banged shut and boot heels thumped heavily across the porch. Seeing the vehicles leave, Blaine Harney ran to the yard to check on Judd. It was a cherry's mistake. Gunfire flashed from where the muffled voices came and the big rancher toppled like a chain-sawed tree.

A match struck where the gunshots came from and the rag wick of a Molotov cocktail being lit revealed Freddie and another man huddled close to the house. I set the pail down, shouldered the Remington and squeezed the trigger. Nothing. I squeezed again. Nothing. I pumped in a fresh cartridge. Still nothing. The firing mechanism on the old gun had finally jammed after so much use.

The clicks caught the attention of the two men. As they looked up, I dropped the rifle, grabbed the handle of the tin pail, and flung it as if tossing a horseshoe. The pail arced across the clearing bottom first and thudded at the two men's feet. The airplane fuel came out in a multihued wave and splashed them. Freddie was holding the lit Molotov cocktail. He shrieked and immediately shovel-passed the bottle of gas to get rid of it. It struck the other man and the wick flared as it came in contact with his fuel-soaked clothes. He erupted in flames. I drew my pistol and tried to find Freddie in the fire's glare, but he'd leapt backward to save himself and disappeared.

I momentarily flashed on the burning trees that had ringed the waterhole where Wanda Manybaskets had dunked herself. The ignited man was trying to slap out the flames with his hands, but like the ancient junipers, there was nothing I could do to save him. I chased after Freddie, leading with my revolver. I had to stop him from getting inside where Elena hid.

As I turned the corner of the house, I made a cherry's mistake of my own. Freddie was lying in wait with a spade that had been left in the flower bed. He swung it and the flat part of the blade caught me square in the chest. It knocked me flat on my back and the revolver out of my hand. The pyro changed his grip and brought the spade guillotining toward my neck. I rolled away and got to my feet. Freddie chucked the spade like a spear. I ducked it and rushed him before he could draw his gun, driving him into the front yard with my head buried in his stomach while bearhugging him. We lost our footing and fell hard.

Freddie tried kneeing me in the crotch, but I blocked him. As we rolled over, Elena began calling from the top window.

"Blaine!" she cried. "Blaine, are you all right?"

A human torch ran toward the house screaming. He collapsed and the flames shooting from his body ignited the wood siding.

"Get out of the house!" I shouted as Freddie began driving his fist into my ribs. "Get out! Fire!"

Freddie sprayed spit in my face as he laughed hysterically. "Girlie's going to fry."

He broke my hold, jumped to his feet, and went for his gun, but it had been knocked out of the holster. I rolled onto my knees near Blaine who was lying next to Judd. I scuttled toward them, searching for their weapons.

Freddie dashed toward the fallen men too. The big rancher had landed on top of his rifle, but Judd's pistol was still in his grasp. Freddie and I dove for it and both got our hands on it. The firebug elbowed me in the bridge of my nose. Lights flashed. Skyrockets exploded. Thunder rocked my head. I got to my feet and fought to keep from blacking out, but the deafening roar grew louder.

Everything around me began to swirl. Dirt and gravel stung

me like shotgun pellets. Freddie was standing too and aimed Judd's gun at me when a dark cloud passed over and the sky split apart. Rain dumped and its force knocked us both to the ground.

"Tuhudda!" I shouted.

Only it wasn't a cloud returning the old Paiute rainmaker's gift. I recognized the roar of a twin-engine B-26 bomber from my Vietnam days. The silhouette confirmed it. The payload it dropped was not munitions but thousands of gallons of water. Flames hissed.

I searched for Freddie. He was flailing around in the yard turned into a mire looking for the gun. Unlike my dream of Daisy and Danny Manybaskets, my boots didn't stick as I sprinted toward him. I jumped on top of him, driving my knees into his back, jamming my forearm against his head, and pushing his face into the mud.

Lights kept flashing and now sirens were screaming. Someone yelled my name. Pudge was running from his pickup as the bar of Christmas lights flashed. Two more sheriff's vehicles sped down the drive and skidded to a stop behind his.

The deputy put a meaty paw on my shoulder. "Hold up there, son. You've knocked the fight clean out of him. Let me have him now." He jerked Freddie out of the mud and snapped handcuffs tightly around the firebug's wrist. "Didn't your mama ever teach you not to play with matches?"

I wiped the mud from my eyes and struggled to catch my breath. Deputies were scurrying around searching for more gunmen, though I figured they'd all have cleared out by now. Elena bolted from the house.

"Blaine!" she cried and fell to her knees beside the rancher's body.

Pudge and I exchanged glances. I shook my head, but I shook it too early. Blaine groaned in response to Elena's cry.

We rolled him onto his back. His eyes fluttered open. "Is the Rocking H still standing?" he wheezed.

"Scarred, but unbowed," I said.

"I owe you."

"What for? You would've done the same."

A deputy took Freddie from Pudge while another applied a field dressing to the bullet hole in the rancher's side. Pudge grimaced at the smoldering body beside the house.

"Reminds me of Iwo," he muttered.

"The air tanker," I said. "Colonel Davies?"

"Yup," the old lawman said, and gave me a quick rundown on what transpired after Gemma had dropped me off. She called him as soon as she got home. Pudge issued an all-hands alert to Burns emergency teams and then tried calling the Rocking H, but the lines had already been cut. He contacted Colonel Davies at his lookout atop Riddle Mountain and told him what was up. The colonel radioed the US Forest Service to scramble an air tanker. When he spotted the red glow from the fuel tank I'd ignited, he vectored the converted B-26 in by radio.

"Lucky for you, the pilot's a Vietnam vet too," Pudge said. "He flew that aircraft over there, why he hit the target smack dab on the bullseye."

"And knocked me flat doing it," I said.

"Son," the old deputy drawled, "you live in ranch country long enough, you learn never to look a gift horse in the mouth."

31

Pudge hauled Freddie to jail while another deputy transported Blaine to the hospital. I borrowed a pickup and headed home to the old lineman's shack where a hot shower waited. I let the water pelt my skin and rinse off the muck while wishing it could also wipe clean the memory of watching men die.

I thought about the times my squad had returned after a firefight. Everyone had their own way of dealing with what happened, be it a case of courage or cowardice, having killed someone or seeing a comrade die. The essence of war was to strip away our humanity so we could perform inhumane acts upon fellow humans. The challenge was to reclaim it afterward. Some of the men would stand under a shower like I was doing now to try and cleanse themselves of their rage, fear, or guilt. Others would clean their weapons as if removing every speck of gunpowder could erase all the effects of their actions on the battlefield.

I did what my trainers told me no squad leader should ever do, and that was to learn the names of my men's loved ones. Knowing them, they warned me, would make me hesitate to send my men into harm's way. It was one thing to be responsible for risking their lives, but quite another to be responsible for the collateral damage to their families. Yet I prompted my men to tell me, and after every fight, I'd go from man to man and ask about their wife or girlfriend or parent or child by name. I'd urge them to reread their loved one's latest letter and look at the snapshots sent from home. It was in those personal, private moments where they realized they hadn't lost their capacity to love or be loved.

The hot water finally gave out. I turned off the shower and grabbed a towel. Exhaustion settled in and the narrow bunk beckoned. As I dried off, I thought about how far I'd come since Vietnam and how I was slowly regaining my own humanity since moving to Harney County. I was remembering how to love, to laugh, and even how to tell a joke. But then the phone rang and I knew a call coming at the midnight hour meant no sleep nor escape from a basic truth. Along with all the good in humankind also came evil.

Orville Nelson was still awake. "I finally reached Loq on the radio," he said when I answered. "Stand by while I patch him in."

A click and a buzz later, the *Maklak* came on. "I caught up to Wanda Manybaskets. She's with the Parkers."

"Where are you now?" I said.

"Outside the Bright Rivers treatment place. I was about to go in when Orville radioed."

"What have you learned so far?"

"I don't have time to talk. It's time for action," the mohawked Marine said.

"Wait. Don't sign off. We buddied up, remember?"

"But I'm here, you're there. Who knows what they're going to do to her now that they got her."

"Busting in there will get you busted. Wanda went to

Spokane voluntarily. We have no proof the Parkers are connected to Daisy and Danny's disappearance or what their involvement is with kids from the reservations. They could be working for government agencies as far as we know even though they told me they weren't. If the feds vouch for them, they'll have the law on their side, not us."

"But they're going around it."

"What makes you say that?"

"Something I learned when I stopped by their church, New Faith whatever. It's a cinderblock storefront that looks like it was a discount shoe store at one time. The windows are soaped out. The sign is the stick-on kind."

"Not all churches have stained glass and gold altars," I said. "Did you talk to someone?"

"A woman was walking through the front door when I pulled up. I followed her in. There's some folding chairs, a scratched up table, an office in the back. The door to it was open and the woman was talking to a man standing on the other side, told him she needed her money. The man said to wait, he'd go get it. I asked her how come he was going to give her money and she said it was pay for being a foster parent. Told me the church served as a go-between with the welfare agency."

"You mean, the agency pays the church and the church pays her?"

"That's right. She said the church set it all up for her. Got her approved by the welfare agency people without her having to meet them and steered kids her way. The church acts as the agency's boots on the ground and takes a cut for doing it. I bet a sizeable one."

Orville was still on the line. "The monthly allowance for a foster child varies from state to state, but it is calculated to cover only the basic necessities such as food and clothing," he said. "The amount is minimal by design to discourage people who might take advantage of the system. A foster parent would be hard pressed to make a profit, and even less so if the Parkers were taking a percentage."

Loq scoffed. "Unless they cut corners at the kid's expense to make a buck, like dressing them in rags and dishing them cold cereal at every meal. Maybe the Parkers are padding the number of kids they're overseeing, getting paid for three for every two. They're the ones filling out all the forms. They could write down anything."

I asked how much money the woman said she was getting.

"She didn't give up any numbers, only that it was better working through the church because they paid in cash and she didn't have to deal with nosy agency folks. Meaning no one was making sure she was doing it by the book."

"How many children is she taking care of?"

"As many as she can get. From the look of her, she's not living in any mansion with lots of bedrooms either. I told her I was interested in getting in on it, but only wanted to foster native kids. She said that'd be easy since there were plenty to go around. See, that shows the Parkers are funneling kids from the reservations into their scheme."

"We'll need proof."

Loq blew out air. "I knock down the door to Bright Rivers, I'll get proof. Confessions too. I brought rope for thumbs."

"Hold on. Did you also talk to the man who worked at the church?"

"Yeah, after he paid off the woman. He was like a quartermaster. Didn't think about the war raging outside the supply tent, only how many new uniforms he had to issue. I told him I knew the Parkers and he said I'd just missed them. I took a chance and drove around looking for Bright Rivers. It's tucked in a medical office building on the banks of the Spokane River. I got there right when the Winnebago was pulling up and saw Wanda and the Parkers go inside."

I asked the FBI hopeful what he'd learned about the treatment center.

"I am afraid not much," Orville said. "Bright Rivers is registered as a private mental health facility. The chief of staff is listed as Dr. Louis Seymour. He is a psychiatrist licensed by the State of Washington. I located a research paper credited to him. I have only read the abstract. It summarized a study he conducted on treating aggressive behavior in adolescents by increasing the dosage of psychotropic drugs."

"Another reason for going in now," Loq grunted. "They'll shoot Wanda full of dope to keep her quiet once she realizes they're running a scam."

"Beside getting her out, we need to learn where foster kids from the reservation are being housed," I said. "We need a plan for going in Bright Rivers and not getting anyone hurt while we're doing it."

"You're too far away to help."

"I can be there in three hours."

"What did you do, steal Judd Hollister's Shelby?"

"Gemma can fly me. Pick me up at the airport."

"Take a cab. I'm not leaving my post in case they move Wanda."

"Then keep your head down until I get there. See you in the tall grass."

Loq hung up without saying another word.

I asked Orville if he was still on the line. He was. "Do you know where Pudge is?

"Deputy Warbler is in the interrogation room with Freddie Sanderlin. There has been a major development. If you need to speak to him, you will need to wait until he is finished."

"Okay. Did you get anywhere tracking down an address for Charley Pony Blanket?"

"That has been a challenge. The telephone company said it will be easier to identify the location once they process his aunt's bill and they can cross-check it for the origin of the collect call."

"That'll take too long," I said.

"I know. That is why I impressed upon them the need to apply an alternative method for searching their computerized database system."

"And how did you do that, tell them how to do it or tell them you were an FBI agent?"

Orville hesitated. "It is better if I neither confirm nor deny that. Suffice to say, the telephone company has assigned a data technician to the search. I expect to hear from him tomorrow morning. Wait, it is already tomorrow."

"Let me know as soon as you hear. Try giving Charity Liveslong a call too and remind her to ask Charley for the address if he calls again."

"Would you like to hear what is happening with the arson and robbery investigation now?"

"No time. I got to get to Spokane."

I pulled on some clothes, jumped in the borrowed pickup, and lead-footed it to the Warbler ranch. I let myself in. Gemma was sitting up in bed reading a book titled *The Brave Cowboy*. It was written by Edward Abbey.

"I thought *Desert Solitaire* was his only one," I said by way of greeting.

She looked archly over the top of the book. "This is an earlier novel, and hello to you too. I'd heard you survived."

"Your father called you. Sorry, I was going to but—"

"You're not finished playing cops and robbers, is that it?"

"Not quite, and neither have you if you want to fly me to Spokane right now."

Gemma flung the book aside. "I've always wanted to fly into a big city airport at night. Radar. A control tower. Multiple runways. I hope there's lots of commercial jet traffic too. What I wouldn't give for some ground fog. Come on, what are we waiting for?"

"You might want to put on some clothes first."

While Gemma got dressed, I went to the kitchen. As I searched for a biscuit or, better yet, a piece of frybread, November shuffled in from her bedroom. A striped Pendleton blanket was draped over her shoulders and beaded moccasins peeked out from beneath the hem of her skirt.

"What are you looking for?" she said.

"A snack. Don't worry, I'll find it myself. You can go back to bed."

The old healer tsked. "This is no time for sleep. Wanda Manybaskets' babies are calling for her."

I started to ask if she could hear them, but thought better. "Did you hear Gemma and me talking just now?"

"I told you before, eyes find children waiting to be found, not wagging tongues. I have already put food in a bag for us to take."

"Us? But Gemma is going to fly me to Spokane."

"Yes, it will get us there much faster than our own two feet can carry us."

"Have you ever flown with Gemma before?" Her head shook no. "Ever been in an airplane at all?" Again she shook her head. "Flying can be scary."

She crossed her arms beneath the blanket. "I have seen the brown world from high above many times."

"How?"

"When *Kwe'na'a* takes me in my dreams. Eagle flies high. His wings are strong. I see what I need to see through his sharp eyes. He misses nothing. We go now."

A minute later the horse doctor joined us in the kitchen. I said, "November wants to go too."

"Finally," Gemma said. "I've been trying to talk her into flying with me ever since I got my license."

I knew a lost battle when I saw it. "Okay, but you two will need to stay with the plane when we get there."

Gemma plotted the flight path as the plane warmed up. The distance was a bit over 300 air miles. We were in luck. Tail winds blowing out of the southwest would give our airspeed a much needed boost. I sat in the copilot seat. November sat behind Gemma. We took off without a hitch and gained elevation quickly. The route took us directly over Burns. I was expecting to see large swaths of burned-down buildings in the glow of the streetlights, but the damage looked minimal.

When we were clear of Burns, the lights on the ground became far and few between. We passed over the rugged, forest-clad Blue Mountains. The plane's single engine droned on for another half hour before the next sizeable patch of lights appeared in the distance. They were shining from the town of La Grande to the east. Soon we were flying in darkness again. I took solace in all of the black emptiness. It told me there was still plenty of middle-of-nowhere for those who chose to live in it or needed to, like me.

"By my calculation, we've crossed into Washington," Gemma said. "It's all rolling wheatfields from here on out. When we near Spokane, I'll be pretty busy talking with air traffic control. See you on the ground."

I checked my field watch. It was 0230. It seemed a lifetime since I'd gotten into Judd's car with him, but, at the same time, it felt like only a few minutes had passed. Combat was like that too. It distorted all sense of time. My men would always check their watches after a battle, sure they had broken.

Air traffic over Spokane was practically nonexistent in the

predawn hour and Gemma put us down without much of a
bump. As we taxied to the part of the airport reserved for private
planes, she used the radio to call for a taxi. I tried to mount an
argument that I was going to Bright Rivers alone, but gave up
when the horse doctor pulled a LadySmith .38 from her flight
bag and slipped it into her jacket pocket.

"Everybody needs backup," she said. "Even you."

Bright Rivers wasn't far from the airport and the taxi let us
off beside the *Maklak's* white pickup with the duck and fish
emblem on the door. The cab was empty. So was the gun rack.
The Marine had already moved out.

32

The front door to Bright Rivers Behavioral Treatment Center had a brass nameplate on it. I tried the knob before pressing the buzzer. It twisted freely and the door opened to a waiting room with chairs along the walls and a table stacked with copies of *Reader's Digest*. A thin, gray-haired man dressed in a baggy security guard uniform sat on the other side of the reception counter. He stared at Gemma, November, and me over a gag made from his tie. He was buckled to the chair by his utility belt and his hands were tied behind him with shoe laces.

"Now we know where Loq is," Gemma said.

"Let's go find him," I said.

I led the way down the hall. Closed doors on both sides lined it. Some opened into offices, others into exam rooms. They were unoccupied. A few doors had small windows made of wired glass that looked into dimly lit hospital-type rooms. Each was equipped with a single bed. The first was empty. A person was sleeping in the second. It was hard to tell if it was a man or a woman beneath the blankets. The door had a deadbolt with no key in it.

We continued our search. Someone was asleep in another locked room. Another was empty. I looked into the final room that had a wired glass window in the door. A woman dressed in a nurse's uniform was bound to a chair by first aid tape. Another strip sealed her mouth shut. When she saw me, she screamed for help with her eyes. A man lay slumped on the floor beside her. He wore a uniform too and his hands were taped together. The rise and fall of his chest told me Loq had only knocked him out.

The last door on the right had a brass nameplate instead of a wired glass window. Dr. Louis Seymour was etched in script. I opened the door and we walked into a plush office. The walls were paneled in rich, dark wood and hung with paintings. Oriental rugs covered the floor. Thick burgundy drapes were pulled shut. A bald man sat tied to a chair behind a massive mahogany desk. Terrified eyes darted behind the lenses of his silver-frame glasses. A gag of white cloth prevented him from crying out.

Arabelle Parker sat tied to a chair beside the big desk. Along with the same dull blue dress and white apron I remembered from before, she wore a gag. Cameron Parker was standing on the balls of his feet in the middle of the room. His black suit jacket was heaped on the floor. Strips had been ripped from the tail of his shirt to create the gags for his wife and the doctor.

Parker couldn't brush back the boyish lock of hair that had fallen across his forehead because his arms were raised above his head. Ropes that had been slip-knotted around his thumbs were tied to the blades of a ceiling fan. The blades were turning slowly and each rotation reeled in the ropes and yanked Parker's arms higher. He was like a ballet dancer trying to keep en pointe. Sweat poured down his brow and dripped from his wispy beard.

"You made pretty good time," Loq said. He was leaning

against the wall. His shotgun was propped next to him and his Winchester was slung over his shoulder. He pointed the skinning knife at Parker. "He insists they're do-gooders and everything's on the up and up. I'll see if he sticks to that story when he and the wife swap places."

"Where's Wanda?" I said.

"He won't cop to it. I waited two hours before I decided it was time to infil. I breached their perimeter and questioned the night watchman. A nurse and an orderly too. Nobody was willing to talk."

"Maybe Wanda's in one of the hospital beds," I said.

"She's not here," Parker gasped, struggling to stay on his tiptoes. "I told him. She left."

Loq squinted at him. "I never abandoned my position. I never saw her leave."

"I told you there's a service door in the back they use for deliveries," he whined. "She must've gone out that way."

"If I start slicing off fingers, you going to stick to that story or you going to tell me where you stashed her?"

Arabelle Parker tried to scream but choked on the gag. Trying to catch her breath made her convulse. Gemma went to her and untied the gag. She patted Arabelle's back and then began rubbing it. "Breathe. Slowly. In. Out. There you go."

When she was finally able to speak, Arabelle said, "My husband is telling the truth. Mrs. Manybaskets left. She was angry when we told her we did not know where her children were. She did not want to take Dr. Seymour's medical advice either."

I glanced at the doctor. It looked like he'd wet himself. "We know you drove her here," I said. "Where did you pick her up?"

"She found us," Arabelle said. "We went straight to our church when we got home. Mrs. Manybaskets arrived there later. It was obvious she needed medical help. The poor thing was very distraught and shrieking about her children. She accused us of hiding them. We called Dr. Seymour. He agreed to meet us here."

"I've been to your so-called church," Loq said. "It looks like a bingo hall without the bingo cage and coffee and cookies table."

"Ours is a humble house of worship," she said with a bow. "We are servants to the indigent."

"That doesn't make it right for you to steal kids and cash in on misery," he said.

"You don't understand!" Parker shouted. "We don't profit from children. We save children."

"Yeah, I heard that one before. By killing the Indian in them."

Parker stumbled as he tried to keep ahead of the ceiling fan that continued to reel in the ropes. The fan was winning. I approached the *Maklak*. "Cut him down."

Loq's long mohawk was waving from the downdraft of the spinning blades. He jutted his jaw. "No way."

"Cut him down before his shoulders pop out of their sockets. He'll pass out from the pain and choke on his own vomit. No one needs to die here."

"Not until he tells me where Wanda is."

"He's a civilian. If he knew where she was, he'd have told you as soon as you looped a rope around his thumbs."

"He's holding out."

"No, he's not. He's soft."

"He's got to pay for taking Indian children away from their moms and dads."

"And if he broke the law doing it, he will."

Loq glared. "You mean white man law. He'll get away with it."

"I'll see that he doesn't. Pudge will too. Come on, cut him down. We'll get more reliable intel out of him that way."

.

Loq's glare burned brighter and the blade of the skinning knife flashed as it moved in my direction. I recognized all the signs of a man who'd been asked to fight in a war where there were no rules—rules that would've prevented him from having to wage a war within himself over there and now back home. I'd seen glares like his in men's eyes before. I'd seen them in the mirror too.

"You're not my CO," he growled. "And I'm not your Tonto."

It could go either way, but I was committed. I put my hand on his shoulder. "And you're not in 'Nam either. You're home, buddy. You made it back. We both did."

He continued to glare, but after ten, twenty, thirty long seconds, he turned away. The knife swished, the taut ropes plonked, and Parker's arms flopped to his sides. He stumbled forward, but I caught him before he fell. I sat him in a chair next to his wife.

"Okay," I said. "We know what you've been up to. Now it's time for you to explain why you did it. Tell it. Tell it all. About the kids. The foster homes. Wanda Manybaskets. Dr. Seymour and Bright Rivers. All of it. If you lie, we'll know it, and you and Arabelle will both be hanging from the fan."

And so they did. Cameron started at the beginning when he and Arabelle were in the Peace Corps. "We were assigned to a village in the Amazon," he said. "The people were so primitive. It was... Well, they wouldn't listen to us. They didn't want to learn what we had to teach them or do what we told them. They were as helpless as little children, unable to feed or care or clothe themselves."

"We tried our best to help. Really, we did," Arabelle said. "We loved them but they never even said thank you. I would instruct a woman on the proper way to scrub a cooking pot, but as soon as I turned my back, she would take it down to the river and join the other women who were washing up. They giggled like little girls. They were laughing at me."

Parker said they returned home to Spokane before their Peace Corps commitment was up. The couple was discouraged, but remained determined to make a difference. They opened the storefront church as a way to raise money to fund a mobile clinic.

"When we set out for the first time, we did exactly what we planned," he explained. "We visited Indian reservations throughout the Great Basin. We paid for our gas, our food, and slept in the Winnebago. We conducted health screenings, provided information, and helped out with applications for social assistance programs. We never charged a penny for it. But going to all those reservations, seeing how the Indians lived, well, they were so helpless and our efforts seemed pointless."

"It was like the Amazon all over again," Arabelle said. "The Indians wanted to do things the way they had always done them, even when it was not the proper way. They needed help, but did not know how to ask for it or even take it when we offered it, so we took it upon ourselves to make sure they got help."

"By tricking parents into signing their children into foster care," I said.

"You make it sound so dirty," she said. "We were helping them."

"Did you explain the foster care form to them clearly, make sure they knew what they were agreeing to by signing it?"

"We explained it to them in a way they could understand," Parker said. "You need to realize not all of them speak English or know how to read and write. The schools are substandard. The children aren't getting a proper education. They don't eat nutritious meals because they don't have grocery stores. It was all the more reason we needed to get the children away from there."

"No one ever questioned you about the forms you were getting them to sign?" I said.

"Not in so many words once I explained there were free programs where children would be fed and clothed, and their health looked after."

"When did you stop bothering to explain it and begin slipping the foster care form in for them to sign along with applications for food stamps?" I said.

Parker hesitated. I waved him off. "Don't waste your breath lying. We know you did."

"They'd be worse off if we hadn't," he insisted.

Loq looked down his high cheekbones at Cameron and Arabelle Parker "Trouble is, once the kids got taken away, they won't all get back home. They get shuffled to a new place every few months. How they supposed to remember where they came from?"

"You can't blame us for that," Parker said. "As soon as they turn eighteen they can go home if they want, but why would they want to go back living in poverty?"

Loq bared his teeth and started moving toward Parker. Gemma stepped between them. "How many children have you put into foster care?" she demanded. "How many foster parents and how many homes are taking care of them?" When he didn't answer, she said, "There are that many?"

"It's not our fault we can't keep track," he said. "When the welfare agency learned about how many consent forms we were submitting, they didn't condemn us, they commended us. They appointed us as their representative and told us to keep up the good work."

"You got trapped by the success of your own scheme," I said. "If the flow of your consent forms suddenly dried up, the agency would've gotten suspicious and taken a closer look at the ones you either forged or tricked people into signing."

"You don't get it!" Parker shouted. "The welfare agency doesn't need us. They can go in and remove children anytime they want. They're authorized by law."

"And that makes what you've been doing okay somehow?"

"Yes. We get to decide which children to save."

"They would not have a life if not for us," Arabelle said.

Anger surged through me as I listened to them justify their playing God. I took a deep breath and exhaled it slowly. I did it three times.

"What was it about Wanda Manybaskets that made you so determined to get her out of Harney County?" I said. "Was it because you've tricked so many parents into signing away their children, you couldn't be sure she wasn't one of them?" When Arabelle avoided my stare by looking at the floor, I knew I had my answer. "That's it. Then you began to think she might be playing you, that she'd tell the law you'd tricked her. You couldn't risk her doing that."

"We've done nothing wrong," Parker insisted again. "Besides, Mrs. Manybaskets is not well. She needs psychiatric help."

"From the likes of him?" I hooked a thumb at the bald doctor whose eyes were blinking rapidly behind his silver-frame glasses.

"We're fortunate to have Dr. Seymour," Parker said. "Many of the children go through an adjustment period during their transition to foster care. He's providing a much-needed medical service to children who would never have benefited from his expertise if they'd stayed on the reservation."

"They wouldn't need a shrink if you'd left them there," Loq said. He turned to the psychiatrist. "I heard you've been giving kids lots of tranquilizers. How about if I give you a taste of your own medicine?"

The psychiatrist cowered.

I waved at the expensive furnishings and said to Parker,

"How much does the welfare agency pay him to treat a foster kid? How much do you get for the referral?"

Parker huffed. "That's very cynical."

"You know what's cynical?" Loq said. "Thinking you know what's best for a people when you never took the time to learn about their ways." He glowered at him. "Give us the addresses of your foster homes."

"I can't be expected to remember them all," Parker said. "I need my records."

"Are they in your Winnebago?"

"No, I keep them at the church."

I wondered what November was thinking as she listened. Did it make the old Paiute healer have to relive her own experience of being taken from her family sixty years ago and sent to a boarding school by people who thought they knew what was best for her? I turned to check on her. I looked left, right, and behind me.

"Where's November?" I asked Gemma.

"She was standing right here a minute ago. Maybe she went to find a bathroom."

I pulled the heavy burgundy drapes aside and looked out the window. It was still nighttime, but the shine of street lights reflected on the nearby waters of the Spokane River.

"I know where she went," I said. "Come on."

"You two go ahead," Loq said. "I'll catch up after I lock these three in one of the padded cells." I looked at the big knife in his hand. He followed my gaze. "Don't worry, Nick, I won't skin them. And the doc here has already been scalped."

33

The service door opened onto a rear parking lot. A few cars were there, but their hoods were cool to the touch. I figured they belonged to the security guard, nurse, and orderly.

"I can hear the river," Gemma said.

We walked toward it, crossing the asphalt and stepping into a field of threshed grass. As we drew closer, a sound like a washboard being scrubbed joined the thrum of the powerful Spokane River as it ran its course from Lake Coeur d'Alene in the Idaho panhandle, through the city, and west to the mighty Columbia.

I clutched Gemma's arm. "Those are Wanda's baby rattles. Careful, we don't want to spook her into running away or jumping in the river."

"It'll be all right," Gemma said. "November is with her."

We reached the end of the field. The moon was still up. The two women were standing together no more than a foot from the water's edge. Wanda Manybaskets was dressed in white and her hair fell loosely over her shoulders except for the portion she'd hacked off mourning Tom Piñon. She began to sing. The dried corn kernels shaking back and forth in the woven rattles kept tempo to her lilting voice. "Water carries the boat. Water carries the baby. Across the big lake. Toward the big mountain. Swirling, swirling. The baby and boat swirl."

As she sang the lullaby, November joined in with a rhythmic talk-song. The old healer held her hands out to the river and chanted. Most of it was in *Numu*, but I recognized the Washoe words for water baby, *we muhu*, grandniece, *lebík'iyi*, and Young Willow, *Dats'ai lo lee*.

"November's asking Wanda's great-aunt for help," I said.

"Yes," Gemma said. "And, listen, now she's calling Wanda's twins by name, *Dawgakákitgiš* and *Dahá aš*. Calm Water and Rainstorm."

"Daisy and Danny," I said.

The lullaby swirled around me and images from the past few days rushed through my mind along with snippets of the conversation Loq had with the tribal cop in Reno and the ones I'd had with Tuhudda Will and November about water babies.

"The story about the twins having died at birth is true," I said. "Do you believe in water babies?"

Gemma hesitated before answering. "I believe people whose ancestors have walked this land for thousands of years and heard stories passed from one generation to the next generation around a fire beneath the stars know things I'll never know or will ever allow myself to know. But what I do know is, I believe in November. I've believed in her ever since she walked into my life when I was five years old and I'll keep believing in her when she journeys to the spirit world. Do you know what I base that belief in?"

"What?"

"Love. Unconditional love."

I pulled her closer. "What do you think will happen next?"

"One way or another, whether water babies exist or not,

November is going to help Wanda find what she's been searching for the past six years."

"And what's that?"

"The same thing. What a mother and child have no matter what. Their love is unconditional, unbreakable, whether in life or in death."

The rattling, singing, and chanting kept up. The moon was arcing toward its resting spot beyond the western horizon, pulling dawn along with it as it traveled. A thin band of light appeared in the east. Two circles the color of skim milk started bobbing in the water near the bank of the river. Maybe they were created by a change in the reflection of a streetlight or maybe by moonlight as it passed in and out of a cloud. Whatever their source, the twin radiances rippled and wiggled, dove and surfaced. I watched transfixed, telling myself the current was making them move. I also told myself there were things I'd never be able to understand and I'd be okay with that.

Wanda and November suddenly stopped their song and chant.

"We are honored you graced us with your presence," the old Paiute woman said. "Wanda Manybaskets has walked a very long trail to sing you her song. I ask that you give her gifts of strength and courage. Her days in the brown world will be long and she needs both, for she is on her way to becoming a great healer and there is still much for her to do to heal the lost *Washeshu* children and also *Numu* and *Newe* children before she joins you in the spirit world."

November clasped her hands in front of her and bowed. She kept her head down. I strained to listen, to hear anything beyond the sound a river makes as it rushes across cobbles and cracks against boulders and kerplunks into pools. Gemma tensed under my touch, but didn't speak.

Finally, November raised her head and said, "Thank you."

She faced Wanda Manybaskets. "Give them the rattles. Follow the rattles, for they will lead you to medicine that will give you *wegeléyu*—power—so that you too may whisper with souls to help heal those who need healing."

Wanda was holding a baby rattle in each hand. Without questioning, she shook them one last time, kissed each in turn, and then tossed them onto the water. The woven rattles bobbed in place as the band of light on the eastern horizon grew wider and the last stars of the night began to melt away with the moon. Soon the twin radiances disappeared too and the current carried the pair of rattles downstream.

A horn honked. "*Wey heya, wey heya,*" Loq called from the parking lot.

"Over here," I called back.

"I got an address for kids," he said.

Gemma moved quickly and put one arm around November's waist and the other around Wanda's. "Let's go to them."

While the three women were making their way up from the river bank, I ran to the pickup. "Did Parker finally give you something?"

"No. I locked them up and got my rig to drive around here to look for you when Orville radioed. He was trying to get a message to you. He's got an address for that boy from Malheur County."

"Charley Pony Blanket," I said. "The telephone company came through."

"Don't know anything about the phone company. Orville said the boy's aunt called him. The boy had called her collect again and gave her the address where he's at."

"I know he's in Washington. Which town?"

"Right here in Spokane. Just down the street. Charley told her after he ran out when his parents were fighting, a couple stopped and asked if he needed help. They said they could find him new parents and drove him to the bus station and bought him a ticket. He got on and fell asleep. Later, the driver woke him and said it was his stop. When he got off, a woman was there waiting for him. The people who put him on the bus? They were driving a motorhome."

"The Parkers."

"Sure sounds like it."

The three women reached us. We put November and Wanda in the front seat and Gemma and I climbed into the pickup's bed. I slapped the roof of the cab. "Go. Go."

The street leading from the treatment center followed the Spokane River. The neighborhood changed from office buildings to warehouses to a rundown neighborhood of old apartments and ramshackle houses.

Loq slowed and we searched both sides of the street. Not all the buildings had numbers on them. The sun peeked over the horizon and the dove-gray sky blushed like a robin's breast with the arrival of the first rays of a new morning.

"There, on the river side of the street," Gemma said. "That two-story house. The one with the broken shutters."

Loq stopped. "That's the number Orville gave me."

I hopped out. The house was dark except for a dim light downstairs. I guessed it was coming from the kitchen.

"We need to do this in a way that won't scare any kids inside," I said as Loq got out.

"But we got to make sure no one runs off," he said. "If I was a kid and didn't want to be there, I'd rabbit at the first opportunity. The adults might bolt too if they got something to hide. You take front, I'll cover the back."

"Roger that."

Loq took off and disappeared between the house and its neighbor.

"It's you and me, Gemma," I said. Then I stuck my head into

the cab and told November and Wanda to stay put. "If we all go up there, the people inside won't open the door."

November harrumphed. "Then go already."

Gemma and I followed the walkway from the street. Weeds were growing in cracks and the cement was buckled in spots from tree roots.

"What's your plan?" she said.

"Make it up as we go."

I gave the door a loud knock. I waited a minute and then gave it another. Lights turned on in the front room and the curtains in the window next to the door parted a crack. I smiled and waved at the eyes peeking through it.

"Go away," a man's voice croaked.

"Cameron and Arabelle Parker sent us," I said. "We want to be foster parents like you and they thought it would be a good idea if we met to get tips on how to raise children."

"Come back later. I ain't even had coffee yet."

"Sorry for the early morning visit, but we're picking up two children at the bus station in an hour. The Parkers were insistent we come now."

"What's to learn? They're only kids. You tell 'em the rules and you show 'em who's boss. Now clear off."

I turned to Gemma. "Well, dear, I'll guess we'll have to learn how to take care of children another way." And then I wheeled and kicked the door and the jam splintered and I barged right in.

"What the?" the man yelled.

I grabbed him by the front of his dirty undershirt and slammed him against the wall. A woman's shriek came from the room behind us. The clang of pots and pans being thrown echoed. Footsteps shuffled and a doughy woman wearing a tattered robe filled the doorway. Loq was right behind her, pinning her arm behind her back. The *Maklak* steered her forward, spun her around, and plopped her on the couch. I shoved the man next to her.

"Don't move," I said.

The woman shrieked, but her caterwauling was quickly drowned out by the wails of police sirens. Tires screeched out front and shoes thumped. Two cops in blue uniforms burst in, one high, one low, fanning the room with their service weapons.

"Freeze! Police!"

"Now, officers," Gemma said calmly. "I can explain everything."

"Hands where I can see them," one cop barked. "That means you, lady."

A third policeman followed them. His collar sported captain's bars. He walked up to me. "What's your name?"

"Nick Drake," I said. "There's a boy being held here from—"

"Oregon," he said. "Charley Pony Blanket. It's why we're here. We got a needs-assist call from Harney County sheriff's about him and you. They alerted the FBI too since the boy was taken across state lines. A team from the Bureau's Spokane office is on its way. Where is he?"

"Ask them." I pointed at the couple on the sofa.

"What about it?" the captain said.

"We don't know nothing about no pony's blanket," the woman said. "The kids here are foster kids. We take good care of them and got all their paperwork."

"That's right," undershirt man said. "I'll go get it. We keep the folders in there." He nodded toward the kitchen and started to push off the couch.

"Sit back down," the captain said. "I didn't get these twin bars for being stupid."

The woman mustered up righteous indignation. "You can't treat us this way. We got rights."

"Yeah," undershirt man said. "We got us rights."

"We'll see about that," the captain said.

More noises came from the kitchen. One of the cops went to check it out. He returned a minute later ushering in November and Wanda Manybaskets.

"They were coming in the backdoor," he said.

"Who the heck are you?" the captain asked.

"They're with us," I said.

November tsked at the police captain. "Why are you wagging tongues down here when the children who need to be found are up there?" She pointed to the ceiling.

The captain looked at her and then at me. I shrugged.

"Look," Gemma said. "Wanda found the baby rattles. They must have washed up on the riverbank in the backyard."

The three cops became fixated on the Washoe woman in white as she glided past them, holding a rattle in each hand, shaking them softly, so softly that the dried corn kernels rubbing against the inside of the woven willow strips made a sound no louder than the whisper of wind blowing gently through grass.

"Where do you think you're going?" the captain said, but made no move to stop her.

Wanda reached the bottom of the staircase. "Children," she said in a voice akin to a mother humming a baby to sleep. "Children, your parents miss you. They love you. It is time to go home."

She made no move to climb the stairs as she kept shaking the rattles. We all stared at the top of the staircase that ended in a darkened landing. Finally, a face appeared in the gloom. It was a little girl's. A few moments later, another face joined hers. A little boy's. Two more children crowded beside them.

"Come, children," Wanda said. "You are safe now."

The first little girl took a hesitant step, and then a second, and then came flying down the stairs two at a time. The others quickly followed. The four threw themselves at Wanda and grabbed her legs. She hugged them so close it was hard to tell where she stopped and they began.

"Is one the boy from Oregon?" the police captain asked me.

"No. He's older. He must be too frightened to come down."

"Do something, Nick," Gemma said.

"Wanda, call for Charley," I said. "Tell him his Aunt Charity wants him to come live with her."

Wanda spoke his name so softly that I didn't think anyone hiding upstairs would be able to hear her, but then a boy stepped out of the umbra and into the light. He had a pug nose and a gap between his two front teeth.

"I am Charley Pony Blanket," he announced. "And I will go home forever."

"Then you shall," Wanda Manybaskets said, and he scampered down the stairs and hugged her tight along with the others.

We spent the next few hours at the Spokane Police Department, taking turns being questioned by the captain and two men who wore dark suits, white shirts, and narrow black ties. Loq was the last.

"I thought I was seeing Orville in double," he said as he exited the interrogation room.

"The FBI should be so lucky to have him," I said. "They wouldn't even have a case if he hadn't done the homework and sounded the alarm."

Gemma sat next to November in the waiting room they'd put us in. "Will they charge the Parkers with kidnapping Charley?" she asked.

"It'll be up to the FBI," I said. "The captain told me he'd sent a couple of squad cars over to Bright Rivers and arrested them. I told him about the forms and he sent someone to New Directions to retrieve the Parkers' files. The FBI will have a lot of evidence to sift through."

"Did you tell him how the Parkers and Dr. Seymour came to be locked in a room?" she said.

"I told him the truth. I didn't do it and I didn't see who did."

"What did you tell him?" she asked Loq.

"He didn't bother to ask. We mostly talked about 'Nam. He's a leatherneck and served in World War Two like your dad. Where's Wanda?"

"She's down the hall with the children," Gemma said. "A woman from Spokane's child services department arrived and Wanda is helping her sort things out. Where the kids came from. How to reach their parents. That sort of thing. It's going to take some time to get all the children to where they belong."

"Hm," he grunted.

"The captain told me we're free to leave," I said. "If there's a trial and we're needed as witnesses, he'll get in touch."

"I don't know about you, but November and I are ready to go home," Gemma said.

"My rig's parked outside," Loq said. "I'll give you a ride to the airport."

We stopped by the room where Wanda Manybaskets was. Charley Pony Blanket was there with the other four children. The woman from child services said we could take him with us as the FBI wanted him repatriated with his aunt as quickly as possible.

November and Gemma hugged Wanda goodbye. When it was my turn, Wanda hugged me and whispered in my ear, "I always knew you and Loq would not give up helping me find all my children."

Charley Pony Blanket squeezed between Gemma and

November in the pickup's cab as Loq drove us to the airport. I sat in the bed by myself. The route followed the Spokane River for several miles. I watched the river's waters sparkle under a sky unblemished by smoke and haze. My thoughts touched on lots of things that had occurred during the past few days, but whenever they started to circle around how two woven baby rattles had floated downriver and washed up on the bank for Wanda Manybaskets to recover, I blinked them away. The fact that they had was reason enough for me.

When we arrived at the airport, November and Charley climbed into the small plane as Gemma walked around it, conducting a visual and running through her checklist.

"Are you going to drive straight back to Oregon?" I asked Loq.

"There's something else I got to do," he said.

"Such as?"

"Help Wanda. She told me those kids are only a start. There's a lot more who need help getting home too, and she plans to be that help."

"You're not going to quit being a Fish and Wildlife ranger, are you?"

Loq looked down his high cheekbones. "See, Nick, you're asking a question you already know the answer to again."

"Then I'll see you next time the *Nuwuddu* need both our help."

"Until then," he said. "Stay sharp, brother."

Takeoff was smooth and we flew back to No Mountain as the sun climbed higher. Gemma and I were wearing headsets but didn't speak for the first couple of hours.

Finally, she said, "I heard what Loq said to you."

"That he's going to help Wanda."

"That too, but he said an actual goodbye and called you

brother. I've never heard him call anybody that who wasn't Indian."

I looked out the cockpit window and, despite the air growing smokier the closer we got to No Mountain, I could pick out the familiar landmarks of the southern Blue Mountains as they sloped toward the black-topped buttes that poked up from the quilted landscape of Harney County. It wasn't all that long ago I was looking down on a battle-scarred jungle from the open bay of a Huey. I'd been able to survive the Vietnam War because I'd become part of a tribe. Loq had been a member of that same tribe. It was a tribe that transcended all races, all beliefs. We'd put our lives on the line for each other, and that made us brothers for life.

The sun remained unsparing and I spent the next two weeks putting out spot brushfires while patrolling the wildlife refuges in my beat, starting with Deer Flat's islands in the Snake River on the border with Idaho and now finishing up with the Sheldon reserve that was more in Nevada than Oregon.

I was still driving the pickup I'd borrowed from the Rocking H while I awaited delivery of a replacement. My telephone call with Regional Director F.D. Powers after he received word of my requisition for a new rig and weapons went about as I'd expected. The suit from Washington DC, as Loq called him, was long on lecturing me about the need to conform with agency policies while I was short on providing details about how the pickup got torched.

The fact was, I'd been second-guessing my own culpability in becoming the firebug's victim. Part of my doubt was spurred by all the protest marches by the growing Women's Liberation Movement. They got me wondering if dropping my guard when encountering what I assumed was a stricken female on a lonely road in the middle of the night meant I was a male chauvinist too.

"Pigheaded, yes, when you went chasing bad guys all on your own after being set on fire, but a male pig?" Gemma said when I asked her. The horse doctor's ponytail swished. "You're an equal opportunity guardian. Men, women, and animals too. Don't forget, when it comes to black widows, the females have the venom, not the males."

Her father was a little less charitable when telling stories at my expense. Pudge took unbridled pleasure in sharing how I couldn't envision Bettina St. Claire risking a chipped nail to hurl a Molotov cocktail.

"Son," Pudge drawled, "you still got a lot to learn about women. If you'd spent as much time around them as I have, first as a husband and then a single father trying to do the best I can raising a daughter who's got more spirit than a wild mustang, not to mention living under the same roof as that old Paiute healer who's gonna be the death of me yet, you'd have a whole lot more horse sense."

The way the lawman told it, the night he drove Freddie Sanderlin from the Rocking H in handcuffs, the pyro started blaming Judd Hollister for everything from the get-go. Freddie swore it was Judd who tracked him down five years prior when he was living with his parents in Wallowa County when they'd fled Harney County in the middle of the night.

"Freddie told me Judd remembered him from grade school, the whaling he gave the bigger kid, how he torched the schoolhouse," Pudge said. "Judd offered him one thousand dollars to do the same to his parents' house. Paid him too. Freddie said Judd was behind the robbery where he got caught and sentenced to prison. Judd was waiting for him when he got sprung and used him on art heists, including at a fancy hacienda with a view of Camelback Mountain down near Phoenix."

Pudge seemed to relish telling the story slowly. "Wasn't only Judd Freddie blabbed about. He said when he was incarcerated in the state pen, Martin St. Claire was also there serving time. Now, Martin was always going on and on about his wife while he was in the hoosegow, telling everyone how she was more beautiful than a rose. When Freddie got out, he paid Bettina a visit. Turns out he wasn't lying when we cornered him in the gas station and he claimed he was seeing a married woman. Criminals always do that, working a bit of the truth into their cover."

The old deputy clicked the inside of his cheeks. "There was Freddie, sitting in my rig with handcuffs on, knowing he was going down for arson, robbery, and the murders of Mr. and Mrs. Hollister and Hairy Jerry. There's nothing he can tell me to talk down his sentence. Not a single, solitary word. But the thing about a backdoor man is, he can't be trusted. Not by anyone, and especially not by the cheating heart he's cheating with. He sold Bettina out without me even asking. Says she had a thing about lighting fires too, and I don't mean the romantic kind."

He chuckled. "It was Bettina who lit the rival dress store in Burns on fire, not Martin. She browbeat him into taking the rap for her. When she met Freddie, they turned out to be two matches in the same book. Bettina was with Freddie when they lit poor Hairy Jerry's trailer on fire. He said watching it was an aphrodisiac. If you don't know what that is, look it up. Bettina's the one who chucked the Molotov cocktail at you while Freddie stayed ducked beneath the dashboard. And it was her who was going to light all the diversion fires in Burns while Freddie was at the Rocking H."

"But when I flew over Burns, I didn't see much of anything that had been torched," I said.

"The whole town owes Gemma and you thanks for that,"

Pudge said. "Her calling it in allowed us to be ready for it. Had patrols on every street and fire engines circling every block."

"What happened, did someone catch Bettina in the act?"

"Yup. Martin did. He finally wised up she was two-timing him, that he was a fool for having taken the rap for her once and wasn't gonna do it twice. He followed her to the courthouse where she was going to set fire to it. Walloped her with a tin watering can and tied her up with a garden hose. He said he wasn't sorry one bit for turning her in. Said he's looking forward to spending the rest of his life with roses because they're a whole lot quieter and prettier too."

The fastest way home from Sheldon National Wildlife Refuge was to drive east on Highway 140 to Denio on the state line and then north up the Catlow Valley, but I chose to take the longer route. I drove west through Lakeview with a detour to the Chewaucan Marsh. I didn't encounter any vigilantes or a man wearing dusty boots along the way, but if I had, I would've given them a hello from my brother Loq.

It didn't take long to find the wickiup made of cattails alongside the marsh. The blanket that had been woven on a hand-loom with a sapphire lake surrounded by snowcapped mountains on it was still there. I gave a moment of silence for Tom Piñon, and then folded the blanket and took it with me for safekeeping. I was sure I'd see Wanda Manybaskets again some-day, and I thought the young healer would want it as she continued on her mission of reuniting native children with their families.

I drove to the grove of ancient western junipers that grew around the waterhole next and walked up the same game trail as before. Because of the blazing heat, *Nuwuddu* had returned and were treating it as neutral territory again. Several prong-horn and a bobcat were lapping water from opposite sides of the waterhole. Many of the trees bore scorched limbs and trunks, but were still alive. The Paiute believed many things had power, what they referred to as *puha* and the Washoe as *wegeléyu*, and the resilience of the ancient trees was proof enough for me they had plenty of it. I took comfort in the grove's longevity, knowing the junipers would continue to live for another thousand years as long as summers never got any hotter and second people got smarter about controlling what we burned.

It was dark by the time I rolled up to the old lineman's shack. It was still much too warm to use the woodstove and so I found company in cooking dinner for myself and finished reading *Desert Solitaire* over a cup of tea at the rickety wooden table while moonlight streamed through the window. When the last page was turned, I climbed into the narrow bunk and let the words of Edward Abbey lull me to sleep: "The night flows back, the mighty stillness embraces and includes me; I can see the stars again and the world of starlight. I am twenty miles or more from the nearest fellow human, but instead of loneliness I feel loveliness. Loveliness and a quiet exultation."

The song of rain pattering against the windows and pinging on the cockeyed metal stovepipe that jutted from the roof woke me early in the morning. I didn't bother pulling on clothes and boots, but ran outside and stood with arms outstretched, soaking in the long-awaited gift from the clouds. I raised my face, opened my mouth, and tasted the end of the fire season in every drop.

After getting dressed and filling a thermos with coffee and a brown paper bag with squares of cornbread, I drove to Steens Mountain. It was still a few more miles to the top when I spotted Tuhudda Will coming down. He held an umbrella fashioned out of woven aspen branches attached to the top of his walking stick.

I stopped and opened the door. "Hello, my old friend."

"Nick Drake. I knew you were coming before you left. This is so," he said in his slow, deliberate manner.

We turned around and made our way back down the mountain. The steep descent had turned slippery with the rain. I handed him the bag of cornbread squares and invited him to help himself.

"The clouds accepted your gifts and finally gave you one in return," I said as the windshield wipers clapped.

"Their gift is for everyone, *Nuwuddu* and *Numu* alike," he said. "The rocks and bushes and trees also. Everything needs rain in the brown world."

He took a bite of cornbread. It brought a smile to his lips. I wondered what he'd been eating for the past couple of weeks. I asked him if he was surprised it took so long to rain.

"Clouds have no time, for their journey has no start or finish, and their shapes have no beginning or end. Theirs is a journey of change and that is a gift also," he said.

"How is that?" I asked as I downshifted before rounding a steep curve.

"No two clouds look the same and no cloud stays looking the same for long. That is their gift—reminding us there are many trails in this life."

Tuhudda pointed at the rainswept sky beyond the windshield. "Their stories are another gift. When you lay on your back and look at clouds, you see in them what you need to see. Perhaps the face of your father and mother who are now in the spirit world. Maybe the face of the woman you have been longing for. Clouds are like the stories the old ones left us carved in rocks and painted on canyon walls."

"Petroglyphs and pictographs. I've seen many of them in Harney County." I motioned toward the thermos resting between us. "Have some coffee."

Tuhudda unscrewed the top and drank. He smacked his lips

and set his red bandana and shoulder-length white hair bobbing. "Someone has finally taught you how to make it good."

We reached the outskirts of No Mountain. "I'll give you a ride to your camp, but I won't be able to stay. I need to double back and get to the Warbler ranch. It's a special day," I said.

"Every day is special. This is so. How is this one any different?"

"It's election day. Deputy Warbler is running to get his old job as sheriff back."

"He was always a good sheriff," Tuhudda said. "He was always fair to *Numu*."

"I'm going to pick up Gemma and November and we're going to cast our ballots at the polling place at Blackpowder Smith's. After that, we're driving up to Burns to watch the election returns with Pudge and some friends."

"Who?" he asked.

"The young man who works with Pudge, Orville Nelson, and a friend of his, Lucy Lorriaga."

"The brave one who must use wheels for legs. You should teach him how to ride a horse."

"I hadn't thought of that," I said. "Orville would like that."

"And will Girl Born in Snow bring frybread to this celebration?"

"Of course."

"Then I will go also. She makes good frybread. She uses plenty of sugar."

We crossed the cattle guard and pulled up to the ranch house. The rain let up as I got out of the pickup. I looked at the sky and saw a V of geese beating their wings beneath the clouds. They were the first of millions of migratory birds that would pass over Harney County in the months ahead.

November was sitting on the front porch, the striped Pendleton blanket draped over her shoulders. A pile of willow strips lay next to her beaded moccasins. She was swaddling a short board with soft white buckskin and humming as she fastened what looked to be shoulder straps to it. She laced wide strips of buckskin with glass bead designs at the head and foot of the board.

"Don't tell me you're making another *kida*," I said as I looked at the object taking shape in her gnarled hands. "The rain has come. The fires are out."

November looked up and tsked louder than usual. "Your eyes are open but still you do not see."

Tuhudda joined me. "What Girl Born in Snow makes is not for carrying water. It is for carrying tomorrows." He said to her, "It has been a long time, but your fingers still know the way."

"My mother taught me and her mother taught her as hers taught her," the old healer said. "What will be needed cannot be forgotten."

"As I cannot forget when my grandson Nagah was old enough to speak. He said, 'Grandfather, why did I have to ride facing backward when my mother faced forward as she carried me.'"

"And you said to him the same as I said to my daughter Gentle Wind and my mother to me, 'Because when *Numu* first come into this world, they must look behind to see where their ancestors walked if they are to know which path to take.'"

"This is so," Tuhudda said. His face became even more craggy with a smile. "Today is a most special day indeed."

The front door opened. Gemma came out and touched my arm. She looked particularly radiant.

"There you are," she said. "Now I know where you've been. Hello, Tuhudda. Thank you for asking the clouds for rain. Are you coming with us?"

"If it pleases you," he said.

"It does. Everything does. Fall is in the air, spring is around the corner, and Pudge is going to win."

"How do you know that?" I said.

Gemma and November exchanged long looks. Then she looped her arm through mine and started walking toward the pickup. Her eyes sparkled. "A woman always knows about such things, hotshot."

AFTERWORD

In 1978, Congress passed the Indian Child Welfare Act (ICWA). The law was intended to address several inequities. At the time of its passage, 25 to 35 percent of all Native American children were being forcibly separated from families that were mostly intact and had extended family networks.

The children were placed in predominantly non-Indian foster homes, adoptive homes, or institutions. The per capita rate of Native American children in foster care was nearly 16 times higher than the rate for non-Native American children. Many of the children were found to have extreme emotional damage resulting from being wrenched from their families and losing touch with their Native culture.

The ICWA gave tribal governments a strong voice concerning custody proceedings and granted tribes exclusive jurisdiction over cases when the child resided on the reservation or were wards of the tribe. It also gave tribes presumptive jurisdiction over the foster care placement proceedings of non-reservation Native American children.

Despite the law's passage, out-of-home placement continues to occur more frequently for Native American and Alaskan

Native children than it does for the general population. According to the nonprofit National Indian Child Welfare Association, Native families are still four times more likely to have their children forcibly removed and placed in foster care than their white counterparts.

The ICWA also gave Native American families the right to prevent the forced placement of their children in off-reservation Indian boarding schools. At one time, there were more than 350 of these controversial government-funded institutions nationwide. The schools commonly banned Native American children from engaging in traditional cultural practices, such as speaking their native language and wearing traditional dress and hairstyles. Children who disobeyed were punished.

While Indian boarding schools have largely disappeared—the Bureau of Indian Affairs operates only four such schools today—historical psychological trauma remains a daunting healthcare challenge for tribes. The nonprofit National Native American Boarding School Healing Coalition has documented widespread Post Traumatic Stress Syndrome among former students.

According to the group, tribes still face unjust education systems. Grim statistics bear this out. Native American youth have the lowest high school graduation rate and the highest suicide rate in the country.

For more information about these issues, visit nicwa.org and boardingschoolhealing.org.

A NOTE FROM THE AUTHOR

Thank you so much for reading *The Whisper Soul*. I'd truly appreciate it if you would please leave a review on Amazon and Goodreads. Your feedback not only helps me become a better storyteller, but you help other readers by blazing a trail and leaving markers for them to follow as they search for new stories.

To leave a review, go to *The Whisper Soul* product page on Amazon, click "customer reviews" next to the stars below the title, click the "Write a customer review" button, and share your thoughts with other readers.

To quote John Cheever, "I can't write without a reader. It's precisely like a kiss—you can't do it alone."

GET A FREE BOOK

Dwight Holing's genre-spanning work includes novels, short fiction, and nonfiction. His mystery and suspense thriller series include The Nick Drake Novels and The Jack McCoul Capers. The stories in his collections of literary short fiction have won awards, including the Arts & Letters Prize for Fiction. He has written and edited numerous nonfiction books on nature travel and conservation. He is married to a kick-ass environmental advocate; they have a daughter and son, and two dogs who'd rather swim than walk.

Sign up for his newsletter to get a free book and be the first to learn about the next Nick Drake Novel as well as receive news about crime fiction and special deals.

Visit dwightholing.com/free-book. You can unsubscribe at any time.

ACKNOWLEDGMENTS

I'm indebted to many people who helped in the creation of *The Whisper Soul*. As always, my family provided support throughout the writing process, including a ready willingness to rein me in should I wander too far off the story's trail.

Thank you Kenneth Mitchell for alerting me to the unique history of the balloon bomb attack on the US during World War II and the tragedy that befell Archie and Elsie Mitchell and five children near Bly, Oregon.

I'm especially grateful to my reader team who read early drafts and gave me very helpful feedback. Thank you, one and all, including Gene Ammerman, George Becker, Terrill Carpenter, Kim Compeau, Gino Cox, Ben Colodzin, Ron Fox, Marcia Lilley, Cath McTernan, Jeffrey Miller, Kenneth Mitchell, Annie Notthoff, John Onoda, Haris Orkin, and Rhonda Sarver.

Thank you Karl Yambert for proofreading and copyediting. Kudos to designer Rob Williams for creating the stunning cover.

A special thank-you to the Harney County Library's Claire McGill Luce Western History Room and Archivist Karen Nitz.

Additional thanks go to the Northern Paiute Language

Project at University of California, Santa Cruz and the Burns Paiute Tribe of the Burns Paiute Indian Colony of Oregon, a federally recognized tribe of Northern Paiute in Harney County, Oregon.

Any errors, regrettably, are my own.

ALSO BY DWIGHT HOLING

The Nick Drake Novels

The Sorrow Hand (Book 1)

The Pity Heart (Book 2)

The Shaming Eyes (Book 3)

The Whisper Soul (Book 4)

The Jack McCoul Capers

A Boatload (Book 1)

Bad Karma (Book 2)

Baby Blue (Book 3)

Shake City (Book 4)

Short Story Collections

California Works

Over Our Heads Under Our Feet